Black Nightmares To Scarlet Dreams

Imagine if you discovered that one of your ancestors had been a pirate and you were named after them. You also find a sword that belonged to them; wouldn't that be something? That is exactly what happens to Rose Scarlet. At first it's exciting but when an American arrives claiming to be the descendent of Blackheart; the pirate that Captain Rosie Scarlet was in love with, her whole world turns upside down.

Blackheart hung for his crimes but Rosie was spared the gallows. Jack Bracken is a troubled man looking for answers but it is a dark power that has brought him to England and the demons unleashed are only the beginning.

CARA ALDOUS

BLACK NIGHTMARES TO SCARLET DREAMS

© Cara Aldous 2007
All rights reserved

www.lulu.com

www.dougdazesummer.com

This book is sold subject to the condition that it shall not, by way of trade or otherwise, be lent, re-sold, hired out, or otherwise circulated without the publisher's prior consent in any form of binding or cover other than that in which it is published and without a similar condition being imposed on the subsequent purchaser.

ISBN **978-0-9556849-0-6**

Black Nightmares to Scarlet Dreams is a work of fiction. The characters and plot are entirely fictitious and any resemblance to persons living or dead is coincidental and unintended.

Prologue

"...Black turns to Scarlet, Scarlet to Black,
The season's in turmoil, time to come back,
Black, back, Black, back,
Back to his true love, always look back..."

His head swam as he tried to open his eyes. Reality was slipping and he realised the thing that held his arms tight and kept his body from moving was a heavy rope bound several times around his body. He struggled and kicked out but his feet too were bound at the ankles. Instinctively he yanked his head as he arched his back.

Bright lights swam across his green eyes and they darkened. So, the men had finally found the courage to mutiny and had left him for dead. It was only a matter of time before the King's men found him. He heard a moan from behind. His beloved Rosie too! The mutineers had signed their own death warrants.

"Rosie! Rosie!" he whispered.

She made no reply. He struggled with all his strength but the ropes were fastened hard and fast. He would not have expected anything less from the very men he had taught and bullied and terrified until they knew everything there was to know about sailing the seas. His breath caught in his throat and he felt the bile rise as he thought of his beautiful ship The Phoenix sailing without him at the helm. He would have vengeance! Frantically he searched in the dim light for his sword but it too had been taken from him.

Raised voices carried on the wind and he stared into the dark inviting waters that lapped at the wooden deck of the dock. With all his strength he tried desperately to lift Rosie so together they could disappear into the depths but the post was solid, holding them fast to their fate. As long as he had breath in his body he would fight; he would fight each and every one of them to the death if it meant his beloved Rosie was safe.

The voices drew nearer and faces loomed. He thrashed and spat and kicked and hissed at them. He cursed each and every one of them and promised them that soon they would be begging to die…

"Sir! Sir!"

Black Nightmares to Scarlet Dreams

His eyes flickered open. The airhostess was above him, holding his arms down. The passenger next to him was pinning him down; his chest felt as though it would cave in with the pressure.

"Sir! You must calm down! We will have to restrain you and the police will be notified and waiting for you as soon as we land! Please! Calm down!"

He looked into her eyes and she into his. Her gaze faltered and she looked away. A smile tugged at the corner of his lips. He stared at the man restraining him. He too looked away and dropped his hold.

"I'm sorry," he spoke softly, "I…I don't fly too well. I had…a bad dream that's all. I'll be fine now, I promise. No more trouble."

They left him alone, the man turning away and the airhostess returning to her duties. He pushed back in his seat. He was exhausted as he pulled the flimsy airline blanket over his shoulders. He would not risk falling asleep; it would still be some time before they landed in England. Time to think; he shivered and shook away the threatening darkness as the plane skimmed over the clouds taking him ever closer to his beloved Rosie.

©2007 Cara Aldous

Chapter 1

An English summer is usually a damp and depressing one but this season was such a spectacularly blistering one that even the sun-worshippers sat in the shade and proclaimed it too much. It was the hottest one ever recorded. Every living thing wilted and tired in the unrelenting heat.

There was no respite when evening fell; as day and night merged into a never ending struggle to work and sleep, people began to lament the wet seasonal summers of past and prayed that soon they would see glorious rain again.

What should have been a time of fun slowly became a nightmare during which a few died through heat exhaustion and the very young found it hard to play in the humid and claustrophobic air. Work became an effort and an eerie silence descended over the school holidays as more and more people stayed indoors, only venturing outside to earn a living or buy essentials. As a result shops were quiet and streets largely deserted.

In one such quiet, unassuming little shop, Rose Scarlet sat behind the counter; the hum of electric fans behind and in front made her curly red hair even wilder than usual. She sipped from a lukewarm bottle of water which had been ice-cold only ten minutes earlier. The door was shut to keep the outside heat at bay and for once Rose was glad of the lull in trade. She wiped her brow and pulled her hair into a ponytail. As she leaned on the counter she toyed with the idea of shutting early. Saturdays were usually her busiest; lots of children's parties and students' fancy dress.

The shop boasted a rail of costumes and several shelves full of small toys and novelties. There were wigs, and a whole selection of balloons in varying shapes and sizes. But the things which sold the best, and were of the most interest were her prized collections of Pirate merchandise.

Across two walls were the cheap, fun things; plastic swords, skull and crossbones, hats and scarves and plastic hooks. And on a wall of its own were the authentic section; costume (based on eighteenth century clothing), several Jolly Rogers based on genuine ones (deliberately distressed as though flown for centuries) and a large wall-mounted display of genuine swords and cutlasses; battle-worn weaponry in all its glory.

Though the authentic stuff sold less frequently it did, nevertheless, sell. Rose had been amazed at the interest generated when she first opened and even more astonished at how many of the more expensive items actually sold. She had several regular collectors now that kept her business afloat and, along with the huge turnover of kid's party things, she was able to indulge her passion for Pirates. She loved to watch the children's and collector's faces alike each time a new item appeared in the shop.

Rose stepped down off her stool, and was about to lock the door when it was pushed open. Hot air instantly penetrated the shop. A young mother and son entered and Rose sighed, wishing she had locked the door sooner.

The mother took her time, picking out a scarf and eye patch whilst her son looked up eagerly at the sword display. Rose watched as his mother tried to convince him to choose from the plastic ones and groaned inwardly when he began a high pitched wail. The mother smiled weakly at Rose who took a sip of the bitter water before moving slowly along the counter to where the boy stood.

"Well now, young master," she began, in a thicker West Country brogue than usual.

Startled, the boy stopped crying and stepped back, his eyes wide and bright.

"Tis a sword yer after, is it?"

Shyly he nodded.

"Then I have jus' the thing."

Black Nightmares to Scarlet Dreams

She selected one of the mid-priced plastic cutlasses and fingered the 'blade' menacingly. "This ere sword was owned by none other than Cap'n John Butcheremall, the most feared Pirate in all the world!"

She smiled as she rung up the items then stood at the door and with a flourish waved her customers out. Wilting in the heat she longed to get home but before she could finally close the door it was again pushed from her grasp. Rick Drummond, proprietor of Drummonds Beds and Furniture strolled in. Rose sighed and put the closed sign up and the latch down before anyone else could walk in. Rick settled himself as comfortably as a large man could in searing heat. He balanced precariously on her stool in front of the counter. Rose leaned back on the glass top and took another swig of her disgusting drink, pulling a face as she did so.

Rick had been the owner of Drummonds for many years. His father built up the business from scratch and Rick had left school with few qualifications due to too many days spent in the shop and not enough at school. With the death of his dear old dad, the shop became his and he now sold as much tat as he could manage to get his hands on. For all his lack of education he was an intelligent man, married to his long-suffering Ruby for the best part of thirty years. He was a regular visitor to Rose's shop, and haggled with her frequently, mostly over the swords.

"Closing early, Rosie? Little Rosie having a half day, eh?" he chuckled.

She forced a smile, "Not much point staying open in this heat."

He shrugged, "Thought about it myself this morning. True as I'm standing here, Rosie. I said to Ruby, 'Ruby' I said 'Ruby, it's a sorry time we live in if I close up because of the weather. Got a load of sun lotions to shift too…"

Rose smiled; he always had something on the side to shift. It amazed her how he always managed to sell so many items unrelated to furniture.

"…Even when we had that really cold spell, you remember Rosie? When we had that sheet of ice, covered the whole ground it did! Slipped all over the place! But people came in then. Why does a little bit of sun stop 'em? Beats me, Rosie, beats me. Like that old proverb, isn't it? You know the one about the sun and wind..."

Rose smiled again and shook her head and nodded in what she hoped were the right places. It really was too hot for this, and she tried to focus her glazed-over eyes on him. Unusually he wore a short-sleeved shirt with no tie but these were his only concessions as he still wore the heavy suit trousers which made him even sweatier than normal. His pot belly hung over his waistband and threatened to burst open the buttons. Sweat dripped down his neck and dark patches grew under his arms. His blond fluffy hair which made him look like a hideous baby matted to his head and Rose shuddered as she lifted up her own damp hair. She smiled and waited for a break in his conversation.

When none came she interrupted, "Sorry Rick, I don't mean to be rude, but…"

Obligingly he struggled to his feet and tugged at his trousers and shirt. As he turned to go he glanced up at the sword display. "Don't s'pose there's a chance today?" he began but Rose shook her head firmly.

It had become almost a daily ritual of his to hold one of her swords; the Scarlet family heirloom. He often tried to buy it but it was the one thing not for sale. Not today, not ever. And especially not in suffocating heat, when she longed to be home with an ice-cold glass of wine. She ushered him quickly through the door and slammed it shut.

She felt guilty at having been so rude, but it was the only way sometimes. Otherwise people took advantage.

'Walk all over you they do!'

Her mother's voice pierced the heat. She would have hated the weather, insisting on Rose looking after her in case she had a 'bad turn'. Thankfully her mother was no longer around. Guilt surrounded Rose. She was far too ungrateful and never satisfied with her lot; Mother had often told her so: she was a terrible daughter; the worst and Rose believed every word.

She had been an only child and was still so afraid of being on her own. She had grown up alone, though not spoiled; Mother had been consistently hard on her and ordered her life even into adulthood. Her father had been a quiet and unobtrusive man who adored his daughter and when he died Rose was left alone and without an ally. Mother leaned on her more and more, earning only pity and resentment in the ensuing years.

Rose opened her shop with a small inheritance left by her father. Mother, jealous at her daughter's new independence, tutted and moaned that no man would ever want her. Rose, with growing confidence, had responded that no man would ever have the chance. This seemed to shock Mother into an awful silence that went on for days. It was emotional blackmail which wore her down over the following years. By the time Mother died Rose was a pale shadow of herself.

The sword caught her eye as she tugged the shutters down. It dazzled in a shaft of sunlight which pushed through a small chink. It stood out above all the others; it always did.

She had found it by accident, the day of Mother's funeral. She had climbed up into the large attic in her childhood home, thinking it ideal for storage; her little backroom in the shop becoming way too small. It was also a chance to escape the false appreciation of a person who, when alive, most people crossed the road to avoid.

She enjoyed hurling old boxes and cases full of rubbish and junk down through the hatch. It was liberating and she had been pleasantly distracted by a large trunk hidden behind them. On prising open the lid she found notebooks and papers and, under it all, something wrapped in an old cloth. On closer inspection she discovered it was a large sword. She had sat for a full hour, forgetting the wake below, and sifted through the papers which had belonged to her father.

Intrigue turned to excitement as she discovered an ancestor; Rosie Scarlet who had captained the Pirate ship The Phoenix. She had ruled the seas with a man on her arm and sword in her hand; the sword

Rose had found; the sword which now took pride of place on the wall of her shop.

*

Rose gazed at the sword, marvelling at the way the sun caught it. She studied the detailed complex moulding on the golden handle depicting a fiery bird. She thought back to the time it came from. Back to the deck of a ship; blades crossing and blood spilled by its sharp edge. She shook herself at the sound of the clashing metal and glanced fearfully around.

Quickly she switched off the lights at the back of the shop, crossing double time to the door in the gloomy light, the dark corners closing in. Hands shaking she fumbled with the door catch and gasped as the heat hit her simultaneously with the harsh glare of the midday sun.

She stumbled past the closed shops along the quiet street. The butchers shop had closed at ten, having gratefully sold all his meat for the many barbecues. The greengrocers had closed early too, all salad gone. A young man emerged from the newsagents carrying a bundle of thick Saturday papers. She passed the post office, its brown blinds pulled down in every window, looking like a huge parcel waiting quietly for Monday morning to come. All around was silent.

She crossed the deserted main road, the tarmac sticky beneath her feet. Her pace quickened as she turned the corner onto Oak Avenue, large oaks standing serenely with not a leaf stirring. She counted each tree as she passed, reaching out to touch as she had done so many times as a child on her way home from school.

©2007 Cara Aldous

She stumbled at the third tree, heart racing and breathing laboured. She knew what was happening, knew the signs only too well. But the panic which welled inside her had not surfaced for many years, not since Mother died. Her head swam with the dizziness and nausea. She swallowed hard and pushed on, the urge to be home and safe greater than the one to stop. She blindly stumbled from tree to tree, finally reaching the centre one which marked the turn onto Oak Grove and home.

Chapter 2

Rose tried to compose herself as she hurried; her focus the enormous oak tree standing on a large grass island in the centre of the road, guarding her house. Oak Grove was a cul-de-sac where she safely played as a child, and where she now lived with her best friend Sam.

After Mother died Sam moved in and between them they renovated the entire house beyond recognition. Even the neighbours had been amazed at the transformation from a tired old period house to a modern and bright home. The front door was now red and the garden planted with brightly coloured flowers. Once the alterations were done Rose felt able at last to look upon it as a happy and comfortable place; home again.

She hurried along past familiar houses. A shout made her jump and she turned to see Stanley Knox jogging up behind her.

"You all right, Rose?" he asked, looking concerned.

Stanley or Babe as his family and friends called him (owing to the fact that to some he was a bit of a babe but to others a complete baby) was twenty-six years old and infatuated with Rose and Sam. Although he was miles younger than their forty years he was convinced they could and, moreover would, teach him a thing or two and so inevitably tried too hard whenever he met either one.

He lived with Sandra and Ernie Knox and was the definitive Mummy's boy. He wandered around with his head in the clouds and told anyone who cared his big plans to have a high-powered job, classic car and beautiful woman all by the time he was thirty. Being a trainee supermarket manager was about as far as he had got. Rose wished he would pass by and go play on his Playstation.

"I saw you leaving the shop. Finished early?" he panted.

She tried desperately to steady her breathing but felt faint so instead nodded. She sat down and breathed deeply, knowing really she should carry on. Her head swam and her heart thumped so loudly she was sure he could hear every beat. As she clutched the wall she felt herself sway. Babe's face instantly drained of colour as he grabbed her arms to steady her.

"I…I'm fine," she gasped. *Leave me alone!*

"I don't think you are, Rose," he said, oblivious, "Here, let me help you."

Let Sam be in, please, please let her be in.

Black Nightmares to Scarlet Dreams

Once inside the safe environment of home Rose collapsed on the sofa. Sam fetched a glass of iced water. Rose took a few sips but felt uncomfortable with Babe there. She listened, detached, as Sam and Babe chatted and wished he would leave so she could lie down and sleep; it was the only thing which would help. The panic attacks had begun after Mother's death and though she had visited the doctor several times, since all he ever offered were pills whose side-effects were worse than her symptoms, she had developed ways to overcome the attacks herself; to a degree. Through her own coping mechanism, when one came on she tried to stop it by humming a tune or breathing steadily to induce a calmer state. Today's attack, though, had been different and more intense than before.

"Must be the heat," Babe was saying, "She looked terrible…"

"Oh no, no, it's a panic attack – she gets them a lot," Sam replied, "Though its ages since the last one."

Samantha Tranter was Rose's best and only friend, and had been since their first day at Secondary school when both stood lost and lonely in the enormous playground. Rose had grown and shone through their friendship and away from the suffocating confines of home life but Sam was quiet and withdrawn. Then puberty hit. Once fully developed Sam embraced her ripeness with such vitality that the boys didn't know what hit them. Rose, on the other hand, was awkward and shy as womanhood gripped and never really blossomed in the same way. While Sam could, and often did, have any boy she wanted, Rose had only ever wanted her ideal man; her knight in shining armour to come and save her from her boring life. The fact he may never exist didn't once cross her mind but in forty years she had yet to meet him.

*

Rose woke, calmed in her quiet house. She found Sam sitting on the decking outside the back door, glass of cold wine in hand. Sam smiled and passed her a glass.

"Feeling better?" She asked but didn't wait for a reply, "So what brought it on?"

Rose took the wine and thought for a moment. She didn't know what had triggered the attack only that she was very frightened. The sword prayed on her mind and the horror which overtook her as she thought of it threatened to hit. She took a couple of deep breaths and a small sip of wine. Her head swam.

"I think maybe I should put it somewhere else. I mean, it isn't right is it? Having it on view like that? I mean, anything could happen!" All her words came out at once.

Not for the first time she felt the danger that surrounded her pirate sword and the threat was all too real.

"What? What are you talking about?" Sam frowned.

Rose blushed, "Oh, that sword I keep in the shop."

"What, your pirate's sword? Why, what's happened? Has someone tried to steal it? Oh my God Rose!" Sam was concerned and it would definitely explain the panic attack.

"No, nothing like that – but it is dangerous! Surely even you can see that? It gives me the creeps, thinking about all the blood it's spilled!

And it's my ancestor's too; that's what makes it all so real!" Rose gripped her chair hard, "It has to go away, where I can't see it any more. That explains why they kept it hidden away from me. I was named after her; maybe I am her!"

"Stop it Rose! You're freaking me out! What the hell is going on?"

Rose took a large gulp of wine which made her head swim even more. She began to tell the story of how she found the sword. It was a story Sam had heard many times but she sat back and listened as friends do as Rose told how she had rummaged through the attic. How she had enjoyed chucking out all the rubbish and junk which her parents had hoarded over the years.

Sam always thought it sad how people's possessions are thrown away when they die because they no longer have a meaning. To the Scarlets the things which their daughter had so readily disposed of had held a multitude of sentimental memories for them. Each picture or ornament, every item of clothing, which was lovingly stored in the attic, had been special to them. Maybe that was why Rose had enjoyed getting rid of it all; her memories had not been as brightly coloured as her parents.

The sword and papers relating to the Scarlet family history had been the only things which Rose had kept and for a short time after she had become obsessed with her namesake: Captain Rosie Scarlet. It was all coming back to haunt her. Rose tended to act rashly if she felt threatened and would take flight in a moment. Sam wished she knew what to say to put her mind at ease.

Rose fell silent. A black cat appeared at her feet. Another came from around the side of the house followed by a ginger tom; a small, unassuming man brought up the rear. They made their way to the decking, just stopping short of climbing the steps to where the girls were sitting.

"Good evening, ladies."

"Hiya Aubrey," Sam was relieved at the interruption; it was great timing from their neighbour.

Aubrey Twissell stood his distance from them and shuffled from side to side as he listened to Rose taking up the story once more. Sam, hoping to distract her, tried to make light remarks and lift the mood but she continued; her words bitter and angry. Aubrey remained oblivious to Sam's concerned looks and simply listened, straight-faced and deep in thought.

"…And it's not just the sword," Rose was saying, "It's the other things too…"

"What other things?" Sam sat up.

"You know; the flag from her ship – The Phoenix. Oh and the letter about Blackheart the Pirate, I told you ages ago!" Rose waved her hand dismissively at Sam.

Sam demanded to know more; it was the first she had heard about these things, although she did recall Rose showing her a flag several months ago. Only she had thought it something to do with the shop and was, at the time, concentrating on much more important things such as should she sleep with her boss at the factory or not? (In the event she did but with huge regret as now he was threatening to stop her overtime if she didn't repeat the performance).

Aubrey interrupted, asking to see the items. Rose disappeared into the kitchen and emerged several minutes later with a bulging carrier. She tipped the contents onto the patio table and pulled from the pile the piece of black material which Sam recognised as a flag.

Unfolded it revealed skull and crossbones inside a red silhouette of a female with a black heart in the centre of that. Rose spread the flag across the table and Aubrey adjusted his glasses as he stepped forward to take a closer look.

"Yes, very interesting," he remarked, "This red outline obviously signifies Captain Rosie Scarlet. This black heart must be, well, Blackheart. And the skull and crossbones would indicate a pirate ship…"

"Yes, it's so obviously hers isn't it?" Rose sounded relieved that someone else saw the connection besides her. "What else do you think?"

"What about the letter you were sent too? What does it say? Who's it from?"

Sam frowned as Rose produced an air mail envelope. She snatched the letter before Aubrey had chance to even look at it. She opened it roughly and scanned down the page. It was the rantings of a lunatic and she paused, worried that Rose had kept this to herself. It was small wonder she was teetering on the edge of sanity what with the heat as well. It was enough to send the sanest person nuts. Rose glared angrily at her as she handed it over to Aubrey. He read it carefully, pondering over each phrase. He rubbed his chin and looked up at Rose, obviously concerned that such a naïve and vulnerable woman should receive such a vitriolic letter yet keep it concealed from even her closest friend. He handed it back to Rose and shook his head.

"Have you told the police?"

"Thank you, Aubrey…See! Even he thinks whoever sent this must be a nutter! Why the hell didn't you go to the police with this?"

Rose listened to the concerns voiced by her friends and turned away. She looked down at the envelope in her hand, at the American post mark and smiled.

"What could the police do?" she asked them, "In case you haven't noticed the letter comes from America! Besides, it's not a weirdo who wrote this, it's someone who knows what they're talking about. Blackheart was the man my ancestor loved. Of course I don't believe he's returned from the grave seeking revenge – that's a load of rubbish obviously! But I do know he was one of the cruellest pirates that ever lived. He's well documented if you know where to look and I'm sure I could find out more…"

"Well, you know, if you looked it up on the Internet there's probably a site devoted to both Blackheart and Rosie Scarlet" Aubrey replied shyly.

Sam stifled a giggle; it was all a bit surreal. Aubrey was at least eight years younger than them but his dubious taste in fashion contradicted his age, and surfing the net was something she couldn't imagine him being capable of. He wouldn't seem out of place in the 1800's, yet he was a mine of information and had to get it from somewhere; even if he was a bit odd. His cats followed him everywhere and in his thick black-rimmed specs, constantly muttering to himself in his thick West Country burr, he made an amusing sight in the neighbourhood. But he was kind and harmless enough.

"I expect" he continued, "That Blackheart, though I don't expect that was his real name, is probably very famous indeed and maybe more so in The States than over here."

"Really?" asked Sam, turning to Rose, "So why didn't you mention him before and, anyway, what was his real name?"

"Jack Bracken."

Rose answered quietly as though saying his name out loud would summon up the devil himself. Aubrey was surprised she knew so much already but then he supposed she got plenty of information through her contacts in the trade.

"What do you know about him Rose?" he asked.

"Nothing much, only that he and Rosie Scarlet were married and sailed The Phoenix together."

Aubrey stayed for supper. His interest in Rose's past was such that Sam was afraid he would stay the whole night. But Rose, exhausted emotionally and physically, and with pirates and swords swimming around her head, asked him to go home and check out the internet for her. With glee at being able to help his pretty neighbours he gathered his cats and hurried off home, the animals needing little coaxing with the promise of supper in the air.

*

Once again the night brought no relief from the heat and Rose felt dizzy with the combination of wine and pirate stories. She tossed and turned in a restless, haunted sleep as The Phoenix loomed into her dreams...

> *"...Storm that turns the ship through sea,*
> *Bring my lover back to me,*
> *Churning, burning, yearning bright,*
> *Bring him forth this heated night..."*

The Phoenix lurched and swayed as the sea, churned up by a thunderous storm, threw it round and around. Swords flashed and blood dripped and the moans and cries of men as they fell into dark water swirled inside her head.

The masts above her creaked and groaned deafeningly. She looked up at the ominous wooden beams as rain poured onto her face and stung her eyes.

"Rosie! Rosie!"

She turned to see the outline of a man, sword in one hand, and the other outstretched. She reached out to him and called his name but no sound came. A huge wave engulfed him and dragged him under the bubbling surface. Rose screamed and crawled toward where he fell but she too was dragged into the sea. Water poured into her lungs and nostrils as she fought for breath...

She awoke with a gasp. She released the cover from her tight grasp, her face wet with sweat and her hair damp and matted across her forehead. Trembling she reached for the lamp but before she could click it on light filled the room. From outside came the sound of the oak tree creaking and groaning. Disorientated Rose thought it might be raining but hope turned to horror as she heard the unmistakable sound of blades scraping wood and realised the air was still much too hot and sticky for the weather to have changed.

Frozen with fear she could neither move nor speak. She listened hard as strange noises accompanied by men's voices resounded in the street below. Her eyes closed as tears began to flow and she managed to slip beneath the sheets. She lay trembling and wished for morning to come. Hot and stifled she began to cry, quietly at first then noisily as huge sobs shook her whole body. The noise outside died and the room filled once more with the deafening silence of darkness. Exhausted, Rose drifted back into a dreamless sleep.

©2007 Cara Aldous

Chapter 3

Loud voices broke through her heavy sleep waking Rose much too quickly. Sluggish and confused she dragged herself over to the window. In the street below several of the neighbourhood had gathered by the oak tree, all talking at once; their raised voices shrill and excited.

The trunk of the tree was obscured by the crowd who fussed and pointed toward whatever blighted the ancient oak. Rose thought she could see something on the trunk but unable to make out what exactly she grabbed her dressing gown and hurried downstairs to join them.

Some turned in her direction as she drew nearer but she was oblivious to their stares. She gasped in disbelief and mounting horror at the sight that met her. Someone had carved deep into its old wooden trunk. It frightened her yet she could not help but admire its beauty; so intricate and painstakingly carved, curiosity overcoming the shock. An outline of a bird gazed out at her with familiarity, its hollow eyes aflame in the morning sun. She stifled a scream, the panic rising; she had seen this carving before. As she staggered forward, her knees threatened to give way. Babe, standing nearby with his parents, managed to catch her before she fell. He helped her down onto the kerb then stepped back.

"My sword!" she gasped.

"Rose?" Babe sounded puzzled and a little scared.

A murmur rippled through the gathering as it became clear that Rose may know who was responsible for this mindless act of vandalism. Sandra Knox tugged at her son's shirt and obligingly he moved away. Rose's face was white with fear. Sam, quietly watching now stepped forward, concerned and confused. Could Rose honestly know the person responsible? There certainly seemed to be a connection for she too had seen the carving before, only it was golden and adorned the handle of a sword. But how and, moreover, why would anyone want to carve a copy into their tree? Whoever had done this wanted them to think Rose was responsible, or stir her up. Perhaps it was the sender of the letter; the postmark had been dated only one month ago.

Sam became aware of the murmurs of disapproval rippling through their neighbours as they closed around them both. Rose sat quiet and ashen as the circle grew tighter, feeding her claustrophobia. Mavis Simkin, an old and respected resident stepped forward as their self-appointed spokeswoman. Sam had always mistrusted her sense of community but Rose always went out of her way to be polite. Mavis was one of those women who knew everyone's business, whether you wanted her to or not, and Rose always pointed out that this was useful as you never know when you might need someone like her. Sam, though, was wary of Mavis Simkin; she saw a gossip who liked to stir up trouble between neighbours. This point was about to be proved as Mavis jabbed a bony finger at a dazed Rose.

"Rose Scarlet, I might have known! What did you want to do that for, eh? Ruining a lovely tree that's stood here hundreds of years? I bet it's something to do with that weird junk shop of yours; yes that'd be it! It's that blinkin' junk shop!" Mavis finished triumphantly.

She looked around for approval and was rewarded with nods and grim faces that spurred her on.

"So what are you going to do about it? Nothing, I'll bet! You young ones are all alike, you all…"

"Shut up." Rose spoke quietly.

"What…?" spluttered Mavis, unused to being interrupted.

"You heard – shut up!" Rose replied louder.

"Well really!" Mavis turned to her audience, "Did you hear that? Never, in all my years, has anyone spoken to me like that! Not even my Arthur, rest his soul, would even dare talk to me in that tone! Fifty-five years I've lived here and never has anyone been so downright rude! If your mother was alive today…"

"Shut up!"

Rose was incensed at the woman's insensitivity; Mavis knew only too well how difficult Mother had been and how hard it had been for the young Rose growing up. She struggled to her feet and turned to face her accusers. Some shifted uncomfortably as she looked in turn at each one of them.

"I won't even try to pretend that I could be responsible for such a beautiful thing. Yes, it would be good advertising for my 'junk' shop. After all, I do sell Pirate things and this is a copy from a Pirate sword. A very good copy too. But no, I didn't do it though I wish who had would come forward so I can shake their hand!"

She turned and ran for the house, leaving behind the mutterings of surprise and tuttings of condemnation; Mavis Simkin stood in the centre of it all.

"Oh hell!" Sam muttered.

*

By midmorning the street was deserted, the heat already unbearable as Rose, Sam and Aubrey stood just a few feet behind the tree with the offending carving out of view. Sam and Aubrey between them had managed to placate most of their neighbours and Aubrey, in his caring and careful way, had even managed to satisfy Mavis that Rose had nothing to do with defacing the tree and had been equally shocked as much as the rest of them. And as that also explained Rose's out of character behaviour, Mavis went home contented, offering to make a cake to cheer her up.

"In the end though," Sam said, with a twinkle in her eye, "I just told them you were completely mad and they said that would explain a few things..."

©2007 Cara Aldous

Rose gaped in horror at her friend; sometimes it was impossible to tell if Sam was joking or serious. She hoped it was just a joke but it would explain the peculiar looks she got earlier as she passed some of her neighbours.

Aubrey had examined the carving closely once everyone had gone and was commenting now on how like a ships figurehead it was. As she glanced fearfully at the tree Rose shakily told of her nightmare and the sounds that had accompanied it.

"Oh that," shrugged Sam, "I heard it too; you didn't dream it."

"So I'm not going mad after all?" she asked, shaken that no-one had mentioned it before.

"No, 'course not! It was a hell of a bloody racket and everyone must have heard it. You'd think they'd put two and two together…"

"So you think that had something to do with the carving?"

"Quite possibly," Aubrey interrupted; "Though I don't really see why anyone would do such a thing…" he trailed off as he too looked in the direction of the tree.

His face turned white. He began to tremble as he stared at the oak.

"Aubrey, are you alright?" asked Sam, concerned; she was beginning to think she was the only sane one there.

"You look like you've seen a ghost!" Rose tried to sound light-hearted, dreading the reply and not daring to follow his gaze.

Slowly Aubrey raised his arm and pointed at the oak. "I think I have," he whispered.

Rose and Sam slowly turned to see a young man standing next to the tree, carefully examining the carving. Even from a distance they could tell he was good looking. Rose thought his profile was handsome in the extreme; the sort that existed only in romantic fiction and airbrushed film stars. He wore a tight fitting t-shirt and baggy jeans covered his long legs. He discarded his cigarette and stood back as though admiring the carved bird.

"Hey!"

Anger brought Aubrey to his senses at the total disregard for their beautiful tree. The grass around its roots was parched as straw and something like a lit cigarette could send the whole lot up in flames in an instant. It wasn't enough that it could probably die from being carved in this weather; it could end up burning to the ground and taking all their homes with it too.

The young man turned and grinned broadly in their direction. It was obvious he had made an impact; he had watched the morning's events from his window though no-one had paid him any attention at all then – too busy blaming the beautiful Rosie to notice a stranger in their midst.

Though it was evident to anyone with half a brain that the noise made as he moved in during the night was so easily a cover along with the huge removal vans parked around the tree blocking the whole thing from sight. Coincidence – huh?

*

The stranger walked over to them after stamping hard on the cigarette butt and apologised for being so careless. Rose smiled weakly at him as her heart pounded and her knees threatened to buckle under her.

Not a panic attack, she told herself, *just a gorgeous man.*

Too young for her though but cute and with a sexy American accent to match; not surprising her stomach was doing somersaults along with the butterflies. The young man spoke to Aubrey but he did not acknowledge him merely continued to stare. Unfazed the American returned the stare. Rose felt uncomfortable and cleared her throat loudly to break the silence.

"Um, my name's Rose," she said awkwardly as she held out her hand.

He took it gently, turning his intense green eyes on her. Up close he was by no means perfect and had a small scar above his top lip but something about him made her knees buckle and her heart flip. When he smiled his eyes twinkled and she blushed furiously, feeling seventeen again.

"Of course you are," he spoke softly, barely audible.

Sam watched as her best friend melted before her eyes. She didn't like this man one iota. Yes, he was okay looking and yes, his American accent was super-sexy but there was something about him which did not quite ring true. She was convinced he had something to do with the tree; and the flag and letter could quite easily have come from him too. It was much too much of a coincidence. She tapped his arm to break the spell on Rose and he swung round to face her.

Unnerved she took a deep breath, "Who the hell are you?"

"Your new neighbour," he replied coolly.

"What?" she wanted more; a name would be a good start.

"Your new neighbour," he replied again.

"Your bloody name?" she demanded again.

Aubrey replied, "Jack Bracken I believe."

The young man smiled in surprise, "Yes, that's right. Jack Bracken; moved in last night. Do you know me? Have we met?"

Aubrey said nothing. His colour drained again and he stumbled forward, the heat and shock combining to make his head spin. Jack caught him and between them he and Rose helped Aubrey home; a reluctant Sam following behind.

The cats stayed at a close distance and gathered around their master as he slumped into his favourite threadbare armchair. He wiped his face with his large white hanky which he pulled from his trouser pocket and studied Jack as he did so. Unperturbed Jack stood stony-faced, his arms by his sides and his head high. Rose felt suddenly obliged, standing in Aubrey's front room, to introduce them all. Jack nodded at them as they muttered curt hellos.

As Rose disappeared into Aubrey's kitchen to busy herself Sam seized upon the opportunity to question Jack once more.

"Where are you from?" she fired at him as soon as Rose was out of earshot.

"The States," he replied calmly fixing her with his eyes.

She coughed to compose herself; this was going to be difficult. "Why move in so late? Couldn't you wait till morning?"

"I had a long and tiresome journey and wanted to be in as quick as possible, okay?"

"No, it's not okay. You made a load of noise last night, totally freaking Rose out as well as annoying the rest of us…"

Rose rushed in and handed a glass of water to Aubrey; she'd heard everything.

"Uh, I didn't freak out, thank you very much!" she turned on Sam angrily, embarrassed by the way she made her feel two feet tall; it was Mother all over again.

"I'm very sorry if I scared you," Jack took Rose's hand gently in his, she blushed and he knew he had her.

"Its okay, no problem – I wasn't really scared. Just a nightmare – and the heat, you know!" she stammered.

Jack smiled and she melted into the carpet, "Well, if everyone's okay? Only I've got loads to do…"

"Oh yes, like what exactly – post another letter? Carve another tree?" demanded Aubrey jumping to his feet, his queasiness vanishing under his need to protect his neighbours.

"I don't see that what I do is any of your business…" Jack faced Aubrey, his fists clenching.

"Oh but it is if it's to do with scaring my good friends and neighbours! Is it, by chance, anything to do with Blackheart?" Aubrey stood his ground even though his knees trembled; he hoped it was not noticeable.

Silence fell on the room as the two men stood facing one another. Aubrey and Jack were of similar age and height but that was where the similarities ended. While Aubrey behaved and dressed like a man twice his age, Jack had the arrogance and swagger of a man ten years younger.

Aubrey studied Jack's face closely in the vain hope that he had hit a raw nerve. He tried to out-stare him but Jack's cold green eyes were so dark and frightening that he turned away. Stepping back he trod on one of his cats who hissed and spat. He bent down to placate the animal but as he picked it up it hissed and growled and leaped from his arms. Totally shaken and nerves fried Aubrey sat down hard and looked up into Jack's sneering face.

"He was a cruel and evil man," he muttered, totally defeated.

Jack sighed and moved toward the door. He stopped briefly and turned, "Yes, he was," he replied quietly before leaving them all in stunned silence.

*

Half an hour later, bewildered and astonished, Rose and Sam stood behind Aubrey peering at the computer screen in front of them. He clicked open a folder and excitedly showed them why he had been so overwhelmed when he had first set eyes on Jack. He explained how he had set about researching Rose's flag and had typed in Blackheart into the search engine which had brought up several sites.

"The first few were interesting enough but had no real information about him but," he continued as he deftly clicked the mouse, "The next one I tried was perfect!"

He clicked on the gallery tab which was now slowly bringing up a picture. The three of them watched intently as a copy of a painting slowly came into focus before their eyes.

"Hell!" Sam muttered and Aubrey nodded in response.

"I know, it's rather eerie, isn't it?" he replied.

Rose gasped in disbelief as, there on the screen in front of them, stood a pirate captain proud and arrogant looking back at them. He had a sword in one hand but the other side of the picture was missing. Without a doubt, the man watching them from the screen, with cold green eyes and a scarred lip, was their new neighbour Jack Bracken.

Chapter 4

Rose left early the following morning. Although she had endured another restless night she was not so disturbed now that both Aubrey and Sam had heard the blades and seen the light. They had discussed it at great length and all agreed it had something to do with their new neighbour and Rose's nightmare was not real. They had spent half the night discussing it. Jack Bracken was a mystery and Rose felt inexplicably drawn to him. When he had held her hand she felt an electric shock as they touched and was sure he had felt it too by the way he looked deep into her eyes and her very soul. Aubrey had warned they were cold and evil eyes and was convinced that, because Jack looked like Blackheart he must in some way be related to the pirate.

"And yet..." he said, "Jack Bracken could not possibly be his real name. It's too much of a coincidence!"

She pulled the front door to with a click trying not to disturb Sam who was still sound asleep. Jack's door opened suddenly stopping her in her tracks as she heard raised voices. Without thinking she stepped up into the doorway and pressed hard against her closed door. A man stepped onto Jack's path and turned angrily to face him; Jack himself was hidden from her view.

"You have been paid handsomely and Mister Roland expects results!" the man barked.

"And he'll get them," Jack replied, "He just has to be a little patient."

"Mister Roland has very little time and even less patience as you will find out to your cost! I expect to collect it from you no later than tomorrow…" the man turned and began to walk slowly up the path.

"Tomorrow? No way – that's crazy I only just got here…" Jack protested.

"The Sword of Aramoth is such a prized and rare possession that there is only a very small window within which it can be moved and sold. If we do not have the sword then the deal is off and…" the man hesitated, "If you value your life it will be here tomorrow."

"Are you threatening me? 'Cause I know all about the map – Roland's real reason for wanting the sword…" Jack stepped forward menacingly.

The man stopped in his tracks and turned; a little unnerved at finding himself face to face with Jack. Neither showed any sign of moving until at last the man turned to leave once more.

Black Nightmares to Scarlet Dreams

"I don't scare easily," Jack hissed at him, "And I certainly don't do anyone's bidding but my own. Roland will get what he wants but at a price. And if you want it by tomorrow then you must help me…"

He stepped up to the man's side and bent his head in a whisper. The man listened and nodded before climbing into the back of a waiting car. Rose had not noticed it before but its engine was running and she wondered how long it had been sitting there and, more importantly, whether the driver had seen her; he might tell the man who in turn could tell Jack.

The car sped off with a screech and Rose hesitated as she watched it disappear at the end of the road. She stepped slowly onto the path and was horrified as she came face to face with her new neighbour. He smiled at her and winked and she lowered her eyes to avoid his piercing stare. Realisation dawned that he had known she was there all the time for he was not in the least bit surprised and leaned on the wooden fence separating their gardens as he continued to stare at her. She blushed and turned away, feeling for all the world as though she were in one of those nightmares where you're naked and you've nowhere to hide. Feeling suddenly small and stupid she ducked her head and mumbled a quick goodbye as she rushed up the path and onto work. The sound of his laughter followed her as she fought back burning tears which pricked at her eyes.

*

Jack watched her leave, aware that he had upset her. He cursed his own stupidity; Rose was possibly his only ally in the street and he had to be careful. He knew she had heard some if not all of his conversation but it did not deter him from his plan; she could not possibly have understood. Besides he could easily win her over, she was no threat but her two friends might be harder to fool. Aubrey had hated him on sight and Sam seemed to dislike him too so he would have to tread very carefully whenever they were around.

He grinned as he thought of Rose again; she was very beautiful and he was drawn to her. Her innocence attracted him to her and he was going to enjoy seducing her; it would be easy money for once.

"...The time is ripe,
Listen to its word,
Take heed it is time,
Return to the sword..."

Darkness eclipsed his thoughts and his head begun to swim. He shook violently; he needed to lie down for a while but he had no time now. He cursed his bad luck at having picked up some sort of virus. Something had hit him hard once he had landed in this God forsaken country.

But little did he realise that the darkness had begun long before he left home and it was the darkness which had drawn him to England and his destiny. The darkness would show him the way.

*

Black Nightmares to Scarlet Dreams

As she hurried along Rose thought about Jack; he was exciting and dangerous and this attracted her to him. Usually Sam fell for his type and she avoided them like the plague but Sam had taken an almost instant dislike to him yet she was drawn inexplicably to him. She wanted to hate him, wanted to so much because she was sure he had something to do with the carving and the flag and letter. But she was fascinated by him, spellbound by his uncanny likeness to Blackheart.

She thought back to the picture; even though it had been grainy she felt certain she would see Captain Rosie Scarlet stood by Blackheart's side in the original painting. She had to check it out as soon as she could. Maybe Aubrey could find the complete version of it somewhere on the internet. Impossibly romantic thoughts of the two descendents brought together to rekindle the love of their ancestors appealed to her dreamy nature. Perhaps they were destined to be together and Jack Bracken was the one she had been searching for all these years; finally, she may have found the love of her life.

'*No good will come of your daydreams my girl! No-one will ever want you!*'

Her mother's shrill words broke into her thoughts of pirates and star-crossed lovers and she blushed. Maybe mother had been right; after all she was forty and in no way near settling down, not even a hint of a proposal had come her way. Sam on the other hand had been engaged several times and even kept the engagement rings as souvenirs. Rose, however, had been on very few dates; none ever matched up to her dreams. In fact no man had lived up to her ideal, until now.

She reached the end of Oak Avenue and, pondering this last thought, stood waiting to cross. At a break in the traffic she automatically stepped out onto the road. Halfway across a car swung away from the pavement and made a u-turn, nearly knocking Rose over in the process. Frightened she raced to the other side and fell to her knees behind a parked car, panting hard. The car which had almost hit her disappeared into the distance with a screech of tyres. She was certain she had seen it somewhere before. She was almost sure she had seen it only that morning. Shakily she turned toward her shop and headed up the High Street. As she drew nearer she became aware that things were not as they should be. When she reached the door to her shop it stood slightly ajar; the lock had been forced. Slowly she pushed the door hard with her outstretched hand. It swung open, lighting up a small patch of darkness inside. Sun shone in through the opening and she could just about make out the counter.

Tentatively she stepped inside and shouted out, "I've called the police! They're on the way now! So…" she trailed off, feeling ridiculous.

She strained her ears in the gloom and listened for a sound. Nothing. She moved behind the counter and looked wildly around; anyone could hide in the dark corners or behind the till. Quickly she flicked the switches and the shop filled with fluorescent light. Satisfied nobody was in the main part of the shop she ventured forward and peered into the gloom of the back rooms. The storeroom was dark but she thought she could see someone or something. She called out again but there was no sound so carefully she stepped through to the back. The switches were situated on the back wall here too and she made a mental note to get them changed. There had never been a problem before but it was becoming increasingly clear how dumb it was to have to walk through a dark shop to get to them.

As she approached the shelving just inside the storeroom she froze. Horror mixed with nausea rose in her throat and she swallowed hard. A man lay on the floor behind the shelving, his limbs sprawled. She opened her mouth to scream but no sound emerged as fear rooted her to the spot. She wanted to turn away but couldn't. She wanted to run but instead was terrified by the sight of the man still and quiet. A morbid curiosity overtook the terror as she looked a little closer at the body. His throat had been cut from ear to ear and the blood that oozed onto the storeroom floor glistened in the half light. She gagged and stumbled back, her legs gaining strength enough to turn and run out of the shop, down the High Street, and into Drummonds.

A young couple stood in the middle of the showroom admiring a leather sofa and chair. Rick stood next to them extolling the virtues of buying this particular suite. His patter was well rehearsed and he was in full flow as Rose burst in. Normally she waited while he finished with his customers. Normally she waved and he nodded and she would go and chat to Ruby. It was sacrilege to interrupt him mid-sale; unheard of. But this was an emergency and she could not wait.

"Rick!"

He nodded but continued his sales pitch.

©2007 Cara Aldous

"Rick!!!"

He turned and frowned, "Tell you what, sir, madam; the two of you have a think. I've got a couple out in the storeroom. Don't leave it too long mind, sold one only yesterday and a lady came in just a minute ago looking to buy. Shouldn't wonder she'll be back before lunch…Anyway, you take your time. I won't rush you and as you're good customers of mine I might be able to knock a few quid off…" Rick smiled and nodded at the couple.

They smiled and nodded at him in return before exchanging knowing looks. He whistled as he walked away from them and led Rose to the bottom of the store out of earshot of the couple.

"One born every minute, eh Rosie?" he chuckled, "Now, where's the fire?"

His smile faded as he took in her white face and shaking hands. He listened quietly and carefully as she explained about the car and the broken door and the dead body lying on her storeroom floor. Without waiting to hear anymore he called to Ruby to take care of Rose and the shop, and he hurried quickly out with his mobile phone clamped to his ear.

*

On reaching the shop he was aghast to find Rose had left the door wide open. The shop was in darkness as he entered and he crossed the small floor space as deftly as one accustomed to the layout. The shop flooded with light and he did a quick mental stock-take before stepping into the back room. Sure enough a man lay dead on the floor and it was obvious to anyone, even a layman like himself, there was nothing could be done for the man. Quickly he exited through the shop and out onto the pavement, with a valuable item tucked under his arm for safe-keeping. Carefully and swiftly he popped the boot of his car which conveniently for him today sat in front of Rose's shop; his own space at the rear of his store being occupied by his delivery van. It was definitely his lucky day in lots of ways. All the while he looked around to make sure no-one had seen what he was doing.

But in his haste he failed to notice that someone was watching; someone whose anger was burning and bubbling. Someone he would not knowingly want to make an enemy of; someone who could and would destroy him.

*

Having been calmed by Ruby and feeling she ought to see if he was okay Rose found Rick standing grim-faced outside her shop, waiting for the arrival of the police. She felt a little better that he too had seen the dead body for it had crossed her mind that maybe she had imagined it all. She had begun to feel that she was going mad, completely nuts. Now and again she glanced up and down the road looking for a flashing light and listening out for a siren. She was amazed when a white Ford pulled up quietly at the kerb and two very ordinary looking men got out and pulled out ID. They disappeared into the shop once satisfied nothing had been touched. Several minutes later the two men emerged, hard-faced and angry.

"A word sir, madam, if you don't mind," one of them spoke as the other gestured toward the shop.

It was more an order than a request and reluctantly Rose and Rick followed them in. They stepped through into the little storeroom which was now flooded with light. The dead man remained on the floor but was faint as though he were a ghost. Rose gasped and Rick frowned as one of the officers put his hand out. The image of the man was now on his palm. Carefully he lifted out a projector from a shelf and pointed it at the floor once more.

"I grant you, with the lights off it does look like someone's dead. But…Didn't either of you think to check?"

Rose shook her head and embarrassed, Rick muttered an apology as he glared at her. She shrugged and gave him a silent sorry with her eyes. It seemed that she had been the object of a sick practical joke. Either that or someone was trying to send her insane; it was certainly working as paranoia crept in and the panic took over.

"But, how do you explain the broken door?" Rose asked as they sat sipping hot sweet tea at the counter.

It had been the policemen who suggested the tea to calm her down when she had started to hyperventilate.

"Well, you have been broken into, I'll give you that. But my guess is you disturbed them when you arrived and they ran off empty-handed; simple as that. Mind, you might want to have an alarm installed? And those lights are in the wrong place. If you'd only switched them on you would've seen it was only a projection…" said one of the officers as he looked around him.

"It was pretty good though. And very realistic too. Though why anyone would want to do that I don't know. It was such an elaborate thing and no point to it. I mean, nothing was taken was it?" asked the other.

Rose looked around her aware that was the one thing she hadn't checked. At first glance all the stock seemed to be there. She quickly scanned everything, doing a mental stock-take; the cheap items were all in order as were the flags and clothes. Her eyes rested on the sword display. At a fleeting look nothing had seemed out of the ordinary. How on earth could she have missed that? It was glaringly obvious. There was a gap. A huge gaping hole. She cried out in dismay and rushed over to the wall where she began to push things off shelves and pull clothes from their hangers. She scoured the floor in case it had fallen. But it was gone.

"Oh my God, no!" she sobbed as she sank to her knees.

Rick knew immediately what she was looking for; the sword. Her special, priceless sword. He opened his mouth to speak but stopped as she began to rant and rave. Most of what she spoke was incomprehensible but it was apparent that she thought she knew who the culprit was; seems she had a new neighbour who had possibly sent her some threatening letter a month ago. So Rick stayed quiet and when she had finished, he calmly explained to the two officers all about her family heirloom.

"And this 'priceless' antique was hanging here, on the wall, for anyone to take down? For anyone who cared to touch it – hold it and everything?" they asked incredulously.

Rick nodded grimly. Rose nodded too, embarrassed at her own stupidity. It was obvious to anybody that she should have kept such a thing under lock and key. Obvious to her too now that it was gone. The officers were also surprised that she had kept what amounted to a dangerous weapon in such a reachable place. Though very young children could not possibly get at the display, others could. Any maniac could have walked in off the street and massacred them all in the blink of an eye. She slumped forward as the officer began to severely reprimand her. She knew she had been stupid, knew she was irresponsible too and she didn't need anyone to point it out. A sob escaped her lips and the policeman stopped. To lecture now was futile so instead he sighed and asked her to describe the sword though by now it would be miles away if not already out of the country.

"It has a gold hilt – handle," she began and faltered, "On it is carved a bird. It's a phoenix. She captained The Phoenix. That's why it was…a phoenix…It was passed down through the Scarlet family. Generation after generation hid it…And now I've lost it! Trust me!"

She began to cry. Rick put a hand on her shoulder. He looked wretched. The policemen, uncomfortable, stood silently surveying the shop. They turned to one another and shrugged in unison. Both knew it would be impossible to find such a sword. But each hoped that it would surface and be returned to the poor unfortunate woman who sat at their feet in tears. They moved toward the door.

"We'll see what we can do, Miss," said one kindly.

"Though I don't think that'll be much to be honest," added the other hastily.

They nodded acknowledgements at Rick as they turned to leave. Clutching desperately at straws, Rose suddenly remembered the conversation she had overheard that morning outside her home between Jack and the stranger. It was his car that had tried to run her over.

"Jack Bracken!" she shouted at the officers, "It wasn't him; I know it wasn't him! But he may know who - the man he was with this morning! He talked about a sword I heard him! And he tried to run me over!"

"Then you'd best give us this Jack's details and a description of this man too," said the officer frowning.

Both men sighed as they came back into the shop and sat at the counter. One flicked open his notebook as the other began questioning her once more. This was proving to be a very long day.

©2007 Cara Aldous

Chapter 5

"Well I can't say I'm surprised. I wouldn't put anything past him! Especially in view of who his supposed ancestor is! I knew he was a nasty piece of work soon as I saw him!" Aubrey snorted with such venom that Rose was taken aback.

She was sitting in his front room sipping from a cup of strong sweet tea which had been made in the old-fashioned way with loose tealeaves and a strainer, poured from a china teapot. The matching cup and saucer were bone china and made delicate chinking noises each time Rose placed the cup down onto the saucer. Her hands shook just as much with the worry she might chip the china as with the events which had happened that morning. She had relayed all word for word; from the conversation overheard on her doorstep to the 'dead body' in the shop and the missing sword.

Now, as she sat thinking about it all, she realised that the sword mattered more above everything else; the other frightening incidents of the day paled into insignificance and it wasn't the monetary value of the sword either, rather the sentimental worth. She had rushed straight round to Aubrey's as soon as the police had left. Rick had offered to wait for the locksmith to fix the door; she couldn't face staying there a moment longer. Not able to face a barrage of questions from Sam probably followed by an almost definite 'told you so' she had opted instead to find solace with Aubrey. She smiled inwardly as she thought of how she hurried past Jack's place, head down; finger's crossed; wishing he was not involved. She had repeated it a hundred times just like she used to when she was a child. That way it would be so.

She had hoped Aubrey would look at the theft of her sword in the same level-headed way with which he viewed every situation. But his obvious glee and delight at even the remotest possibility Jack could be involved threw her off balance and she wondered if perhaps she had made a mistake in coming to him for help. An uncomfortable silence descended on them and for a while all that could be heard was the chinking of the china and loud ticking of the huge clock which sat proud and alone in the centre of the mantelpiece. Every sound was magnified. Aubrey spoke first, breaking the silence as he voiced his thoughts aloud.

"What I don't understand though, is why he stole the sword in such a cruel way? It doesn't make sense."

"No, it doesn't, does it? I mean all he had to do was just take it or even come into the shop and take it when the shop filled or something."

She sat forward; glad at least that Aubrey had let Jack off the hook.

But he hadn't, "More like something," he murmured, "If he'd asked you would have handed it over with a smile and a kiss."

"No, I wouldn't!" she lied, "Besides, we don't know it was Jack took it, not for sure."

He paused, "Not for certain, I agree. But it was you Rose who first accused him of taking it; you who overheard his conversation. You, Rose, who saw the car outside his house, the same car you say that very nearly ran you over. And besides all that it is you, Rose, who Jack clearly has an unhealthy interest in…" He stopped, embarrassed; he had gone too far.

She blushed at his accuracy, feeling secretly pleased that what she saw in Jack's eyes as he gazed into hers, Aubrey had also noticed. A faint smile tugged at the corner of her lips and her stomach did back flips.

*

Aubrey felt sheepish. He knew he was old-fashioned and boring to a woman like Rose but he had a soft spot for both her and Sam. He was a good eight years younger than both of them; probably the same age as the American but knew it seemed more like ten years older. He knew he was no pin-up but lived in hope that one day she might see him differently; that one day she might fall into his arms and finally see what she and all the other women were missing. A peck on the cheek would be enough to carry him through for a while but that was looking less and less likely. There was such an obvious attraction between Rose and Jack but one which he could not fathom. He was angry. Angry that Jack's youthfulness and American charm had won Rose's heart in a way he, Aubrey, never could. But also hopeful that once she saw through the chat and the macho bullshit, she would see Jack Bracken for the phoney he most assuredly was.

Rose only believed they were close because their ancestors love for one another had spanned the centuries. Aubrey scoffed at such rubbish; it was only a matter of time before Jack Bracken or whoever he was showed his true colours but until then Rose would remain under his spell. Anger seething he jumped to his feet and began to pace the room; he had to find a way to force Jack Bracken to show his hand.

*

Rose watched as Aubrey moved back and forth. The cats which had been reclining on the arms and back of his chair stretched their claws and backs and jumped down to join him. She stifled a giggle and pushed the comedy of it all to the back of her mind. This was no time to burst into hysterics; she needed to think calmly and clearly and pull back from the brink of panic she was teetering on the edge of. She went over the events once more, piece by piece, as she had relayed them to the policemen. And, just like the policemen, came to the conclusion that there was no hard evidence that Jack Bracken had anything to do with it at all. He may have some odd friends but she knew very little about him to be able to make any informed opinion. And there was no proof that he had even been near her shop. After all, he would have passed her, wouldn't he? Aubrey believed him to be responsible just because he was better looking and American. Aubrey hated all things American, when it suited. Suddenly he stopped pacing. The cats jumped to attention at his feet and waited patiently. Rose held her breath. An idea was brewing and she somehow knew she wouldn't like it.

"What we need is proof," he said, "So we have to search his house and get it."

Rose did not like it and stared reprovingly at him. He ignored her and began again to pace up and down. This time the cats, bored by this game, went back to their places on the chair. Rose watched them before turning her glare back to Aubrey.

"What I think is Jack slipped into the shop when you ran along to Drummonds after finding the 'body'. He could have slipped in and out, unnoticed that time of the morning. And it was probably his visitor who set up the projector and his visitor who came back and picked him up again. All this was done before Rick or you even stepped foot outside Drummonds. It's quite obvious, when you think about it, isn't it?" Aubrey finished triumphantly, expecting her to be pleased.

"If it's all so obvious, how come the police didn't think so?" She asked, angrily, "How come they said I should stay away from Pirate movies and books for a while, eh? Not for my health, was it?"

"That was uncalled for," Aubrey agreed. "But the police, Rose, are so snowed under with paperwork these days that it's not in their interest to investigate something that's pure conjecture. It's much easier to hand out a crime number for the insurance and file it away."

Rose caught her breath, "Oh, Aubrey! The insurance! I haven't notified them yet!" She buried her face in her hands.

"Don't worry, we'll sort it," Aubrey placed his hand awkwardly on her head and patted her hair, "I'll make another pot of tea then we'll call the insurance people…And then we'll pay Jack's house a little visit."

Rose stiffened but Aubrey continued, "I really do believe that Jack Bracken has plenty to hide, not least your sword. I think he's responsible for sending you the flag and letter. I also believe he's responsible for the carving on the oak as well as the stealing of the sword. And it all somehow comes back to Captain Blackheart – he's obviously trying to frighten you."

"But why?" Rose asked pointedly, "What has he got to gain from that?"

Aubrey went over to his computer which sat humming, its screen flickering, in the corner. Swiftly and adeptly he clicked onto several programmes before beckoning Rose over to join him.

"Do you remember the picture I showed you the other night?" he asked but did not want a reply, "Well, I found a copy of the complete one…"

Rose watched in amazement as another part copy of the old oil painting materialised onto the screen. This time it was bigger and much, much clearer. Blackheart stared out of the screen at them, his emerald green eyes cold and cruel. He wore long black boots and breeches with a long black greatcoat billowing behind him. On his head sat a black tricorn hat, locks of dark long hair flowing beneath. His lips curled into a wicked smile and a scar cut down from his nose to his lip. Rose breathed in sharply. Yet the right-hand side seemed to be clearly cut off and she longed to see the whole painting.

"Yes, it could be Jack today, couldn't it?" Aubrey smiled up at her, "The coldest and cruellest Pirate that ever lived! Look at the sword, though."

Rose could not take her eyes from Blackheart's gaze; it fascinated her. "Where's the whole picture?" she asked, "I thought you said you found the complete one?"

Aubrey shook his head sadly, "Couldn't find that, I'm afraid, I meant to say a clearer one. But don't worry, I'll find it! Still a few hundred more sites to try! But, the sword Rose, the sword; look!"

Sure enough; the sword held in the left hand of Blackheart could have been the same sword that had been in Rose's family for generations; the same one that was stolen. Even she had to agree it was too much of a coincidence.

*

Several hours later Rose stood in Jack's silent, empty kitchen. Sam had agreed to be in on the whole stupid idea and had coaxed Jack into going to the pub with her on the premise of getting to know all the things about Rose that her best friend would share with him. Whilst Sam whisked Jack off to their local, Rose and Aubrey had broken into and entered unlawfully his home. Rose was desperately unhappy about the whole thing and only agreed to go along with it so that she could prove his innocence. The kitchen was clean and clinical and looked barely used. There was not an ounce of clutter on the worktops, unlike every other household in suburbia. The cupboards contained little more than the basic pots and pans found in most rented accommodation, and there was no food, not even a ketchup bottle. In fact it looked more like a house between tenants.

Annoyed at not having found anything in the kitchen Aubrey stomped down the hall and into the front room. Rose followed gingerly behind, afraid at any moment Jack would return home and discover them. She held her breath at every sound and her heart threatened to burst from her chest it pounded so hard; this was not good for her. She hummed softly; she couldn't afford a panic attack now. She followed Aubrey through the open door but as she stepped inside the front room she stopped in amazement.

The floor was littered with papers and books. Some had been sorted into higgledy-piggledy piles. Aubrey was knelt in front of one such pile, leafing through it. He stopped long enough to take out a pencil and notebook from his jacket and flipped it open ready. Reluctantly, Rose knelt and began to carefully look through a large pile near the door. They sat for almost an hour sifting through the multitude of papers. Rose was getting cramp and increasingly agitated; she knew they were pushing it if they stayed much longer. There was nothing even remotely interesting to her, only maps and pictures of places she did not recognise.

Now and then Aubrey would murmur and nod to himself and furiously scribble on his pad. He showed a printed sheet to her but it meant nothing; only a list of internet sites, most of which she knew he had already tried himself. She urged him to hurry up and absently turned her attention to a pile she had not yet looked through. She ran her fingers up and down the papers and stopped. There appeared to be something small tucked in the centre. Carefully she lifted the top papers off to reveal a notebook identical to the one Aubrey was using. She picked it up and flicked it open. Several familiar words jumped out at her; Blackheart, The Phoenix, Captain Rosie Scarlet and something about a Sword of Aramoth. Her heart sank as her eyes alighted on her home address written on a page of its own.

"Aubrey, I think this could be what you're looking for?" she whispered.

Aubrey reached out and took the pad off her. His face lit up as he scanned the pages. The handwriting neat and tiny, so much information was crammed into the small book. His excitement mounted as he flicked over the pages. Rose glanced at her watch; they had been there over an hour now and she was increasingly worried they would be found out.

"Aubrey, we really should…" She began but he was too engrossed to hear her, "Aubrey! Come on! Put it back and let's go!"

"Hmmm?" He looked up and saw her motioning at her watch.

Rose watched open-mouthed as he closed the notebook and, instead of putting it back into the pile, slipped it into his pocket. Then, horror mounting, she stared aghast as he tore off sheets he had written on from his own notebook and stuffed them into his pocket. Carefully he placed his now empty pad in the centre of the pile and covered it back up with the top layer of papers.

*

Black Nightmares to Scarlet Dreams

Rose sat in her kitchen, her heart finally slowing to normal. Well, normalish; it wasn't every day she broke into someone's house and robbed them. Her face flushed as she thought first of what they had done then of what they had uncovered. Jack seemed to have had plans for her well before he even arrived in England, according to Aubrey. She sighed and reached a hand into her pocket; Aubrey had not been the only thief. Carefully she placed a card down on the table in front of her and peered at it closely. It was a postcard reproduction of the painting Aubrey had found of Blackheart. But this painting was in its entirety.

In it Blackheart stood proudly, as before; one hand gripping a sword, but the other wrapped around a woman. The woman wore a beautiful silk gown of ruby red and a rose in her deep red hair. Her long flowing locks cascaded over her shoulders and she stood proud and defiant by the side of her man. Rose was looking at a carbon copy of herself.

Rose shivered as she tried to look deep into Blackheart's cold green eyes again; how could a woman love such a man? Unable to focus on him for long she turned her attention to the sword. Although it was difficult to make out completely, Rose was certain Aubrey was right; it was her sword.

The two pirates were Blackheart and Rosie Scarlet; doubles of Jack and her and, as she gazed at the ancient lovers she made a promise; first thing in the morning she would go and see Jack Bracken and confront him with all she knew. No more running away, no more burying her head in the hope it would all disappear. And maybe, just maybe, Jack would open up to her.

Chapter 6

Unable to settle into a longed for comforting sleep, Rose woke in the early hours; her thoughts turning to Jack. Her usual insecurities and inability to believe in her own decisions had weakened her determination to such an extent that having it out with him had turned into hopefully having a quick chat, but only if he felt like it. She silently scolded herself. Aubrey stealing Jack's notebook without a care to what he would do when he found it gone had thrown her off course completely and, the more she thought about it, the more she realised that they had, in fact, entered and stolen extremely unlawfully. Jack could have them prosecuted if he wanted and neither of them had a leg to stand on. Quite simply put: they were in the wrong.

She sat up as the sun rose and rubbed any sign of sleep from her eyes. She considered that Jack must have realised by now that they had been in his house. She felt upset by the thought he would think her a common little thief. How he saw her seemed to matter and she tried in vain to push ideas of love to the back of her mind. She should be angry; it was possible he had used her in some way. He had almost certainly scared her and pretended to like her. She stopped. Why would he even bother? He had no need if his sole purpose had been to get her sword. Thoughts and ideas whirled around her head; maybe he did like her. After all, she liked him; for her it was love at first sight.

    Loud whispered voices floated up to her open window. Carefully she climbed out of bed and moved to see what was going on. Jack stood on his path; shaking hands with the stranger she had seen yesterday. In the stranger's other hand was an object which he seemed to struggle with. It hung by the side of him and he had great difficulty holding on to it. It was narrow and made a metallic clunk as it dropped down onto the path. Jack hushed the stranger angrily and pushed him toward the gate. The metal sound shuddered through her as she fought back tears. The object was so clearly a sword and, though it was wrapped in cloth, Rose knew it must be her sword. Her heart sank and she turned away from the window.

*

Jack wanted Mr Roland's heavy to leave quickly and quietly. He had hoped the deal to be done before Rose had any idea of what was going on, but his stomach knotted as he caught a glimpse of her curtain move. He could not be certain she had seen anything but had to find out for sure. Quickly he ushered the man into his waiting car but, relaxed that his job was now done, the man was in no hurry to go. As he chatted and laughed, Jack nodded in reply though his attention was on Rose's window. As far as the man was concerned, Jack had his cash and the job was done. Jack knew differently. He knew once the sword was in Mr Roland's hands, he would realise it was not the Sword of Aramoth. This was why it was so important to keep his cool, say nothing. Sweat formed on his upper lip and his hands shook as finally the car pulled away. He had to see Rose. He watched the car until it turned the corner out of view. He turned around and his breathed out sigh of relief caught in his throat as he spied Rose looking accusingly at him from her bedroom window; she had seen everything.

*

Rose tried desperately to focus her eyes on the carving of the phoenix on the oak; anything to stop herself from thinking about what she had seen. She stifled a sob; it would be a lasting reminder of her sword. She watched tearfully as the stranger drove off with it and rued the day that Jack Bracken had walked into her life. She tried fruitlessly to read the number plate but her eyes were so blurred with tears that she could only make out the letter Y and even that she was unsure of. She shut her eyes tightly and clutched the curtain which was now tucked around her. Tears streamed down her cheeks and she felt useless and wretched.

She opened her eyes and blinked hard against the bright sunshine flooding into her room, gradually focusing on Jack. To her horror he was standing at the top of her path looking up at her. As he opened the gate she panicked and, without thinking, rushed down before he could reach the bell.

Flinging open the door she came face to face with him. She stumbled back aghast as he leaned in and brought his face up close to hers.

"We need to talk," he whispered into her hair.

His warm breath sent a shiver through her and her heart raced at both the excitement and fear of being so close to him. Suddenly aware she was only dressed in her short nightie, she tugged at the hem, wondering why on earth she hadn't put her dressing-gown on. He looked down at her breasts and she instinctively moved her hand up to cover them.

"It…It's not convenient right now," she stammered, "Sam's in bed…

"No, she's not – I watched her leave an hour ago," he said with a smile.

"Yes, she is, she must be," Rose was shaken, "She's on the late shift…"

"I saw her leave over an hour ago…" Jack repeated.

Rose blushed, furious at her stupidity for putting herself in such a position. She should have checked Sam was in before opening the door. She heard her mother's voice berating her for being so irresponsible; he could be a dangerous man, after all she knew nothing about him. Yet instinctively she felt safe. He moved closer and she could feel the heat of him through her whole body. She longed for him to take her in his arms but instead stood back to let him in. She steered him toward the kitchen then raced up the stairs two at a time and dressed hurriedly.

Black Nightmares to Scarlet Dreams

*

"...Time comes near,
All becomes clear,
Black is coming back,
Back to claim to truth..."

Jack stood in the kitchen quietly contemplating his next move. The darkness descended on him every time he thought about Rose and what he had done to her. Maybe it was shame; something he knew plenty about. Shame had dogged him throughout his life. Shame had gotten him into no end of trouble. It ran in the family.

He could hear Rose moving around upstairs. He knew he scared her and that she was upset and angry with him. If only he could tell her; he was sure she would understand. He listened to her footsteps on the stairs and smiled as she entered the kitchen.

*

Rose smiled confidently trying to conceal her feelings; inside she quivered like jelly. She moved past him and put the kettle on, clattering cups and spilling coffee which instantly gave her awkwardness away. As she poured the boiling water into the cups she became aware of his eyes burning into her. Avoiding his stare she offered a cup to him but, to her dismay, he did not take it. She placed it next to him and sat at the table, warming her hands on her own steaming cup. She took a sip and looked up at him. She had to stifle an anxious giggle; he stood with feet apart and hands behind his back like a captain on the deck of his ship. She found herself wondering what it would be like to kiss those full lips and have those strong arms envelope her.

"So," she said at last, "Talk."

"I had an interesting evening last night, with Sam – How about you? Did you and – Aubrey isn't it? – Did you both have an interesting evening too?"

Rose blushed but said nothing. She didn't think he really wanted an answer, besides he was the one who owed her an explanation. She waited to hear his apology for stealing and selling her sword. Her silence confirmed what he already knew.

"As I thought. Well, let me bring you up to speed on a few things. First off, my name's Jack Bracken and I moved to this country in search of my ancestors. One of whom was Captain Blackheart, the notorious pirate who hung for his crimes."

"He was married to Rosie Scarlet, your ancestor I believe? Small world, huh? For that really is all there is to it – coincidence. I was as blown away as, I guess, you all were." He stopped and raised his eyebrows.

Rose nodded and lowered her eyes, shutting out his unnerving stare.

"It's said they were deeply in love," he continued, "So much so that he would do anything for her – even die. He certainly killed for her."

His quiet tone altered as he threw back his head and laughed, "Love! Hah! Is it love that leads one to betray another? Is it love that watches as he heads for the gallows?"

Rose shifted uneasily in her seat as he ranted, anger contorting his handsome features. His green eyes grew cold and dark and suddenly she was afraid. She cursed inwardly at her cowardice, and at Jack for making her experience a multitude of feelings in so few minutes.

"He loved her! That much is certain," he spat angrily, "But did she love him? She stole his heart – she stole everything!"

"Just like you did!" she snapped back.

He stopped and looked at her, his expression softening for an instant. He frowned inwardly and shrugged. He put a hand up to his head and massaged his temples as though his head ached. After a while he continued, quiet and subdued.

"Anyhow, as I said, though I am Blackheart's descendent meeting you and moving into the same street as you is nothing more than coincidence. Pure and simple. I even done a load of research on our ancestors and the ship they sailed together. But," he stopped and grimaced, "You already know that, don't you?"

"What? I…I don't know what you mean!" Embarrassed Rose stared at the brown liquid inside her cup. "Seems we're equal on that score," she muttered.

"It's no good denying it, I know what you did," he shook his head sadly, then spoke softly to himself, "I like you; am drawn to you; am in love with you. I can see in you what he undoubtedly saw in her."

"I…I don't know what you mean!" Rose whimpered, not quite believing what she was hearing; her heart beat faster and her palms sweated.

©2007 Cara Aldous

"Really? Really, Rose? Not a clue, huh?" he paused, his eyes twinkled, "Then let me refresh your memory..."

Rose shivered as he smiled at her. She knew what was coming and felt powerless. She was frightened of him yet wanted him badly. She was confused; disorientated. Here she was sitting in her own kitchen being accused of stealing by a thief – that was rich!

"…My notebook, which contained all my research, has disappeared! Not only that it has been replaced by a book belonging to someone called Aubrey Twissell. Now, how do you imagine that happened? Maybe I should pay him a visit? Perhaps I can beat it out of him?"

Rose jumped to her feet and stood facing him, with chin raised and anger in her eyes. How dare he try to intimidate her! How dare he come into her life, turn it upside down, steal her sword and threaten her friends! She looked defiantly into his eyes; and melted.

*

Meeting her gaze Jack moved so that his face was inches from hers. Her body shook with anger and he shivered with anticipation. He wanted her, wanted so badly to take her in his arms, to protect her. But, in her eyes, he was the threat. His head swam as the darkness descended once more and he stepped back from her, turning away.

> *"…Your love has fled,*
> *Your love was dead,*
> *Black is back,*

Black Nightmares to Scarlet Dreams

Avenge my Black..."

*

Rose felt dizzy with the power she seemed to have over this volatile man. He could not keep her gaze and had backed down. Now it was her turn to make him squirm.

"Well, what about you?" she began, shakily at first then stronger as he hung his head, "You stole my sword! Don't think I don't know – I saw you! This morning! Giving my sword to…to…"

He turned very slightly and peered over his shoulder at her through his lashes. Then he spoke, so quietly that she could barely hear him.

"It's mine."

"What? What did you say?" she had to grasp the side of the sink to steady herself for the onslaught.

"The sword is mine," he spoke louder as he turned to face her. "I stole nothing from you."

"No, no! You…you're wrong! The sword was, no, is mine! The Scarlet family have kept it hidden for years! How can it be yours when it has been in our attic since before you were born?"

He moved in closer. His face so close she could feel his breath, smell his aftershave. She could see the stubble on his face, the beads of sweat on his forehead. The darkness in his eyes had lifted and they shone, deep and green. So deep she was afraid she would drown in them. Hypnotised by him she was completely and utterly under his spell.

"The sword," he said quietly and brushed her lips with his, "Is mine."

The kiss jolted through her body like a bolt of electricity. Surprised, Rose stumbled back and felt his strong arms grip her tightly. Her hand instinctively touched her mouth and she shuddered; this time with pleasure. Shaking, she reached out and touched her fingers to his lips. She followed the line of his scar and it was his turn to shiver. He tightened his grip and she gasped at the crushing intensity of his hold. He kissed her again, slowly at first then hungrily as she responded. A murmur escaped his lips and he tried to pull away.

"Don't," Rose whispered, "Don't stop."

He sighed deeply and buried his face in her neck, breathing in her sweet scent.

"I've waited an eternity for this," he said softly as he began to kiss her neck.

Chapter 7

Aubrey was troubled. What he had discovered in Jack's notebook worried him. He knew Rose liked Jack and she had seemed touchy when he kept the notebook. He was certain she would question anything he found simply because she had thought it wrong to take it in the first place. He turned another page and sighed heavily. He placed it on the arm of his chair, moving to the window to think. He peered out onto the deserted street.

A fan hummed behind him moving the hot air around the small room. He looked out at the cloudless blue sky; the weathermen could predict no end to the ghastly, oppressive reign of sun. The evenings continued to be unrelenting, the air still and suffocating and as unbearable as the days were long.

Aubrey's usual summer routine of watering his garden had begun in earnest at first. But the heat and subsequent hosepipe ban prevented him from doing even that small task now and the time on his hands had become intolerable. He scanned his garden where a multitude of colours should have been but only a handful of withered flowers now hung their heads. Even the shrubs and bushes which lined his borders struggled to stay upright. His garden, once tidy and beautiful, looked messy and unruly, only the weeds capable of survival in these desert conditions. No longer able to bear looking at the brown mess he turned his attention to his mewing charges.

Lovingly he poured ice cold milk into several saucers and watched a few moments as the cats gladly lapped it up. Then he made himself some iced tea and returned once more to the notebook in the hope of finding something; anything to recriminate Jack Bracken and something which Rose would have to believe.

The first few pages had contained around thirty or more websites with small notes about each one: Sword of Aramoth; Eighteenth Century Pirates; a reference to Captain Blackheart; and Captain Rosie Scarlet. One page was headed 'Blackheart and Scarlet' and told the story of their love and how they came to captain The Phoenix. Legend has it they met when Rosie Scarlet, dreaming of a life at sea, dressed as a man and joined the crew of a merchant ship bound for the Caribbean. Blackheart's band of pirates attacked the ship and she was discovered. But, instead of using then discarding her as was his usual wont with women, Blackheart was so impressed by her courage and vigour that he spared her life. They became inseparable and pretty soon lovers.

They wed amid much furore from the crew of The Phoenix; women were considered bad luck and so as a rule banned from the ship.

But Blackheart was cruel and feared, and few argued with him and lived. His crew were made up of desperate men wanted for crimes against England and The Crown yet they followed Blackheart without question, benefiting financially from his evil notoriety. Their greed for gold and riches kept them content to a degree. All who sailed the Eighteenth Century seas knew his reputation and feared him. Blackheart was the cruellest pirate of them all. Yet Rosie Scarlet fell in love with him.

Aubrey shuddered as he imagined Jack Bracken's cold green eyes, penetrating his very soul, crushing his will to a pulp. He put the notebook to one side and pulled a handkerchief from his trouser pocket. He mopped the cold sweat from his brow and, removing the heavy-framed glasses which dug into the sides of his nose, wiped his eyes.

Picking up where he left off he began to read how Blackheart had become obsessed with Rosie Scarlet; his jealous rages erupting every time a man dared to look at her. One instance recorded was of a young shipmate who smiled at Rosie as she passed by then made a playful grab for her. The man had his arms sliced off then was thrown to a watery grave tended by the sharks circling The Phoenix. It was rumoured that sharks followed her wherever she sailed in the knowledge there would be plenty of fresh meat.

Aubrey gulped down his iced tea and tried to read on. His thoughts turned to Rose. If Jack really was a descendent of Blackheart's he could be extremely dangerous. It was apparent by the way he had written down every word of the vicious and bloodthirsty exploits of the dreadful pirate that he was proud to be a relative. Aubrey feared that Jack was in awe of the pirate and, maybe, even believed himself to be the reincarnation of the man. He certainly had Blackheart's cold eyes and the scar on his lip; Blackheart's caused by a lucky swipe from a victim before the poor wretch met his fate by a fatal blow from the pirate's sword. Jack's probably caused by a simple accident or even self mutilation. It was quite possible he simply may have been born with it.

Whatever the reason his likeness for the pirate must have fuelled his obsession and no-one, not even Rose, could fail to notice the uncanny resemblance. The two were centuries apart yet almost identical in looks. Could it be they were also identical in temperament? Aubrey shivered at this, the cold creeping up through his body; goosebumps erupting. He must find something that would show Jack for the cruel person he without a doubt aspired to be. He had to prove to Rose that to fall for Jack Bracken would probably be the last thing she would ever do. Aubrey read on carefully.

The words mingled into one and he had to put the book down again and his thoughts turned bizarrely to his dear old mum. She had been a cruel and domineering woman; just as Rose's mother had been yet the two women, so much alike, hated one another although both had been too hypocritical to say so. His mum had been strong and overbearing and would allow him very little life away from her and the confines of their home.

As he began to grow and develop so her heart had conveniently grown weak. Many a time she had clutched at her chest when Aubrey should have been on his way out to meet a girl. On the odd occasion that he called her bluff he had found it impossible to concentrate and would inevitably end the evening early to rush home. Word soon got around that he was a mummy's boy and, coupled with his deteriorating eyesight and, consequently, looks his luck with girls vanished much faster than it had begun. His clothes were from jumble sales, but had been okay by the standards of the late eighties. Unfortunately, the thick glasses he was eventually required to wear were the only things females focused on and gradually his confidence, along with the opposite sex, vanished completely.

As he got older he settled himself into work which satisfied his need for company. He also attended evening classes which mum actually approved of and as a consequence didn't object to his leaving her one evening a week. This was on the proviso that he returned home promptly afterward. Gratifyingly he found he had an aptitude for computing and gained qualification after qualification, enabling him to earn good money from home too.

He handed mum his wage packet every month for his keep and in return she continued to provide his clothes. By this time he was past caring where they came from, although he had an inkling they were still from jumble or charity shops. Oblivious to her oppressive behaviour Aubrey happily settled into the life they had together.

Mum had raised him alone; his father a dim and distant memory having walked out when Aubrey was just two years old. So, with Aubrey her sole focus, she brought him up to respect women and never to use or abuse them but also, most importantly, to look after his mum. Aubrey coped admirably with her suffocating him, even into adulthood when any normal young man would have rebelled. Mainly he thought it cruel to abandon her the way his father had and so put up with her domineering behaviour unquestioningly.

She died one winter's night, passing peacefully as a storm howled and he had been blissfully unaware until he took in her second cup of morning tea and noticed the first one remained untouched by her bedside. Once she was buried he felt freer than he ever had but being a creature of habit continued to live in the only way he knew how. The only concessions being that he now shopped in M&S and his money was his own to do with as he pleased; which was to put it away for a rainy day that was still yet to come. Over the years he had amassed a small fortune.

Rose too had suffered many similarities to Aubrey and, in his opinion; they should have been well suited. Although he was eight years her junior he was more mature than his peers and had a lot to offer someone like her. But she could not see past the glasses, hair and clothes either. It never occurred to him to try to improve his outward appearance; buy smarter glasses and trendier clothes, get a haircut rather than a 'short-back-and-sides'. Instead he contented himself with being Rose and Sam's friend too. He knew they laughed at him; making fun of him behind his back.

As he read on through Jack's notes; the scribbling of an obviously tortured mind, he wondered how Rose had failed to see the insanity of their smooth talking charming egocentric American neighbour. He began to scan the pages speedily, fed up with reading about the increasingly sickening escapades of Blackheart the Pirate.

"Is there nothing to show he was human?" he muttered.

His eyes fell upon something. At last things were starting to become interesting. The crew of The Phoenix fed up with Blackheart's obsession with Rosie and believing her to be the curse and ruination of them all, mutinied. The Phoenix had put ashore for some much needed repair and provisions; they were beached somewhere along the coastline of the Bahamas. One night, after a bout of particularly heavy drinking the crew, empowered by rum and overwhelmed by superstition, rounded on Blackheart and Scarlet. They were caught unaware as they slept and were roped together, though none of the men had the stomach to mete out a punishment of their own. They left them ashore, tied to the wooden landing of the nearest Port as The Phoenix set sail with a new command.

The British governing body of the Colony had been astounded the next morning when they discovered their captives. At once two of the world's most notorious pirates were imprisoned and Blackheart sentenced to be hanged. Rosie Scarlet, as was required by law for a woman, was put to trial. On discovery that she was pregnant and, not wanting to appear as brutish as their enemies, the authorities ruled that she be saved the gallows.

Aubrey paused; this would confirm Rose's family connections. Aubrey had used her father's research and managed to trace the family line almost back to Pirate Rosie. Now he had the missing piece to complete it. That would mean also that Rose was a descendent of

Blackheart too. He shook his head sadly at the implications; he wrongly or rightly believed insanity was genetic and Jack was almost certainly unbalanced. His line of thought took him to the conclusion he wanted; if Rose found out that her and Jack could be related it would most definitely stop her from entering into a relationship with him. At the very least it was worth a try although he would have to cross reference and check the details, to be one hundred per cent certain.

Excited, he read on. Blackheart was hanged by the neck for all to witness and his body hung in a gibbet at the harbour mouth to warn other Pirates of the fate that awaited them. It was recorded that he muttered curses under his breath at his mutinous crew, the judge, the hangman; promising his ghost would haunt them all for a thousand years before dragging them down into the pits of hell with him. Many had been unnerved by his steady, quiet words. But none more so than his beloved Rosie whom he vowed a never-ending revenge upon, cursing her family for eternity and promising his ghost would never rest until a suffering equal to that which he had endured was visited upon her; her children; and her children's children.

The writing stopped. Quickly Aubrey flicked the pages, hoping to find more. He hoped that Jack had written his own curses and thoughts, but that would be too good to be true. He was in no hurry to tell Rose any of the awful, horrible things her ancestor Blackheart was responsible for. Even though the things he had learned so far could turn her against Jack it would also, undoubtedly, give her nightmares. And she was having those already.

Black Nightmares to Scarlet Dreams

Halfway through the book he found more but it was nowhere near as interesting. He glanced at a page that spoke of buried treasure and dismissed it for the fantasy it was. Only in books of fiction and films did such a thing exist. Another page was devoted to a sword called 'The Sword of Aramoth'. This was supposedly the sword belonging to Blackheart. It was said to be a prized possession and never left his side.

"How come he didn't use it against the mutineers, then?" Aubrey chuckled aloud.

It was no surprise to read the now familiar description of a golden hilt bearing the head of a phoenix; the same bird now carved into Oak Grove's old tree. There was a sketch of the sword too, drawn by someone adept and artistic. He flicked over the page and drew his breath at a simple lined drawing, each one numbered. It was the phoenix again but this time undoubtedly a template for the carving of the tree. So Jack had been responsible after all. Aubrey chuckled with glee; he couldn't wait to show Rose. He faltered; Rose might not listen to him though. What would really work was if he could get Jack to confess it all right in front of her. She might not look at the notebook or believe anything he, Aubrey, told her but if it came straight from the Pirate's mouth so to speak.

The rest of the pages were largely empty so he tossed the notebook down onto his chair while he tried to come up with some sort of plan. The black cats settled together in the warm seat he left and pawed at the pad. Smiling, Aubrey bent down to move it and noticed something written on the very last page. He picked it up. Two telephone numbers were written in full. From the code they were most probably American. The first had the name *ROMAN ROLAND* written next to it. That was the same name Rose mentioned she had overheard. Someone Jack was working for perhaps. The second said simply *FRANNY*. He picked up the phone and, after consulting his phone book, dialled direct.

"Roland Enterprises; which department do you require?" The woman was polite and professional.

"Um…Sorry," Aubrey was not prepared so stumbled on, "I…I'm not sure – Is this…um…What do you do, exactly?"

The woman sighed. "Antiquities, memorabilia. Export and import of…" she chanted.

"Oh, uh…I think maybe I've got the wrong…Sorry! So sorry to…"

The line fell dead. But the call had provided him with something; proof that Jack had the means to dispose of a stolen sword. He dialled the next number, excitement mounting. It proved just as interesting. It belonged to Franny Luckheimer: Agent to the Stars. She sounded bored and no-nonsense so Aubrey decided to change tack with her and be honest; to some degree.

"I'm trying to get in touch with one of your 'stars'," he paused for effect, "His name is Jack Bracken, around thirty, tall, dark hair, green eyes…"

She cut him short. "Sorry, hun, nobody by that name on my books."

Black Nightmares to Scarlet Dreams

Hoping she wouldn't hang up he ploughed on, "Are you sure? Bracken might not be his 'stage' name. He's got a scar on his lip but is quite handsome, I suppose." He gritted his teeth.

"No, honey; you got the wrong agency...Hold on..."

Aubrey was about to thank her and hang up when her voice suddenly jumped up an octave.

"Hold on! Did you say he has a scar? Above his mouth? And, he's gorgeous? Green eyes, brown, tousled hair?"

Aubrey sighed inwardly; obviously it took her a while to register things and there really was no accounting for taste. He swallowed hard, "Yes that sounds like him."

"Jon Black is his name! Not what you said! He's working on location at the moment. What do you want him for?"

"Well, actually, I..." Aubrey grabbed at the first thought that came to mind, "Actually I'm in England and I caught his performance the other day..."

"Oh my God! Jon's in England? This is so exciting! Hold on, when did you say you saw him? Did he give you my number...?"

"Well, thanks for your help, must go...Bye." Hastily Aubrey replaced the receiver.

His hands shook and he prayed that the call couldn't be traced back to him. He leaned his head on the chair and steadied himself. So, Jack Bracken was an actor. Or Jon Black was an actor and Jack Bracken a pseudonym. Why the deception? Oak Grove was hardly the centre for international organised crime. Was it? A small, uninteresting, some would say sleepy, area of England could be the perfect cover. Even your neighbours have no idea what goes on behind closed curtains. But the very public tree-carving and sword-stealing was hardly discreet; it was all so baffling.

The cats rubbed impatiently around his legs, desperate for their tea. Getting up he moved slowly to the kitchen in thought and lifted the bowls onto the counter. Jon Black was unstable – fact. He used bizarre means to steal – fact. Rose had some connection with all this – fact. Rose was in love with Black. He stopped, trying to clear this last thought from his mind and focused instead on dishing the meat out carefully and equally into the bowls. Glancing up out of the window he hesitated; from his window he had a clear view of his neighbour's garden and right in front of him, sitting on their deck, was Rose and Sam…with Jack. Quickly Aubrey scooped out the last bit of meat and unceremoniously dumped the dishes onto the floor, much to the cats' disgust.

He dashed out of his backdoor, his mind racing with all he had discovered about the stranger in their midst. It was a great opportunity, too good to miss and now was as good a time as any to out Jon Black. Rose would know exactly what he was: a con-artist and a thief. He approached the fence at break-neck speed and the three of them turned to face him. Rose smiled at him but Sam seemed tense and she shook her head at Aubrey as though she could read his thoughts and wanted him to stop. Determined, however, he leaned on the fence confidently.

Black smirked and put out a hand and tenderly touched Rose's face. Aubrey watched in dismay, his confidence slipping as Black pulled her close and kissed her gently on the lips, savouring every moment. His cold green eyes fixed unflinchingly on Aubrey and he knew that Black had won this battle. Defeated, he nodded to Sam then turned and walked steadily back to his house.

©2007 Cara Aldous

Chapter 8

A shaft of sunlight fell across the bed and Rose stirred. Sighing blissfully she nestled into the pillow, her hair falling over her face. As she pushed her curls back out of her eyes she became aware that she was not alone. She blinked as she started to focus on, by now, very familiar green eyes staring back at her. She smiled warily.

"...The time has come,
To search the earth,
T' will be undone,
Once Black is back..."

They lay together, their bodies entwined, as the ship rocked gently from side to side. The only sounds were the waves lapping at the hull and the cries from the gulls overhead. When the female was discovered the men immediately set about roping the plank to the side from which she should walk to her death. But he had seen the fear in her eyes and desired her; they had been at sea far too long and he needed the scent and feel of female flesh against his own to keep the madness at bay.

She had been a willing lover and as he watched her sleep he knew he could not let her go. The men would object but The Phoenix was his and aboard it his word was law. Any man who did not agree to Rosie staying would walk the plank themselves. That would stave off their bloodlust for a while. As soon as she awoke he would take her officially as his bride. He watched her stir in her sleep and her eyes flicker open. Love replaced fear as she smiled at him knowingly. Yes she would consent to be his; no words need be spoken aloud...

*

Without moving, Jack smiled back at her and continued to study her in wonderment. They stared at one another until Rose giggled nervously, breaking the spell. Two weeks had passed since their first kiss; two whole weeks of a fast moving, fast paced relationship and she was still dizzy with excitement. She was in awe of him yet a little scared too; they were after all strangers and she knew very little about him.

"Hi, sweetie," she whispered hoarsely.

"Hey, honey," he replied softly.

She raised her head slightly, to take him in fully. He was stretched out by her side propped up on one arm, the other reached out gently touching her cheek and she shivered. His smile was fixed and almost manic, as though he were fighting some inner turmoil.

Disconcerted, she smiled back at him and they remained motionless until Rose stretched and turned away to look at the window.

"How long you been there?" she asked, not meeting his gaze.

"Not long."

When his answers were short and clipped it was going to be a very long and difficult day; that much she did know. It was also going to be another hot one too by the look of the clear blue sky outside. She sighed and rolled onto her back, gazing at the ceiling. She thought back to their first kiss which seemed like an age ago now. Her stomach flipped as she remembered how they had made love for the first time. The urgency to be close had overwhelmed them both and they had practically torn one another's clothes off in the frenzy. The first time had been fast and urgent but what had followed since was slow and sensual and mind-blowing.

Rose bit her lip and turned to face him, longing for him to make love to her again, willing him to read her mind. During their first night together he told her they were destined to be together; Rosie and Blackheart's love had spanned the centuries and were reawakening their souls. The romantic in her wanted so desperately to believe him.

*

Jack reached his arms around her and pulled her close. His kiss lingered tenderly before he sighed, resting his head on her chest. She responded by wrapping her arms around him, pulling him to her and gently stroking his hair. He sighed deeply and buried his head further, breathing in her sweet scent.

Black Nightmares to Scarlet Dreams

He wished the moment would never end but knew inevitably it would; and soon. The darkness swirled inside his head. It was there most days now but was strongest whenever he was close to Rose; even thoughts of her made his head swim. When he was with her his dreams mixed with reality until they blurred into one living nightmare. He wanted to scream with the pain it caused, wanted to run away back home and hide out the rest of his days being a walk-on in some low budget B-movie. He wanted to end things, to put a stop to it all.

Mr Roland had been conspicuous by his silence. Jack half expected one of his trained apes to show up any time now. Expected a beating at least. But there had been nothing. Maybe the sword had not yet been recognised for the fake it was. However he knew it was only a matter of time before Roland's heavy came calling again. He had to tell Rose everything; before it was too late.

He let her hold him a while as she ran her fingers through his hair and softly hummed. Finally he pulled away from her, raising himself up on his elbows and looking deep into her eyes.

"What?" she smiled.

"Nothing…" he smiled back at her; the truth moments away.

*

Outside in the hallway Sam padded along to the bathroom. They heard the door close then water running. They listened to the morning noises of tooth brushing and gargling and washing. The toilet flushed then the door opened and they heard her pad back down the hall. Moments later there was a tap on the door, it opened and Sam's head popped into view. She stiffened at the sight of Jack. To irritate her further he planted a kiss on Rose's neck and nestled into her breasts.

"Cuppa?" she asked curtly as she turned and headed back down the hallway.

"Do you want one?" Rose asked but Jack shook his head.

He looked up sheepishly at her and grinned. She melted whenever he did the little boy lost thing. She kissed his forehead and he relaxed into her ever so slightly as he hungrily returned the kiss.

*

Rose lay back on the pillow and smiled. She felt warm inside and deeply satisfied. Jack curled up next to her, putting his head on her shoulder, and arm around her naked waist. He seemed troubled and slightly agitated and, frowning she kissed him softly and stroked his hair slowly and carefully. Usually this calmed him; usually their love-making calmed him but this morning was different. It was as though he wanted to say something but every time he was on the verge he would sigh and hold her tightly to him. She waited. She dreaded the truth but wanted it all the same.

"Rose, I…I have to…to tell you something," he began at long last, "It's about your…your…Well, I think you know…"

He looked to her for help but she was struggling to remain calm. Yes, she did know, but she wasn't going to make it easy for him.

"Your sword," he continued, avoiding her eyes. He couldn't bear to look. "The one that was stolen…"

Black Nightmares to Scarlet Dreams

A small sob escaped her lips. This was it; he was going to confess yet it was not what she wanted now. Not anymore. She brushed away the tears as they rolled down her cheeks and he held onto her tightly. She leaned her head into his chest and cried. She mourned the loss of her sword and the passing of her father and, at last, the death of her mother. Jack held her, his grip firm yet gentle. He kissed her hair and rubbed her shoulders as he fought with his own demons.

*

"...In time my love
Will come to be,
With time, my love,
My family..."

He knew she would struggle knowing she could never go back to her family. She had cried as she told him of her promise to bring them all great wealth and riches after making her fortune at sea. He promised she would have her fortune and infamy too though she did not want the latter. He promised safe passage aboard his ship and equal captaincy once they wed. He offered his sword up to her if she would bear him an heir. Holding her close to him he vowed she would never want for anything so long as she was his. Slowly he kissed her; they would make love then she could sleep and be rid of her sorrow.

*

They fell back onto the pillows, Rose wrapped in Jack's arms, both hot and steamy from the sex. Slowly and gradually he began to talk. He wanted to tell her everything and have no more secrets.

"Roland employed me because I look like him. Like Blackheart. He was after the sword of Aramoth – your sword, Rose. But, he hasn't got it! Not yet! And not ever if I can help it. Someone else took your sword, that day you…You know. Anyhow, I watched…I so wanted to hold you and tell you it was okay…but…"

"Why didn't you? I needed you!"

"Anyway, like I said, someone else got it. But it's safe – Roland doesn't have it. And he won't have it! I don't know what he wants it for exactly, but there's a whole lot more to it than just being a sword. It's the key to something and, I think, could be dangerous…"

"Dangerous?" Rose lifted her head and looked at him sharply.

"Yeah," he faltered, "It…has something to do with buried treasure. But there's something else lying dormant with that treasure and Roland wants to resurrect it…"

"What rubbish! I haven't heard anything so ridiculous in all my life!"

"I know honey, I know. I know it sounds…Stupid, impossible but…Listen, he hasn't got it and I know who has. I'm keeping my eye on things. I'll get it back for you, I promise." He kissed her nose and she nodded.

"But then," she opened her eyes wide. "If you were employed by this Roland guy to be Jack Bracken but you're not then…who the hell are you?"

"I'm an actor," he stopped. "My name is Jon; Jon Black. I live in LA. But, what Roland doesn't know is that I am related to Blackheart - for real. My ancestor was his brother and that makes me a true Blackheart descendent."

He held her tightly as she tried to relax into him yet she could not shake a tiny niggling doubt; Jack had intended to steal her sword. He was stopped only because someone else had beaten him to it. He proved himself to be both a liar and a thief. She so desperately wanted to believe in his innocence in all that had happened but he wasn't making things easy. She pulled away from him and headed for the shower; she had to think. Within minutes he had followed her. As he moved his hands over her body any qualms she had instantly disappeared and she gave herself to him once more.

It was midmorning when Rose and Sam sat at the kitchen table, finally alone. Rose had been quiet ever since Jack had left that morning and Sam was concerned for her friend. As much as she hated Bracken the last thing she wanted was for Rose to be heart broken by the bastard. She resented the manner in which he had wormed his way into their lives; things had been brilliant when it was just the two of them. But, ever since he had come along, Sam had seen less and less of her friend and more and more of the 'happy couple'.

It was never an issue whenever Sam fell in love (and this happened frequently) because Rose never had to worry about her boyfriends getting in the way. Now, however, the tables were turned and Sam hated Jack with a vengeance for coming between the two of them. She also mistrusted him greatly. There was nothing for it but to talk things over with Aubrey; that's if he was still prepared to discuss Jack Bracken. Back at the start of Rose's infatuation with Jack, Sam felt sure Aubrey was going to say something then; something important. But when Jack grabbed Rose and kissed her, in front of them all, it had seemed to stop Aubrey in his tracks. Since then Aubrey had stayed out of their way, conspicuous by his absence. Sam had a feeling Aubrey had a soft spot for Rose.

Slowly she got to her feet to make a fresh brew. Rose hummed softly and flicked absently through a glossy magazine which normally she pored over avidly. Sam sighed loudly; she missed the sarcy remarks and giggles they shared about the skinny publicity mad celebrities. She sighed again in case Rose missed the first one but it was ignored, the humming unbearable. Unable to stand it any longer Sam slammed her cup down on the draining board, chipping it. Finally, Rose looked up at her friend.

"What's up, Sam?" She sighed and closed the magazine. She knew what was coming.

"I think you know!" Sam turned and faced Rose, a scowl on her face.

"Jack?" Rose sighed.

"Yes – bloody Jack!" Sam shot back. "How the hell did he get in this morning, for a start?"

"He has a key," Rose answered calmly.

"Oh really? And what about me?"

"You have your own key," It was a useless attempt at a joke.

"Oh don't be so bloody smart!"

Rose cringed; it was Mother all over again! She felt angry tears welling. What right had Sam to treat her like this! Why on earth couldn't she be happy for her? Jack was her soulmate. Difficult; yes. But, wasn't the path of true love supposed to not run smoothly? Or was it the other way round? She sighed; she didn't want to fall out with her best friend over a man but she was becoming increasingly fed up with the jealousy. Sam was not her Mother.

"Who do you think you are?" Rose spoke quietly.

"What? I…I…" Sam stuttered; she knew she had gone too far, "I only asked, I mean I live here too!"

"Well, you have a choice…" Rose flicked over the magazine, a page ripped.

Sam bit her lip. Things were getting silly; time to back off. Change tack and Rose may just cool down. If not she could be out of a friend and a home. Maybe if she appealed to Rose's better nature; just as long as Jack hadn't crushed it completely.

"I'm just worried about you, that's all!" Sam reasoned. "I mean, what do you exactly know about Jack? You…you've only really known him a couple of weeks."

"I know enough." Rose answered quietly and shivered.

She remembered when her and Jack had stood in that very same spot together. When he had taken her in his arms and kissed her for the very first time; it was like all her birthdays rolled into one. She had felt elated and completely invigorated. But now those feelings were mixed and muddled. He had told her things that morning she had not really wanted to hear; he had told her all about Mr Roland; a serious collector, specialising in swords. He had heard about one in particular; Rose's sword and he wanted it for his collection. It had a name: The Sword of Aramoth. Jack was employed to take it from her by whatever means necessary.

Her tears had almost brought her to her senses there and then but when he had joined her in the shower, she had given in to him like a silly teenager. And now, as Sam stood there, telling her off, it was the final straw. She felt small and silly. It was a feeling she had known all her life and which fed her resentment each time it happened; Mother had made her feel that way often. She sighed and stood, pushing her feelings aside as usual. Mustering all her energy she reached out and took Sam's hand in hers.

"I love him," she said simply.

A light rapping on the door caught Rose by surprise. She turned, expecting to see Jack grinning at her through the glass but instead it was Aubrey, his face set and determined. Sam was less surprised as she had seen him walk up the path but she was intrigued as to what he had to say.

Hopefully he knew something about Jack Bracken which would bring Rose to her senses.

"Hallo, Rose," he looked sheepish and awkward.

Sam smiled at him but did not speak; she had said enough. Besides there was no way she was going to upset Rose any further; it was her home at stake as well as their friendship. They waited for Aubrey to continue.

"I have something to tell you that can't wait," he said at a rush lest she interrupted. "I have spent some time looking through that notebook – and pretty grim reading it makes too, I can tell you! Anyway, I found out some very interesting things about your…er…boyfriend."

Rose waited, arms folded tightly across her chest. Sam knew from experience that this meant she was angry. She watched her friend closely as she listened to Aubrey. Any sign that Rose was about to erupt and she would put a stop to his revelations. Even if it might mean Rose not finding out the truth about Jack Bracken. Things were shaky enough. Besides Sam could always find out later and together she and Aubrey could decide what to do if anything.

"I think you'll find this interesting Rose! Jack Bracken is not Jack Bracken at all! He's Jon Black – an actor!"

Sam gasped in amazement; this was far better than she could have imagined. Rose remained quiet and thoughtful. The air was thick with the day's heat and Aubrey's words hung in the air. Finally Rose looked up, first at Sam then Aubrey. Sam felt queasy; for the first time since she could remember she could not read her friends expression. Rose's face was closed.

"I know," Rose replied finally.

"What?!" Aubrey spluttered.

Rose took a deep breath. "I know everything about him – and more! Much more than I needed to know! But then, he had to tell me, didn't he Aubrey? He had no other choice. He knew you'd come running straight over here! And you! You love all this, don't you?"

"Well, he didn't have a choice!" Aubrey was indignant, "I have his notebook!"

Sam remained silent and waited for her friend to finish.

"Oh yes, the damn notebook! Well, that's where you're wrong! He didn't have to tell me anything, he could easily have denied it all. He could even have said you made the whole thing up and I would have believed him. You're both wrong - about him – about everything! He loves me and I love him and that's all that really matters!" she stormed.

They stood in stunned silence listening to a distant clock ticking somewhere in the house. Time seemed to stop as each one of them were submerged deep in thought. The hour chimed a distant echo.

"Right, well if you'll excuse me," Rose moved toward the door, her mind made up for her, "I'm meeting Jack for lunch – if that's okay with you two!"

They watched, dumbfounded and stunned. She stormed out of the door and rushed down the path. Sam and Aubrey shrugged simultaneously; any other time Sam would have found this funny. She wanted to cry and, sensing this, Aubrey moved to her side and placed a hand on her shoulder. With one single exchanged glance they silently agreed never to approach Rose directly on the subject of Jack again until they had something more on him; with hard evidence.

*

Sam waited in all afternoon and all evening for Rose. Sitting on her bed in the dark she heard the front door slam and footsteps on the stairs followed by the slamming of Rose's bedroom door. She listened hard but could hear no voices or sounds to indicate anything other than Rose was alone. Aubrey had ranted so passionately about the mystery surrounding Jack Bracken aka Jon Black that Sam had been quite taken aback. It was obvious Aubrey hated him as much as she did. He understood her too. She felt uncomfortable by the way Jack had unashamedly kissed Rose so intimately that morning, when he knew Sam was watching. It made her cringe to even think about it. He was callous and uncaring in his blatant public performances with Rose. For that's what they were: performances. After all, he was an actor and he played his part so well.

A sudden gust of wind blew the curtain up into the air. Sam leaned forward; perhaps the awful heatwave was finally coming to an end. She moved to the window, opened the curtains wide and looked up at the black sky. A rumble of thunder floated in on the wind as it blew in, sucking the curtains out. She reached up and tugged at them, leaning on the windowsill to get a grip. She closed her eyes and felt the cool air blow onto her face. Smiling at her own childish excitement fuelled by the imminent storm she looked down onto the silent gardens below. Being at the back of the house there was no luxury of streetlight but the darkness did not bother Sam; it was rarely completely black and your eyes soon became accustomed. A rustling from one of the gardens caught her attention and she strained her eyes hoping to spy a hedgehog hurrying to safety before the rain came.

Lightening flashed across the sky momentarily lighting up the dark and she blinked, not wanting to believe what she had seen. Lightening flashed again and the sight that met her shook her powerfully. Horrified, she stepped back into the shadows of her room. Tugging the curtains together she peered out slowly, hoping that what she had glimpsed had been nothing more than an overactive imagination. Hoping that the broody night was merely playing games with her head she strained to see in the blackness. Another flash lit up the terrible vision once more and made it sickeningly real.

*

"...Time is clear,
Dark comes the night,
Black is near,
We shall soon unite..."

Jack stood in the garden, feeling the cool air on his face, on his body. Wearing nothing more than a pair of jeans he could feel the cold grass beneath his feet, between his toes, awakening his senses. In his hand was the Sword of Aramoth. He had retrieved it hours earlier. It had been simple enough; the fool had left it in the trunk of his car. Levering it open had been child's play. The vehicle hadn't even been alarmed. But the idiot guy sure would be when he discovered it was gone. But what could he do? Report something he had already stolen as stolen?

Jack smiled as he held the sword aloft, his arms spread wide above his head. The broody night and looming thunder added to his mood and blocked out the demons pulsating through his mind. He would return the sword to Rose but not tonight. Tonight he had other plans for it. Tonight he would play out his nightly ritual but this time with the sword of his ancestor. Once more he would ask the ghost of Blackheart to relinquish his hold on Rosie Scarlet and all her descendents and this time it might just work. This time he had the right sword and Blackheart was in his head, in his mind, and in his body. But worse than that, much, much worse, he was in his soul.

*

Sam watched transfixed; a chill shivered through her spine as Jack stood in the storm, arms outstretched. Something glinted in his hand as the sky lit up; it was something long and sharp, something metal. The fool! He held it aloft as though beckoning the lightening, almost like he worshipped the storm. As the thunder grew closer and louder the lightening became more frequent, lighting up his face, shocking Sam with each manic expression until she could take no more. She wanted to scream, to shout and run to Rose but the terror froze her and all she could do was whimper and shake.

©2007 Cara Aldous

Hailstones began hitting the ground hard but still he did not stop this strange mantra, this weird ritual. The sword swooped and slashed the air, faster and faster. He began to laugh, deeply and quietly at first then louder and more and more manically as the hail fell faster and harder. He seemed unaware of any pain, but must surely have felt it as the hailstones hit his face and body. The wind blew as the thunder drew overhead, its roars shaking the house and foundations. Yet still he did not stop. He held the sword high in the air and shouted, his cries falling silent on the wind; his words drowned out by the thunder. Yet Sam heard what he said. They carried up to her window on a current of air and she cursed him; her every dream now promised to be full of nightmares.

"Black deceased! Black desists! The hour has come, do not resist! The storm will bring an end, Rose Scarlet shall make amends! We soon will wed! She shall be dead! Your will shall soon be done!"

Chapter 9

Rose left quickly and quietly as early as she possibly could the next morning. She wanted to get to the shop and think. It was the only place where neither Sam nor Jack seemed to bother her. It was the one place where she would be able to concentrate completely and decide just what she needed to do next. Everything and everyone crowded her thoughts these days; her sword, Sam, Aubrey, and especially Jack; she couldn't bring herself to call him Jon, it didn't feel right. Besides, he preferred to be called Jack and what if it was a little weird? Who was she to argue?

She also wanted to avoid any awkward questions or accusations which Sam might throw at her. Their friendship had considerably altered since Jack came into their lives but Rose was not unduly concerned; it might even be for the best. For once she could make her own decisions without Sam always thinking she knew better. Now all she had to do was figure out what, if anything, Jack was up to and what difference it would make to any future they might have together. If his original orders had been to steal from her, his new objective had taken a very different turn. He seemed totally obsessed with her, forever touching and kissing her; even in front of Sam and Aubrey which, she had to admit, was becoming more than a little uncomfortable. She found it really embarrassing when he pawed at her. Perhaps it was an American thing but their cultural differences could only widen the gap further between them; a gap which was becoming bigger and deeper by the day.

Both Aubrey and Sam hated Jack and he them; and that was no exaggeration. Granted, Jack's conduct sometimes got out of control and this did scare even her a little. But the erratic mood swings and odd behaviour only went further to prove Sam and Aubrey's theory; he was at best peculiar and at worst mentally unstable.

"NO!" She stopped and shouted it out loud, her voice echoing in the deserted early morning street.

Turning onto Oak Avenue she gazed down along the line of trees, at their unspoiled trunks and shook her head. He could not be mentally ill; she would know if he was - surely there would be other signs. No; he was simply highly strung as most actors are; highly strung and insecure. This reasoning of hers did not sit too comfortably and she tried to think of more excuses for his unpredictability. She had been the first person to show him any stability and maybe it had been too much for him to take. Maybe it was hard for him to understand that she could love lots of people yet be in love with only him. He needed her full attention all the time and she had to admit it was becoming wearing. She was increasingly aware of how he made her feel and, coupled with his jealousy, she loathed the feelings it brought to the surface. It reminded her too much of Mother as so many things often did.

The person who had employed Jack; this Roland man, he was the one who had caused all the problems; it was entirely his fault. If he hadn't been obsessed with owning her sword in the first place, none of this would have happened and, if what Jack had told her was true, he was also very dangerous. Jack was not insane, simply misguided in his choice of employer. Yet she knew, deep in her heart, that if it wasn't for Roland she and Jack would have never met. She knew what she must do to remain safe.

At the main road she stopped and checked each way several times. It had become an obsession ever since that fateful day when she was nearly run over; the day her sword had been stolen. Her breath caught; Jack had already admitted to having watched it all unfold. From the corner of her eye she spotted a car speeding toward her. Without hesitation she raced across to the other side, her heart thumping, and ducked down behind a parked car. But this time there was no screech of tyres just a little old lady behind the wheel of a Ford Fiesta trundling by.

She tried hard to steady her breathing, to keep the panic at bay. Slowly and with the aid of the parked car she got to her feet. She watched the pensioner drive out of sight, and took in deep, slow breaths as she did so. The tightness in her chest subsided as the car disappeared from view and she turned and headed shakily for her shop.

She was angry at herself for letting them win. Though just who they were she had only a vague idea. She hoped and prayed that Jack had not been part of it all, that it had been someone else who had cruelly played their heartless joke on her. Paranoia was starting to creep into her every thought in a wave of conspiracy theories and she was always the victim. Next she would be thinking it was a Government directive; God! She had to stop! It angered her at how anxious she felt whenever she walked the short distance to work now. It was only a few days a week she actually made it in; how the hell she or her business were going to survive she had no idea. Everything and everyone made her feel angry these days.

Unlocking the door her hand began to shake and she cursed Jack and Roland as she took a few more deep breaths. The shop was eerily silent as she quickly made her way to the back and the switches; breathing a sigh of relief as the lights flickered on and lit up the interior. She tried to avoid looking at the gap in her sword display and decided she would change it soon, but not yet, not while there was still a small chance it may come back to her. The door tinkled open and she blinked back the threatening tears as a familiar face smiled a cheery greeting.

"Hallo, Rosie," Rick chirruped.

"Hi Rick," her voice was high-pitched and strained.

"Any news?" he asked hopefully as he pointed at the display.

Sighing she shook her head and turned away as a tear escaped. She brushed her cheek against her shoulder to hide her pain.

"Never mind, eh? Look on the bright side – it was a very dangerous thing and, all things considered, the whole sorry business could have been a lot worse…" he trailed off, suddenly embarrassed as she gawped at him in sheer astonishment.

"How, Rick? Hmm? Tell me how things could be any worse?" Anger brought its own tears.

Sorry for making her cry (he hadn't made a girl cry since infants) Rick offered her his large white handkerchief but she declined with a sniff and a wave of her hand. The tears dripped onto the counter and he watched them slowly forming two puddles. Any minute now they would form one big one and run down the front of the glass and that would be a bugger to clean off; the glass would be smeary for months. He waited for her to calm down, feeling awkward and embarrassed. He thrust his hands into his pockets and jiggled the loose change he had.

Rose sighed, it was not Rick's fault her sword had been stolen. He had been brave and tried to rescue her by taking charge and calling the police. Perhaps he had even unwittingly seen the man who had stolen it. He could have watched him just as Jack had. Rick might know the thief by sight or name even; he knew everyone local who shopped along their little high street. She wavered on the verge of asking him when something in her head screamed, Stop! What if Jack had made it all up? Jack could easily have been the one who had taken her sword.

She offered Rick a cup of tea and they sat in silent contemplation sipping their brew, each glancing at the other and smiling uncomfortably. Both looked up, relieved, as the door tinkled open. Rose's expression turning to one of pleasant surprise as Rick scowled at the sight of the two policemen who now stood before them. They were the same officers who had attended the original break-in and both smiled amiably.

Good news, Rose hoped.

Can't be good, thought Rick.

"Sir, Madam," the man Rose now knew as Detective Sergeant Roberts nodded.

He leaned on the counter and wiped his brow. The heat remained unrelenting even though it was nearing the end of August. Forecasters predicted Britain would experience an Indian summer right through into September. The storm the previous night had not lifted the claustrophobic feeling in the air and DS Roberts felt uneasy as the atmosphere in the shop was just as suffocating.

"Well, Miss Scarlet," he began, "We've some news – now; could be good or bad. Thing is we found a sword. Simms," he nodded toward his colleague.

Detective Constable Simms took up the narrative as he produced a notebook. "On Saturday morning at approximately eight a.m. a consignment was searched and an item recovered matching the description of a stolen sword. The said item was part of a large haul recovered at the Airport and of which one sword is being held at the Station awaiting formal identification."

Rose's stomach somersaulted and churned and flipped in such speedy succession she thought she might be sick. Her head pounded along with her heart and she had to steady herself as the room spun.

Sensing this Rick brought her a cup of water and she sipped it gratefully whilst DS Roberts explained gently that they would like her to identify if it was in fact her sword.

"…Any time would suit, Miss but, obviously for all our benefit, the sooner the better…" he hoped she would feel up to it.

"Today," Rose nodded and took deep breaths, "I'll come along today."

Rose waited impatiently by the door for Rick to leave. She told the two policemen that she would be at the station in half an hour and Rick had listened as she made those arrangements; he knew how desperate she was to find her sword. Yet he seemed reluctant to leave and this made her feel uncomfortable; it was completely out of character. He kicked at his heels, hands in pockets and looked sulkily around the familiar little shop.

Finally he spoke. "Rosie, ah, there…there's something I need to tell you…"

She held her breath; this was it, he was going to tell her he saw a man fitting Jack's description stealing her sword that day. Maybe, even, that he had been threatened; warned to keep his mouth shut. She shook her head and closed her eyes. Her old habit of playing out every worse case scenario had begun again; recently she was doing it more and more. She had actually stopped it after Mother had died; that was her lowest moment when the only way left to go was up yet here she was, spiralling downwards and out of control again. The day was like a giant rollercoaster ride which she couldn't get off, no matter how sick she felt.

She breathed out shakily and waited for Rick to continue. When he did it was totally unexpected and not one of the many scenarios she had foreseen.

"It's not yours, Rosie…What I mean to say is – it can't be, can it? There's absolutely no way your sword is still in the country after all this time, is there? I would say it's long gone. But – and this is a big but – if it is yours it might be better not to admit to it."

"What?!" Rose was shocked.

"I mean – if it is yours then whoever stole it will try again. Let's face it – whoever took it did so in a very nasty way, didn't they? There was no need for that, no need at all!" He seemed distant.

"What are you saying Rick?"

"What I'm saying, Rosie, what I'm actually saying is: say the sword isn't yours."

"Yes?" She looked at her watch; it really was time to go.

"Well, that's it – say the sword is not yours, even if it is!" He smiled at her sheepishly.

"So – let me get this straight, when I get to the police station and the sword they show me is mine – lie! Say 'no, sorry, looks like it, yes! But it isn't'?" Rose asked incredulously; he was unbelievable.

"Um, yes. It's a bit of a bugger I know…" Rick fingered his collar nervously.

"Well thank you Rick for that great piece of advice, I'll bear it in mind next time I try to defraud my insurance company, shall I?" With that she gave him a small shove and locked the door quickly behind him.

*

The bus journey into the city centre only took between ten to fifteen minutes but the intense heat made it seem like forever. The ancient diesel vehicle shuddered and stopped at every single stop along the route only to let a single, solitary person on or off each time. Rose sighed and looked at her watch. She dug into her bag for her mobile; it was time she told Jack her possible news. It took several rings before he finally answered. He was out of breath as though he'd been running.

"Jack? It's me – I...I might have some news soon..." she faltered.

"Rose, honey? Where are you? It sounds as though you're in a tin can..." he sounded distant too.

She laughed at this, "No – I'm on a bus!"

"A bus! Rose, what the hell...?"

"Listen, baby – I can't talk long. I've got some news – they might have found my sword – only might so don't get too excited!" she tried hard to disguise her own excitement.

"They what? I can hardly hear you...Listen Rose, honey, that's great news! But, here's the thing – if it's not your sword just say it is anyway, okay?"

Rose could hardly believe what she was hearing, "What? Lie, you mean?" she felt angry and confused; twice in one day.

"Uh, yeah. Listen honey if it's not your sword but you say it is – then Roland and his musclemen will leave us, I mean, you alone. Don't you get it? If they think the cop's got your sword then you'll be safe..."

Rose fell silent; she knew what he said made sense but there seemed more to this than simply her safety. Rick had just told her to do the complete opposite and the contradictory advice confused her. Her head spun as she tried to make sense of it all. She half listened as Jack pleaded with her to do the right thing; as he spoke her name and called her 'honey' as though that was all he had to do. Actually it was he'd click his fingers and she would come running. Eventually she could take no more and, with a promise to call him the minute she finished at the Police Station, she hastily ended the call before switching off her mobile.

*

A few hours later Rose sat outside the Police Station, staring blankly ahead as the traffic roared by. She rubbed her eyes hard until they stung. She felt numb and shivered even in the heady heat of the midday sun. The fumes from the cars and Lorries choked her but not as much as the shock of discovering that the sword they had found was not hers. The one they had shown her was very nice and normally she would have been excited by it; but it was not a normal day. It was not the Sword of Aramoth. It did not have a golden phoenix on its hilt nor a sharp, swift blade that had spilt so much blood so many centuries ago. So she had shaken her head and sadly but truthfully told DS Roberts that the sword was not hers.

Jack would not be happy with this but at least it had helped make her mind up. It had been his insistence that she lie that brought her to her senses. It was time to finish with him; time to say goodbye before he destroyed her confidence completely. She stood up, reached in her bag and switched her phone on then, thinking better of it; switched it off again and headed to the bus stop. She would tell him face to face. She owed him that much and besides, it was high time she face up to things instead of taking the easy option all the time.

*

Aubrey and Sam marched up Jack's path and banged confidently on the front door. Sam shuffled nervously from foot to foot but knew it had to be done; they had to confront him. They were both fed up with him and his hold over Rose. Sam was sure he had hypnotised her but Aubrey dismissed that idea and said, quite simply, she was afraid of him. But whatever, Jack had to be tackled over his intentions, his involvement with the sword, and all the weird goings on to date. Aubrey and Sam were in total agreement about facing him but, whilst Sam would rather have discussed it further Aubrey had insisted that there was no time like the present.

 They stood on the doorstep, waiting for Jack to answer. In the safe and cosy confines of Aubrey's sitting room Sam had been bold and brave; pulling Jack Bracken or, rather, Jon Black to pieces. Aubrey too had enjoyed the character assassination and it was he who had taken the decision to move it along a pace. So they found themselves stood outside Black's house. But in the cold light of day, hanging around outside his house like naughty school children made both of them very uneasy. His failure to answer the door only heightened their nervousness and anxiety. Aubrey was just about to suggest they call it a day when, as he looked over at the window, the curtain moved.

"Did you see that?" he asked.

"What?" she hissed back.

"It may be nothing..."

He moved closer to the window for a better look.

"What are you doing?" Sam hissed at him again.

Aubrey made no reply. He stooped underneath the window ledge and slowly raised himself up to see better. Mesmerized by what he saw he beckoned for Sam to join him. Concerned and more than a little worried at what she might see Sam carefully positioned herself so she could hide behind Aubrey. She peered through the window. An icy chill crept down her spine and, not for the first time, what she saw froze her to the spot.

*

"...Spirits of the sea,

Spirits from beyond,

Bring him home to me,

Black where he belongs..."

Standing in the middle of his front room, the furniture pushed back against the walls and the floor now clear of all the paperwork and research, Jack stared ahead. He wore a pair of black breeches and boots like the Pirate Captain. His bronzed muscles rippled as he lifted the heavy sword and began his daily ritual. Now entirely materialised the demons whooshed and swooped around his head. He sliced the air with the blade as it swished and whooped. In his mind he condemned

Blackheart for all the pain he had caused; cursed the pirate for the grim fate he had placed upon his descendants.

    If he could just think clearly, if he could just keep the demons at bay until Rose came home. She would soothe him and calm him and then he would be able to think straight. Then he would be able to put things right. He moved around the room as he fought with the closing darkness in his head; struggled to regain control. For a split second the darkness lifted; just long enough to see the horrified faces of Sam and Aubrey staring at him through the window. This soothed him a little and, after holding their gaze a moment longer he moved back to begin his ritual once more.

*

Neither Sam nor Aubrey could move, yet both were aware that their presence had been noticed. They remained transfixed by the skill and dexterity and horror with which Jack manoeuvred the sword. Sam had seen it the night before and now Aubrey had also witnessed the spectacle. Aubrey, meanwhile spellbound, struggled to contain his mounting frustration that Rose was not with them. He knew she would not easily believe the word of two people who openly disliked her boyfriend. But they must warn her all the same.

    He followed Jack with his eyes, hypnotised as the sword swung quickly round and around when suddenly Jack turned, faced them and stopped, the sword still held aloft as he paused and focused on them. Although longing to, Aubrey was unable to turn away. Jack held their gaze, his cold green eyes dull and unblinking. He brought the blade up in line with his nose then narrowed his eyes in warning. Though he was silent this action spoke volumes. Sam stiffened as though ice had crept through her veins. She tried to turn away. A smile flickered briefly across Jack's face before he turned and began to swing the sword in ritual once more.

Chapter 10

Rose sat alone on the decking, deep in thought; going over her visit that afternoon to the police station and Jack and Rick's interference. The door into the kitchen stood wide open and she glanced at the clock on the wall. It was five-thirty and, unusually, no sight nor sound of anyone; Jack was out and Aubrey and Sam were conspicuous by their absence. The cats were wandering the gardens looking for Aubrey and Sam was on the early shift so should be home by now. Oak Grove was hushed, the old tree standing serenely with not even a whisper of a breeze to stir a single leaf.

Rose was fretful and on the verge of tears; the day's events and the fact it hadn't been her sword culminated in mixed emotions and she was trying hard to keep a lid on it all. She was worried about what Jack would say; she agonized over her final dismissal of both the sword and their relationship. Mounting panic gripped her and she took huge gulps of air. She was struggling to keep calm but knew this wasn't the way to handle it. She was in danger of hyperventilating and losing control. Her head felt light and her heart pounded against her chest. The palms of her hands felt slippery with sweat and they slid across the table as she laid her head down on it.

Slow down! She urged herself, *slow down!*

She wanted Jack; needed him but, as when her sword was stolen, he wasn't there for her. He only ever surfaced when he wanted something. He said he loved her and his very public displays of affection went someway to prove this. But sometimes she felt it was all just a show, a performance to him. Sometimes it was way over the top; much too much and Rose had a niggling feeling that it was indeed nothing more than an act. Perhaps it was his insecurities that made him behave so badly; kissing her and pawing at her to get his own way. Even if it were she could not live like this any longer.

Their relationship had become too one-sided. It was Mother all over again. The emotional blackmail, the control, the jealousy had begun to wear her down. If she stayed she was in danger of belonging to him and that would not do either of them any good. She loved him so she would have to leave him; be cruel to be kind. She closed her eyes and strained her ears for any sound that would bring comfort. Traffic hummed in the distance. Birds sang in the trees. The heat was almost bearable after the storm of the previous night.

Soon it would be September and the chill of autumn would be in the air. She longed for the coldness of winter, hoping it would bring respite from the panic attacks. At least then the hot flashes which swept over her entire body would subside as quickly as they came. And her gasping breaths would not be so difficult in a chillier air. Her breathing slowed to a normal pace in the calmness of the early evening as she watched the sinking sun cast pale shadows across the lawn. It was important she stayed calm so that she could talk rationally to Jack. It was important for one of them to remain composed and was almost certain he would be far from relaxed. She sat up as she heard a car pulling into the Grove. It stopped just outside; quite close by. Hoping to find it was finally Jack or one of the others she got up and walked steadily round to the front.

*

Rick climbed out of his car grim-faced. As Rose approached he turned on the charm and a smile that made his chubby features grotesque. Even in the cooler evening air he sweated profusely and his hair matted to his forehead. He wiped the drips out of his eyes with the back of his hand then wiped that across his trousers. He winced at Rose's disgusted expression. It had been a struggle, deciding whether to come or not but he had to see her, had to find out what she had found down at the police station. Or, moreover, what she had said to the police.

He turned and locked his car door, frowning at the damage to his boot where it had been levered open. The insurance company were penalising him for the break-in which was really unfair but, apparently, theft and vandalism were considered his fault. His premiums would shoot through the roof. Ruby had told him he was lucky not to have lost anything. But she hadn't known what he had kept hidden in his boot. He had kept it safe and secure; so he had thought. It was worth thousands;

when the thief discovered what he had in his possession he would flip. That's if he ever discovered its true worth.

He smiled at Rose and nodded as he walked up to her gate. "Hallo, Rosie," he grinned at her inanely.

"What do you want, Rick?" She sighed; he was the last person she wanted to see.

"Thought I'd drop by, see how you got on down at the ol' police station?" he puffed as he leaned on the gate.

Several awkward seconds of silence passed before Rose sighed again and gave in; it was obvious he was not going to go away unless she told him how things had gone that afternoon so she invited him into the garden. Offering him a cup of tea he gladly accepted and followed her into the kitchen. It freaked her out having him in such close proximity and in her home too. Their relationship had always been a strictly business affair and one which should never overstep the boundaries – ever. Quickly she made him tea in one of her smallest cups, handed it to him then motioned him toward the decking. She sat down opposite and watched as he slurped the hot tea. He placed the cup down on the table and studied the pattern closely.

She groaned inwardly thinking he was going to reel off one of his tedious little anecdotes like he usually did; this pattern was painted by the oh-so-boring dynasty of who-gives-a-stuff – that sort of thing. But he didn't and so they sat in silence awhile until finally he could wait no longer.

"How did it go – at the station, then?" he asked.

"Fine," Rose didn't want to give too much away.

"Well, was it the sword? Your sword?" he asked, exacerbated at having to squeeze every ounce of information from her.

"Oh, um, no – No, it wasn't…" she looked into the dregs at the bottom of her cup.

"Well done, girl! Well done! That was a relief..."

She looked up into his pleased face. "No, honestly, it wasn't my sword – for real!"

"Yes, yes, of course. Well done anyway." He winked.

He drained his cup and sat back in his seat. It groaned and creaked under his weight and Rose grimaced as he tugged at the waistband of his thick and sweaty trousers. She longed for a friendly face and wondered where on earth Sam or Aubrey was. Or even Jack; where the hell was he when she needed him? She didn't have to wait long to find out.

*

Jack had been watching them from a distance. He smiled as Rick strained his large frame into the small wooden chairs and Rose slipped easily into hers. Even though she had her back to him he could tell that she was on edge. He was angry with her and enjoyed watching her squirm uncomfortably in Rick's presence. He could put a stop to it at any time and would soon enough but he would let her suffer just a little longer; just enough to pay her back for the way she had hurt him. She had deliberately made him wait to see what she had said to the police. Plus there was the small matter of her friends spying on him.

©2007 Cara Aldous

He had an inkling that she was going to end things between them soon but knew that if he bided his time and perhaps rescued her from the grubby little man leering at her she would be grateful. Maybe she would be so grateful to him that it would make it awkward for her to end their relationship. An evening's grace was all he needed to put things right between them.

The darkness which had lifted after several hours spent in a deep sleep that afternoon threatened to overwhelm him again. He had to hold it at bay. He continued to watch Rose and Rick and the anger welled up inside and simmered as he did so. Resentment and jealousy at another man sitting in such close proximity to his Rose spilled over into fury and this time a red mist descended; the demons swarming in thick and fast.

"...Kill the interloper,
Make him flee,
Then this woman
Come back to thee..."

*

Rick's face paled as Jack leapt over the garden fence. Rose smiled at her white knight coming to her rescue but the initial amusement abated as Rick began to shake. Jack stood behind her and placed a protective hand on her shoulder. She responded by placing her own hand over his and he in turn brushed her cheek with his other.

"What do you want with Rose?" he demanded of Rick.

Rick, still shaking shook his head, "N-n-n-nothing…" he stuttered.

"N-n-n-nothing?" Jack sneered, "Must be something for you to bother Rose at home!"

Rose frowned; how did Jack know firstly who Rick was and secondly that he'd never been there before? Rick stood clumsily, preparing to leave but in a flash Jack blocked his way. He stared him down, his green eyes cold and narrowing, forcing Rick to collapse onto the chair with such force that it visibly bowed. Rose looked away, embarrassed for him but unable to intervene for fear Jack would turn his aggression on her; she had to stay strong and focused on the task ahead and when Jack was in this mood it was best to let his anger run its course. Besides, being cruel to Rick was not something she was particularly against at this present moment; he had made her feel awkward and now it was his turn to squirm. An immature but satisfying thought.

"I believe you owe Rose an apology," Jack hissed in his ear.

"S-s-sorry, Rosie…" Rick stammered, all the while glancing fearfully at Jack.

Jack flinched and shuddered. "Wrong!" he roared loudly, making Rick shudder.

He looked up at him. "W-w-what? I…I d-d-don't under s-s-stand!"

©2007 Cara Aldous

Jack took a deep breath, his nostrils flaring and he spoke so quietly Rick could only just hear him through his throbbing ear drum, "Her…name …is…Rose! Not…" he inhaled sharply, "…Ros-ie!"

Rose felt sure Rick was going to cry; she expected him to burst into tears at any moment, a hideous baby. She was about to intervene, to try soothing Jack's rage, putting a stop to Rick's humiliation when suddenly he eased himself up and out of the chair, pulled himself up to his full five feet two and faced Jack square on. Unnerved Jack remained rooted to the spot, fists clenched. Rose had an urge to laugh; it all looked so ridiculous with their macho posturing. Yet she knew laughter could bring its own problems and it certainly wouldn't improve Rick's present situation which was looking worse by the minute. Rick looked to Rose and she smiled, nodding encouragingly.

"I'm…sorry…Rose!" Rick almost shouted her name in his haste to apologise properly and escape.

"There, that's better, isn't it?" Jack leaned in close, "If I see you anywhere near her again I will kill you. You do understand?" His voice was so low that Rose couldn't hear him, "I know what you did…I saw what you took…And what happened to your car could so easily happen to you…One day when you least expect it I'll be there. And Rose won't be able to protect you then…Understand?" Rick nodded and with a single backward glance in Rose's direction, he turned and walked quickly and steadily out of her garden and out of her life forever.

Jack took her by the hand and led her inside. Upstairs in her bedroom, he slowly removed each item of clothing and lay her down on the bed. He kissed her forcefully; his tongue probing and searching for reassurance and forgiveness. It felt nice and warm and cosy and the best place in the world to be. Rose was confused; he made her feel loved unconditionally yet she knew that wasn't the case. The love and passion she felt for him overwhelmed her and she pushed away any negative thoughts. She felt whole and for the first time in her life she felt like a woman.

She moaned as he covered her neck with gentle kisses, his tongue searching and exploring as he moved lower. She pulled his face back up to hers and pressed against him. She tried to resist; tried to say no but though her head knew it was wrong her heart disagreed. She tried talking to him but somehow it seemed wrong to end things now. To stall him so she could collect her thoughts she began to tell him about the sword at the police station.

"…It was a fantastic sword – I wouldn't have minded it in my collection! You should've seen it, Jack…It was beautiful, and an eagle was carved into the blade. The hilt wasn't that special though –gold with a silver edge…It was still beautiful…Pity it wasn't mine!" she buried her face in his neck and breathed in his smell.

"You should've said it was yours though – like I told you," he chuckled to himself. "No matter - I would've loved to see their faces…"

Rose looked up at him, "Whose, the police?"

He turned his face and looked deep into her eyes. He smiled and kissed her on the tip of her nose. He cupped her face in his hands and kissed her lips tenderly. She thought she would drown in the deep, dark pools of his green eyes. She struggled for air but gave up the fight; she could die quite happily in this moment. She found it so hard to resist him. He had won; for now.

"No, Roland and his gorillas…" he laughed, "I sold them that sword. I told them it was the sword – The Sword of Aramoth. Your sword, honey. Only…"

Rose broke away from his grip and held him at arms length, "Only?"

"Only obviously it wasn't! The sword I sold them – the one you saw down at the station – was mine." He rolled onto his back and reached for a cigarette.

"So…" Rose sat up, "So where is my sword, Jack? Who the hell has it? You?"

"No, baby," he murmured, "As if…"

He looked at her through a haze of smoke; a literal smokescreen. She coughed and swung her legs over the edge of the bed. Reaching for her dressing gown she pulled it tightly around her as she moved to the window. It was late evening and the sky was a deep blue; night had fallen quietly on Oak Grove. There was neither sound nor movement in the street below. Sam hadn't returned home, or Aubrey; she watched the cats pacing round the tree, calling for him. She touched the curtains, barely registering a movement in them, and looked at the orange glow of the streetlamp below.

"How pissed will they be?" she murmured.

"Very." He chuckled.

She turned, "Yes, but how much, exactly?"

"Well," he squinted up at her through the smoke, "Enough to kill me."

©2007 Cara Aldous

Chapter 11

Sam and Aubrey sat quietly together at a table tucked in the corner of The Dog and Duck. They had headed to their local for some much needed alcohol after seeing Jack's creepy show. The sight they had witnessed had set Sam's nerves on edge; she had seen Jack's sword-swinging routine twice now and she feared not only for Rose but for herself too. She had no idea whether Jack had seen her watching the night of the storm but he definitely had this time.

She sipped her pint of cider and closed her eyes as the cool golden liquid slipped down her throat soothing and numbing her senses. Aubrey had insisted she have a brandy first but she refused and at her request he had bought two pints instead. He watched in awe as she steadily downed the first one, draining it to the bottom of the glass. She smiled, desperate to belch loudly but trying instead to let it out discreetly.

"So, what do you reckon all that was about today then?" he asked.

She frowned and shook her head, "Anybody's guess I suppose – Jack Bracken or whatever his name is – certainly does things for effect, don't you think?"

Aubrey grimaced, "I think it was more like a ritual, don't you? It can't have been for a reaction 'cause by rights we shouldn't have seen it. No – it was like a sort of rain dance, only I don't believe it was rain he was conjuring up…"

"Oh, God, Aubrey you don't think it was Satanism?" Sam jumped, "Oh God Aubrey, Rose is in so much trouble! Shit – do you think he was trying to summon up the devil?"

"Who knows what that man is capable of?" Aubrey sighed, then seeing Sam's frightened expression, quickly changed the subject. "You know, I've always liked you Sam. Well, both you and Rose actually…But it's you I like the most. Really like you I mean…We've become quite close over the last few…" He trailed off as he noticed her mouth hanging wide open in amazement.

Sam snapped her jaw shut tight. She looked at Aubrey as he blushed and pulled his glasses off to wipe his face with his fresh white hanky. Properly for the first time ever she saw him. He blinked at her with eyes that were deep dark brown, almost black; his dark hair, without its usual tonne of grease fell forward over his forehead, hanging in curls; his lips lifted at the sides into a permanent hint of a smile and his hollow cheeks, accentuated by high cheekbones sculpted his features handsomely. Sam was in love; again for the first time ever, she was in love. She leaned forward and kissed his cheek. He replaced his thick, black-rimmed glasses and coughed nervously. He tucked his hanky back into his pocket and looked at the table.

"I liked that." He spoke quietly and leaned forward. He kissed her cheek.

"Me too," she replied, shyly.

They finished their drink in companionable silence. Sam couldn't stop smiling and felt energised. Aubrey smiled too, happier than he had ever been before. They got up to leave simultaneously and pushed their chairs in together, laughing at the simplistic way in which their sudden compatibility shone through like a cloudburst of sunshine. But their happiness was short lived as they walked along Oak Avenue hand in hand. Their thoughts turned to Jack and the ritual they had seen. Sam voiced her concerns first, having witnessed his deranged actions before.

"Aubrey, do you really believe he was worshipping the devil?" she spoke in hushed tones, afraid to speak too loudly.

Aubrey stopped, gripping her hand tightly, "No…No, of course not! I don't know what he was doing exactly but I don't think it was devil worship…"

What he actually believed he couldn't tell Sam; not yet. But he had a suspicion that Jack was trying to resurrect the spirit of Blackheart. And one thing he was certain of; they had to tell Rose and bugger the consequences. Jack was dangerously close to the edge. What Aubrey had seen through that window had shaken him up. Jack's cold eyes had seemed to penetrate through Aubrey's soul sending ice coursing through his veins and any man who could do that to another was not of sound mind. If Jack's hold on Rose became too tight then they would never break her free from him. It was for her sake what they were planning but he doubted she would see it that way. It was a little worrying though as they could end up driving Rose and Jack closer together and distancing Rose from them in the process but it was a chance they would have to be prepared to take.

Aubrey suspected that deep down Rose was not that happy with Jack herself and possibly even wanted out of the relationship anyway. But whilst Jack controlled her, getting Rose alone would be the hardest part of all. Sam's friendship with her and their long history together was the only hope. Although usually level-headed Aubrey was sure that evil played a part in Jack's reason to be in England. He couldn't quite put his finger on it but something made the hair on the backs of his hands stand each time they met. Plus the reaction of the cats was enough on its own. Their hackles rose and they hissed and spat whenever Jack was around. Aubrey had made it a rule a long time ago, never to trust a person who his cats didn't like.

They came to a halt under the oak tree and Sam fingered the carving. It was surprisingly smooth and she followed the contours, wondering how on earth Jack had managed to do something so intricate under cover of darkness. She smiled shyly at Aubrey and made to kiss his cheek but as she moved closer he turned and their lips met. He held her face gently with his hand, encircling the other around her waist. They remained locked in their embrace for an age before coming up for air. Both reluctant to break apart they stayed close, and Sam leaned her head against Aubrey's.

She felt elated and a little shocked too; not so long ago if someone had told her she would end up snogging Aubrey Twissell under the old oak she would have laughed in their face. But this was no silly little game; it was real grown-up love. She had at long last come of age. Aubrey pulled away and grudgingly Sam allowed him to kiss her goodnight.

"Stay," she asked.

Aubrey shook his head, "No, not tonight."

"Please," she implored.

He took her hand in his and kissed it, "What we have found tonight is precious, special. We should let it grow and get to know what it's like to love and be loved properly. Then, and only then, will we be ready."

"Aubrey, you are funny," she giggled, "I think that's why I love you." She blushed and smiled shyly.

He smiled back, his whole face lighting up, "Good, because I love you too. Now, goodnight and remember – Tread very carefully with Rose – and Jon Black...uh...Jack Bracken!"

"Okay," she nodded and kissed him again.

*

He watched her skip down the path. Turning her key in the lock, she entered and blew him another kiss before closing the door gently behind her. Slowly she climbed the stairs, stopping at the top and listening hard. From behind Rose's closed door she could hear the deep tones of Jack's voice. She sighed heavily; it would be morning before she got chance to talk to Rose. So long as Jack had gone. Anger welled and she stomped into her room, slamming the door with all her might. Damn the man! Damn him back to the hell he came from! She flung herself down on the bed and buried her face in the pillow. She desperately wanted to share her good news with her best friend. But Rose clearly did not care anymore. Jack was visibly all she needed. The bitterness subsided as Sam replayed her kisses with Aubrey in her head. Each kiss making her stomach somersault and she smiled as she drifted off into a wonderful dreamy sleep.

*

The week passed fairly quickly. Jack practically moved in and Sam out. He seemed to have an idea that Sam wanted to say something to Rose and refused to stray far from her side. He even managed to have a pop at Sam by ridiculing her and Aubrey's blossoming romance. She tried dropping huge hints about swords and rituals but Rose either did not hear or chose to ignore her. At one point Rose was so fed up with the back-biting and bickering going on between the two of them that she turned on Sam, blaming her for causing the rift in the household.

"Oh for God's sake Sam – grow up!" she growled in a blaze of anger, "You're forty – for Christ' sake – act like it!"

By the end of the second week and with Jack seemingly glued to Rose's side Aubrey decided they must have a change of plan. But his idea of frightening Jack off; warning him to stay away, did not sit at all well with Sam. Whilst she now saw Aubrey in a very different light she still found it hard to believe that he could frighten anyone, let alone Jack. He was too gentle a soul.

"It's a good idea," she agreed, "But, how do you plan to scare him off exactly?"

Aubrey considered a moment. "We could hire someone to warn him. You know, like a 'heavy' or something?"

"Aubrey, sweet, I think you've been watching too many gangster films! Let's just say for arguments' sake such a person existed, how on earth would we find him or, come to that afford him?"

Aubrey grinned sheepishly, "Sorry, Samantha. I guess I could try? If I managed to land a lucky punch or something…?"

"Don't even go there!" Sam warned, "No, if you're absolutely sure that's what must be done we need someone who is a bit thick but has the brawn to have a go – and I know just the man…"

*

Babe stood on the corner of the High Street and watched as Rose opened the shop, disappearing inside followed closely by Jack. Sam and Aubrey had asked him to scare Jack off and he'd gladly agreed. It appealed to him, being the big hero and he imagined Rose falling into his arms with gratitude. Sam had sold the idea so well that he really believed he was going to save Rose from Jack's evil clutches. He stood for a while and watched, tapping the cricket bat he was carrying lightly on the ground. It had been his idea to bring along a weapon; Sam hadn't been convinced when she first set eyes on it but he soon managed to persuade her of its necessity. Jack wouldn't know what hit him; literally. Without thinking about the consequences should it go wrong he marched inside the shop; the bat slung over his shoulder.

Rose looked up, surprised, as the door flew open and Stanley Babe Knox stood in the doorway. He held aloft a cricket bat in both hands and looked extremely nervous. Jack glanced up briefly from the newspaper he was reading then returned to it, unimpressed. Rose was astonished to see him, he had never set foot inside her shop before and his awkward demeanour made her more than a little suspicious. She didn't think he was the sort to shoplift but, since the disappearance of her sword everyone had become a suspect; she watched him closely.

He wandered aimlessly around the small interior, picking things up, pretending to look at them, then putting them back without really seeing them at all. The whole time he kept his eyes on Jack who, unperturbed, carried on reading the newspaper. Finally he stood in front of the counter facing Jack head-on; the cricket bat held aloft as though he were going to swing it hard. Horrified by what was happening, Rose called out to Jack but she need not have worried.

Quick as a flash, he ducked away from the oncoming bat and swiftly grabbed one of the real swords from the display. He swung the cutlass around his head and moved so that the tip was pointed at Babe's throat. Babe dropped the bat with a clatter and began to shake. Rose scrabbled to pick it up and found herself caught between the two men.

Jack's eyes were cold and dark and did not flicker. He seemed to not even register her presence and, not for the first time, he scared her.

"Jack," she spoke steadily, "Drop the sword…"

He looked straight through her and she shivered. "Jon Black!" she shouted, "Drop the bloody sword! For God's sake, Jack, drop it!"

*

"…Churning waves,
Blowing sails,
Black is saved,
Come back…."

Rose's voice penetrated through the darkness and he was no longer on the deck of a ship but in her little pirate shop. He glanced around him. The flags hung silently on their rails and the sword display now had two gaps. He looked down at his hand, at the cutlass he grasped. It was held against the throat of a man. He recognised the young man now cowering as one of their neighbours. What was he thinking? He stepped back and lowered the blade.

"I…I'm sorry," he attempted an apology, "He…he tried to…I just…" Trying to explain his actions he held the cutlass up but shrugged helplessly.

He looked at the man and at Rose holding the bat. It dawned on him that this man had tried to kill him; he stepped forward, raising the cutlass to the man's throat once more.

"You tried to kill me! Who you working for?" He demanded.

Babe smiled nervously, sweat glistening on his forehead. How could he answer when he was in danger of being killed himself? He hoped Rose had some control over this maniac. Although terrified he tried desperately to keep his wits about him and searched frantically for a way to escape.

"Not kill you exactly, no..." Babe stopped.

"Then what, exactly?" Rose asked incredulously.

"Just, warn you off..." Babe hesitated; should he drop Sam and Aubrey in it too?

"Warn me off...?" Jack began to laugh, "What – Rose? You?"

He flung his head back and laughed louder and louder. His face distorted into a manic mask of terror as he turned to Rose. He stopped at the look of horror in her eyes and realised with sadness it was over; it was all over. He sighed long and deep and his shoulders drooped forward. He tried to smile but the lump in his throat threatened to explode, exposing his misery at having finally lost her. To fight it off he turned his attention back to Babe. He raised an eyebrow and curled his mouth into a snarl. It did the trick. Babe grabbed the bat from a startled Rose, turned tail, and ran. The little bell jingling wildly as he slammed the door behind him.

©2007 Cara Aldous

Chapter 12

Rose sat at her kitchen table and poured herself a large glass of red wine. Jack had gone home; disappearing under a huge black cloud of depression. He knew their relationship was over but was reluctant to accept it completely and like a petulant child had sulked all the way back to Oak Grove.

Babe's attack had come out of nowhere but she was in very little doubt as to who had put him up to it. Sam and Aubrey were very noticeable by their absence. Sam was with Aubrey she assumed yet she was happy for her. Her friend had interfered many times in her life but, for once, she was glad to have such faithful friends in Sam and Aubrey even if they were somewhat misguided. Rose had been surprised at the ease with which Jack had slipped back into her life again and if it hadn't been for Babe and his daft attack they would still be together. Of that she was certain. And although she had not actually told him it was over; he knew now without a doubt.

Black Nightmares to Scarlet Dreams

Her whole life had been turned upside down from the first night he had arrived and for what? A hunk of metal: The Sword of Aramoth; her sword. And now that it had disappeared out of her life for good so too could Jack. After all, there was nothing left to keep him here. She coughed and swallowed hard, gulping down a huge mouthful of wine in the process. No more of her tears would be shed. Not for her sword, or Jack, or her wasted life. Tomorrow's another day, she thought ruefully as she refilled her glass. A hammering on the front door made her jump, bringing her out of the doldrums; the sooner she forgot about Jack the better. Her heart beat fast as she answered it; Sandra Knox stood defiantly on Rose's doorstep and anger flashed in her eyes.

Sandra Knox was well known for fighting her son's corner. Each and every time he got into trouble with one or another of the neighbours there she was, on their doorstep and armed with the unflinching love of motherhood. Stanley Babe Knox had been a complete little bastard growing up and wreaked havoc whenever he could. Even as a young trainee manager he still found time to upset people. Only lately it had been with his noisy, souped-up car and loud base music booming late at night. Rose stared blankly at Sandra and waited.

"Right you! I want to know what you think you're doing – you and that bloody Yankee boyfriend of yours? My Stanley came home with a humungous red mark all across his throat and said that flippin' bloke of yours did it!" Sandra stopped to draw breath.

Rose seized her chance, "Okay, Sandra," she began, "Your precious son attacked Jack with a cricket bat…"

"He never did! He wouldn't do something like that! Why would he do that? Why, hmm? No, it's that bloody boyfriend of yours! There's been nothing but trouble, since he came! Ruined our lovely tree! And now, tries to have a go at my boy! Well, he's gone too far this time! I shall call the police and let him explain it to them!" Sandra finished triumphantly, feeling the battle had been won.

"First of all, Sandra," Rose began quietly, "if you were really that convinced Jack had attacked Stanley you would be talking to the police now instead of me! And secondly, Sandra, shouldn't you be having this conversation with Jack – again not me?"

Sandra took a step back, "Yes, I…I thought he was here! That's why I came here. Also…Also I…I didn't trust myself to talk to that…that bully!"

"Go away, Sandra," Rose sighed, "Go away and ask that darling son of yours just why he was in my shop with a cricket bat and why he decided to have some practise using Jack's head as a ball? Jack was only defending himself and Stanley got what he deserved."

Sandra Knox turned abruptly and clattered back up the path in her stilettos. Babe stood by the oak tree watching her. Although he had been unable to hear anything said between his mother and Rose he knew things had not gone well for him. Sandra's face was like thunder and this was a rare sight when aimed in his direction. He clutched the cricket bat and closed his eyes as she approached. Before he knew what was happening Sandra had grabbed the bat from his hands and swung it hard. It hit the trunk with a thud and several shards of bark fell onto the ground below. Then in a rage and with a roar she flung it back at him. It landed at his feet.

"Stanley Knox!" she screamed, "You wait till your father hears what you did! I won't be able to help you this time you stupid little boy!"

Babe closed his eyes and ears to the fury of his mother. Several of the neighbours had come out to see what all the fuss was about and a few now were smiling at him. Some openly chuckled at his public humiliation. It was degrading, like a public flogging. This was all thanks to Sam and Aubrey. Where were they now when he needed back up? Where were they when he nearly got his throat cut by that maniac? He had never really been that bright and if he thought about it he could so easily drop them in it. But all he could concentrate on was his mother's shrill voice as she slated him for every single thing he had done wrong in his life. He had almost been killed and she was telling him off!

He hated Jack Bracken for making him look like a fool. Not only had he been made to look weak and stupid in front of Rose but now, because of Jack, he was being made to look stupid in front of all their neighbours too. He watched his mother's lips as they moved rapidly but did not hear any of the words she spouted. He began to giggle nervously at her fast moving mouth; she looked like a Muppet. But he stopped laughing when his mother, mid-sentence, froze and turned very pale. Slowly she turned and he followed her gaze.

*

Jack Bracken stood behind Sandra Knox roaring loudly with laughter. Like everyone else there he found it amusing to see a grown man being publicly scolded by his mother. And unaware that a hush had fallen on the assembled throng he continued, laughing manically. Hushed voices and whispers blew through the crowd, and the breeze through the leaves on the tree added to make a shushing sound that grew to a crescendo and fell as abruptly he stopped. His expression changed in the blink of an eye and he stared hard at Sandra; the sneer on his face so cruel that she turned meekly back to her son for comfort.

Incensed at his mother's distress, Babe rushed forward, picking up the cricket bat from where it had fallen, and flew at Jack. This time he would do it properly, this time it was personal. He swung the bat in the air but, before it could connect with his head, Jack had grabbed it and twisted it quickly and skilfully from Babe's grasp. Babe stumbled forward and fell onto his knees. The watching crowd gasped as Jack kicked him in the small of the back and he went sprawling face down onto the ground. Sandra screamed as he scrabbled round in the dust to face his adversary. Jack stamped hard on his chest rapidly forcing the air out of his lungs. Placing the bat to his throat Jack dug in sharply, squeezing the air from his windpipe, watching intently as Babe began to lose consciousness; Sandra's shrieks becoming nothing but a distant squeak and the neighbours shouts no more than muffled words.

*

"...Yo-ho Yo-ho-ho,
Steal their stores,
And away we go,
Steal their food,

Black Nightmares to Scarlet Dreams

Take their wives,
Yo-ho-ho-ho,
End their lives..."

"Jack – no! For God's sake – no!" Rose's voice broke through the storm and lifted the darkness which had engulfed both men.

Aware that he was surrounded Jack lifted the bat and moved his foot. Babe wheezed and clutched his throat; his breaths great rasping gasps as he spluttered back to life. Jack gazed around at the circle of men closing in and raised the bat once more; he would take them all on if he had to. He was conscious of a tugging at his shirt and smelled a familiar perfume. He turned and looked into the soft emerald gentleness of Rose's eyes and wished she still loved him. He closed his eyes and leaned into her as a sob escaped his lips; he wanted it to stop. He hung his head, no longer caring, unable to stop; the darkness swallowing up the demons and taking them back to the dark depths they belonged. His tears flowed fast as she held him to her, running her fingers through his hair until they subsided. Then, very gently; so afraid she would leave him again, he pulled her close and together they pushed through the throng toward his house and sanctuary.

Sam and Aubrey were standing just a few feet away. They had watched silently as the drama unfolded in front of them. Sam felt guilty and wanted to intervene; to explain things. But Aubrey had stopped her just in time.

"Rose won't thank you," he had warned, "And it's important you appear to remain impartial in this instance."

They listened carefully as their neighbours gathered around Babe who was still lying on the ground. Sandra was screaming hysterically beside him. A few had gone back to their homes, closing their doors; not getting involved. Others were urging Sandra to call the police and have Jack arrested. Mavis Simkin offered herself up as an eye witness. Sam cleared her throat noisily and stepped up nervously to address them, paying particular attention to Sandra.

"Um, excuse me but," she felt sick, "Rose is with him and she'll keep him away for the time being. Listen Babe, Sandra, it's not strictly Jack's fault – is it? I mean, we all saw what really happened: Babe you swung at him with that damned bat again, didn't you? He was only defending himself…"

"Rubbish! He's a maniac!" Sandra Knox was indignant, "He nearly killed my little Stanley! You all saw it!"

Murmurs and nods resounded uncomfortably around the dwindling gathering. Seeing a few more edge their way slowly away, putting distance between them and the trouble, Sam seized upon this to urge those left to also reconsider their positions.

"Do you really want to get involved? I mean, you have no idea who he is, where he came from. He's American you know, they have guns 'n' stuff!" she stopped; maybe she had gone a little too far.

Aubrey interrupted, "What Samantha is trying to say is that we are all of us just as much to blame. Apart from Rose not one of us has tried to make him feel very welcome, have we? Perhaps our lack of compassion has pushed this poor unfortunate over the edge? If we had all done more..."

Several shuffled around looking at their feet; only a small minority now insisting on police involvement. Many muttered they didn't want any trouble brought to their doors, after all; it was the Knox family's business not theirs. The Knox family were beginning to feel increasingly isolated; Sandra wishing her husband would come home and take charge, Babe hoping his mum wouldn't tell his dad.

"The thing is," Aubrey continued, "Rose is in there with him and I think we should wait it out, see what happens in the next hour or so. Because, the thing is, I don't believe she's in there of her own accord..."

"What?" Sam was shocked, "What do you mean?"

"I think she went partly to keep the peace here and partly to comfort him but almost definitely to stop him killing Stanley. I really believe if she hadn't intervened when she did we would absolutely be calling the police – about murder."

A hushed quiet descended; the small gathering contemplating Aubrey's words and what they meant. There was a few mutterings and murmurings but before anyone could speak up Jack's door opened. All turned silently toward Jack and Rose as they emerged. Much of the neighbourhood was in shock yet the human condition of morbid curiosity took control of all other feelings and they stared, unmoving.

Rose stepped out into the sunshine, Jack's hand firmly grasped in hers, momentarily blinded by the brightness. Aware that all eyes were on them she turned away to gather her thoughts, pulled the door shut and walked confidently up the path. Jack staggered after her, half falling half running to keep up. He kept his eyes on the ground, ashamed at what he had done, terrified at what he could have done. He never once thought he was capable of killing and it scared him to think he could have easily murdered Babe in cold blood. Rose was not safe; no one was safe from him. He tried to tell her this once they were safely indoors. He tried to reason with her; if he could attack a stranger like that, who knows what else he could be capable of? It frightened him as he realised it was his dabbling in magic that had probably caused this. He knew his personality had changed; knew he was at risk of actually turning into Blackheart. And if he did then Rose would be in terrible danger.

He pleaded with her to leave him but she had refused to listen. She told him that she loved him and promised she would never leave. She had blamed herself; said it was all her fault. She had driven him to it by confusion and hurt. He hadn't told her about Blackheart's spirit; hadn't been able to explain without sounding insane. She had finally told him she loved him; that was all he had ever wanted. He had a chance at future happiness with Rose by his side and he wasn't about to throw it all away with a stupid confession. He had made up his mind there and then; he'd be an idiot to tell her about his ritual. He would stop. Blackheart would go away and everything would be alright again.

They walked steadily away from the staring neighbours, and her friends; Rose straining to keep her head held high. She focused ahead as they moved slowly but surely along the path. She grasped Jack's hand tightly and had to keep pulling him to her side. She couldn't look back; she couldn't stop for fear she might cry out for help. It had been her decision to save him and hers alone. It was something she would have to live with for the rest of her life. She would have to stay with him now and forever. She tucked an arm around him and he followed, putting his arm around her. They came to the end of the street, turned onto Oak Avenue and disappeared from view.

*

Sam and Aubrey stood as one, enthralled yet amazed at Rose's braveness and clear insanity. Her quest for her true love had culminated in a hypnotic fascination with a man capable of cold-blooded murder. One thing though; he had proved without a shadow of a doubt that he truly was a descendent of Blackheart. He was black-hearted beyond all comprehension and not for the first time since he had appeared in their lives, Sam felt afraid for her friend. She bit her lip so hard it drew blood.

"She looks so awful," she muttered under her breath.

"Absolutely terrified," Aubrey agreed.

©2007 Cara Aldous

Chapter 13

Marching determinedly down Oak Avenue, Rose passed the oaks one by one, counting each one off in her head. She was trying her utmost to keep focused and calm when what she really wanted to do was run screaming and shouting back to her friends.

Jack flagged behind despite his best efforts to keep up; she was like a woman possessed. That was rich; he was the one possessed. He had to take two steps to one of hers and he felt like a small child being led by his parent. His memories threatened to take him back there and he had to shake his head to rid his mind of them; that was one place he dared not revisit. His childhood had been far from happy. Even years of therapy had failed to wipe away the anguish and pain entirely; it was a life he had tried so many times to leave behind. Tried and failed miserably until now.

Black Nightmares to Scarlet Dreams

Rose kept her eyes on the path ahead, not daring to look back for fear she might change her mind. Now and again she glanced at Jack. He hung his head deep in thought; his face troubled and her heart went out to him. Love really was a strange thing and she doubted that she was emotionally equipped to deal with it; to deal with him. But she owed it to him to try. It was true to say she had been more than a little staggered by his violent reaction when Babe had tried to attack him again. But she was also secretly glad that Babe hadn't got the better of him. When Jack had pulled her with him she had allowed him to take her inside his house in the hope they would be able to sort out the whole big mess. She had stood in the hallway, studying him closely as he caught his breath and composure. The tussle with Babe had drained him yet his breakdown, especially in front of all their neighbours, had surprised her.

He had held her at arms length then as his gasps subsided he let go. She thought it odd that one minute he wanted her close and the next away from him. Usually when he was in one of his strange moods he held her so close she could barely breath. She watched him, frowning, but he didn't attempt to speak and so they had remained silent for several minutes. He studied her face closely as though trying to guess what kind of mood she was in. Eventually he had sighed deeply, sitting down heavily on the bottom stair. She had to hold onto the banister for support, her heart racing and the panic welling up inside.

As they waited silently Rose had felt quite surreal; if any outward sign of her panic were visible Jack showed no indication that he knew. With the fear bubbling up inside she leaned her whole weight into the banister, hoping he would continue wrestling with his own demons in ignorance of hers. At last, he spoke but his voice was quietly subdued.

"I...I shouldn't have reacted like that – I know!" His head remained bowed as he continued, "I couldn't help it! You saw what he did –saw what he was like, didn't you? You know what really happened?"

Rose hadn't replied then; she didn't know what to say, what he wanted her to say, so she just watched as her breathing steadied, the banister grasped tightly between her sweaty palms. He studied her for a while as though noticing for the first time that she too was tormented. He reached out a hand to touch hers but flinched, afraid to lay a hand on her.

"If I hadn't done anything he would've hit me you know – probably even killed me!" He had looked at her for support but she gave no reaction.

Steadily she had held his gaze, hoping her face remained closed. She wanted to give nothing away; not even the tiniest emotion. He stared at her, stared right into her eyes but she had simply stared blankly back at him. Then, finally, he had closed his eyes as a solitary tear fell down his cheek. Another formed in the corner of his eye. She watched and waited and clenched her teeth; she had tried her damnedest not to fall for it.

He sighed deeply before opening his eyes. He spoke in a whisper, "The whole thing's a mess!"

"You're not wrong there!" she replied with a small laugh.

"I don't think there's one person I haven't upset or turned against me; all because of a sword and that damned Pirate!"

She faltered, looking at him with surprise. It was the first time he had spoken out against Blackheart and with such vehemence. It was then he had seen a glimmer of something in her face; hope. He seized upon this last chance.

"I don't care about the others though, Rose. It's you I care about, more than anything! Nothing else matters to me as long as I have you…I love you…"

He prised her fingers from their tight grip on the banister and held her hand close to his chest. He entwined his fingers with hers and held her hand gently. She had tried desperately to hold onto the banister and her sanity. It would be pure madness to fall for his charm all over again. Each time it happened she promised herself it would never happen again. But here she was once more; she had wished in that moment they had never met. She loved him too much.

"Rose," he put her hand to his cheek and she felt the wetness from his tears, "Rose, I love you. And I know you love me too. And, even though so many are against us, we'll manage. We have to…I love you and I would die for you, you know that don't you? You know that…"

He had faltered then and she urged herself to close her mind to him, close her ears to his poetic prose but his words penetrated and, like a caged bird, she felt constrained to listen. She was his prisoner; she would always be his prisoner. His love was strong but it was also destructive. They would be together but at a price; her sanity and freedom. Must she always be doomed to a life of domination? Was it her lot in life to always do as she's told? As her mother had once ruled her life so it was Jack's turn. And, as she had once played the dutiful daughter, so now she would play the devoted wife.

"We were meant to be together, Rose! You know that we were meant to be," he kissed her fingers as she shivered at his touch.

She had pulled away from him then with one final attempt at escape, trying so hard to break the bond, "No, Jack – no! We were not meant to be together any more than we are our ancestors spanning centuries in search of love! We were – are – strangers! We know nothing about one another apart from our ancestry and that's hardly relevant to the here and now, is it? You came here because of another man's obsession with a sword and your obsession with Blackheart! And now we're in this bloody mess all because of him! No, correction, you're in this bloody mess – not me!"

"…what about your obsession with your sword?" He was struggling to keep her.

"Oh sod the bloody thing! I wish to God I'd never found it! I wish it had just rotted in the attic with the rest of the rubbish…"

Something had stirred then in the recesses of her memory. So she had focused hard on Jack, standing before her, his head hanging low as tears trickled down his cheeks and onto the wooden floor. She fought the urge to brush them away, held back on the need to hold him to her. Instead she had watched, detached, as he wiped his face with his sleeve and looked up at her through damp wet lashes.

"I do love you Rosie," he had whispered as he leaned forward and brushed her lips with a kiss.

Black Nightmares to Scarlet Dreams

Her resolve shattered in to a thousand pieces and she was lost. She surrendered herself into his arms and together they had sobbed, promising to always be true to one another. Her quest for true love and her belief that her knight would rescue her from her boring, mundane life had been turned completely on its head. Jack was more pirate than knight and, right there and then; she would have given anything to have that old life back. But she must move forward if she was to keep any control. There was only one thing to do; it was time to find her sword and lift the curse that Blackheart had bestowed upon her family. If she gave it back to Jack they may just have a chance at happiness.

*

Jack watched the woman striding ahead of him; his Rose. He had broken her spirit; he knew he had. Their love was so fragile though; it couldn't possibly stand up to any more suffering. He couldn't shake the feeling of helplessness engulfing him. It seemed to wipe everything else out. He must hold onto the fact that his feelings of true love for her had saved everything; him, their relationship, her.

"...On a sinking ship,
The captain stands,
And the crew will die,
They are his hands,
His is law, his is right,
No man or woman must try to fight..."

©2007 Cara Aldous

The darkness descended on him in an avalanche of fear and dread and he couldn't fight it anymore. The demons swirled back into his mind and delved into the darkest corners where they hid. If Rose knew of them she would leave him but he knew her exhaustion weakened her. He would allow her to be angry with him, for a short time. Allow her the luxury of thinking that she had won; that she was now in charge. But no woman had ever had much of a hold over a Black. So passively he followed her. They were heading for Drummonds but he had nothing to worry about; Rick Drummond wouldn't give anything away; he couldn't.

Rose shoved the door open hard and as they stepped over the mat a bell sounded making the shop-keeper aware of their presence. Rose was grim-faced; she wasn't looking forward to this but it had to be done. Ruby was chatting confidently with a customer and half an eye on her visitors. Rose gazed around, looking for Rick. Her eyes fell on the lurid green faux leather sofa Ruby was trying to offload to the unsuspecting shopper. No doubt it was part of a job lot Rick had done a deal on with the manufacturers. Though why anyone in their right mind would want such a putrid thing in their front room Rose could not imagine.

Ruby was doing a great job and was in full swing, the sale almost in the bag, when she became aware of Rose and Jack waiting impatiently behind her customer. Jack was staring at her with his intense green eyes and she faltered. Rose nudged him in the ribs to break the spell and he moved his gaze onto her but the customer moved away; Ruby had lost the sale. She turned and nodded curtly at them, her face strained into a smile. She ushered them briskly into the office at the bottom of the showroom.

"What can I do for you?" she asked with a short attempt at a smile, "And make it quick, I've got business to take care of."

"Where's Rick, Ruby?" Rose asked, looking around the empty office; everything in the showroom had a sale sticker on. Ruby was obviously having a clear out.

She shrugged, "How should I know?"

"He's your husband! Where is he?" Rose demanded.

"I don't know! Gone away!" Ruby replied petulantly.

It was going to be harder than Rose expected. "Where?"

"How the hell should I know?"

"Don't mess me about Ruby! Where is Rick? Has he got my sword?"

Ruby stepped back; she seemed startled, "I really don't know what you're talking about, Rose, honestly! Look, the last time I saw him he said he was coming to see you. That's the last I heard from him."

Rose looked at Jack, "What? But…weren't you worried? When he didn't come home?"

Ruby shrugged again, "Between you and me, Rose, I thought good riddance! You were welcome to him as far as I was concerned…"

Rose shivered, "Me? God, no, you must be joking…"

Ruby smiled and shrugged again.

"Sorry Ruby," Rose said sheepishly, "No offence…"

"None taken! Anyway, he's gone and I haven't heard a thing from him…" Ruby raised her hand and studied her polished nails.

"Really? Nothing at all?" Rose didn't believe her.

Ruby shook her head, her eyes staying on her nails, "Not a sausage!"

"And the sword?" Rose snapped.

"That's all he ever went on about! Rose's sword this and Rose's sword that…Got on my flippin' nerves if you must know!" Ruby kept her eyes down, avoiding their stares.

Jack stepped forward menacingly. "Okay, enough of this crap! Where is he?" he demanded menacingly.

Rose put out a hand to stop him. He shuddered at her touch and she knew he ached for her as much as she did for him. A shiver ran along her spine as he leaned into her and it was all she could do to stop herself gasping from the sheer intensity of her feelings. She dropped her hand to her side and looked at Ruby with pity. The woman in front of her had been attractive once, many years ago. Her hair was redder than Rose's but had a false brightness to it; a copper brashness. Her large bosom heaved with each breath she took and her face and chest were flushed and ruddy. Jack scared her as he once had Rick.

A chill crept over Rose, slithering through her skull, making her feel as though her hair literally stood on end. Jack was capable of most things but, if it came to it, would he really be capable of murder? She tried to run her fingers through her knotted curls but got them caught. As she struggled to free them she desperately tried to think of something to say which would not betray her thoughts to either Ruby or Jack. The bell chimed as a couple stepped into the showroom and Ruby went to them, a smile fixed ready on her face. Without Rick in tow she shone and Rose watched in awe as she moved easily into her sales patter. Jack waited sullenly by her side and Rose knew it was time to leave. They waited in silence as Ruby left her customers and returned to them.

"Look, if you don't mind…" she began.

"Yes, of course Ruby," Rose sighed, "Just one thing…Do you have any idea what happened to my sword?"

"Well, sort of – Rick would only say it was stolen. He reckoned he knew who did it too but he never told me who. Sorry."

Rose shrugged, "Not to worry, Ruby. Listen, when Rick does eventually show up can you ask him to call me? Or perhaps he can call the police, tell them what he knows?"

"I'll try but somehow I don't think he will be back," Ruby replied with another shrug.

Rose and Jack turned to leave.

"Oh, there was one thing – Rick did say something quite strange actually – he said that the sword had been stolen not once but twice! And that the bugger who did it had better watch his back 'cos there are others much more dangerous in search of it now!"

Jack spun round sharply; Rose asked her to explain but Ruby could help no further. Sadly, Rose turned and walked down through the showroom for one last time. She clung tightly to Jack, who seemed visibly shaken. He had stumbled forward at Ruby's words though what the hell it meant to him Rose had no idea. As they stepped out into the brilliant sunshine she breathed in the fresh air. Though it was still heavy the air was much fresher than the stuffy showroom. The stench of cheap leather had made her gag. Their conversation with Ruby made no sense; where was Rick? If he had disappeared Ruby was in no hurry to find him and didn't seem worried at all. Perhaps he had left her before.

"Maybe he had enough of being married to her?" Jack mumbled, "Know I would!"

Rose smiled, "Maybe you're right –but why disappear so suddenly…Jack?"

He guessed what was coming.

"Did you…Did you hurt him in any way?"

"Rose! What do you take me for? I told you – I'm an actor, not a gangster!"

She smiled ruefully, "Sorry, baby, had to ask – You do understand?"

"I guess," he replied sulkily, "I think, maybe, well…Perhaps I could've had something to do with him leaving in such a rush…"

Rose turned harshly on him. "What?"

Sweat formed on his upper lip, "Calm down honey! Not like that. I didn't kill him or nothin'! What I mean is – I saw him do something…briefly."

"When? Where?" She grabbed his arm, "Tell me!"

Jack sniffed and looked around; they were standing outside her Pirate shop. This is where it had all begun. He shrugged, "It was right here, as a matter of fact, I was watching – You ran from here so fast...I wanted to...call out to you...Hold you – You looked so scared! Then I saw him – Rick. He went inside then came out again real quick. Rose, honey, Rick had your sword! Tucked under his arm. I saw him put it in his trunk. I was about to go talk to him when you came back...Then the cops arrived..."

"Oh my God! Then it wasn't that far away...I could have...could have...got it back...." Rose stumbled forward, grabbing his arm.

He grasped her tightly around the waist and sat her down on the kerb. She felt sick, her stomach churning and she had to fight back the rising bile in her throat. She coughed and gulped as he rubbed her back in soothing circular movements.

"Oh my God, Jack," she whispered, "I stood here talking to him, trusting him! Why? Why did he do it?"

"Money, I guess, same as the rest of us," he held her close and breathed her in.

"And," She pulled away, "And you were going to take it! He beat you to it – that's the only reason you didn't steal it from me!"

"I know, honey, but if I had taken it then, I would've given it right back once we got together..."

"How can I be so sure?" She bit her lip to stop the tears from spilling down her face. Her eyes glistened.

"Because I fell in love you," he said as he tenderly kissed her.

He held her tightly as they sat on the roadside. Traffic rolled by nothing but a blur. People stared and walked by. But they were oblivious to their surroundings; the two of them clung tightly together. Jack felt as though his chest would burst open at any moment. He loved her so much but he knew, deep down, it would never be enough. The darkness in his head was now permanently there and although he tried hard to ignore it the headaches were becoming more and more painful. Whenever Rose was close her touch nearly blinded him with pain.

He had figured out some time ago that she was the cause. It had to be the love he felt for her. It was so pure, so powerful and all consuming that it overwhelmed him. The rituals he practised daily to rid her of his ancestor's curse was almost definitely a factor too. It was a dangerous game to play. It was stupid to dabble in the occult and the hex he practised came from a black magic book he had discovered in an old bookstore back home. Several times he had considered finding a priest to rid himself of the ghost of Blackheart once and for all. Well, he would stop now; he had Rose and everything would be okay. He had to believe that.

Rose shivered and leaned into him and he shivered back at her touch. She put a hand to his face and traced her fingers down his cheek, around his nose and down his scar. He trembled and she smiled as she kissed his lips. He stood and pulled her to her feet. Then he wrapped her in his arms and led her toward the relative safety of her shop.

Ruby smiled a wide toothy grin at the couple who had just bought the last ghastly green sofa and silently offered up a prayer of thanks that they were finally rid of the white elephant. She ran her tongue along her teeth; always afraid some of her red lipstick would find its way onto them. She sashayed back to her office. Rose and Jack's visit bothered her; her darling husband had not told her the full truth. It was time to ask him some questions. She picked up the receiver and tapped out the number, taking care not to damage her newly polished red nails. She studied the many rings on her fingers as she waited and thought it about time she had some new ones; with real diamonds this time.

After several more rings her call was answered, "Hello, yes?"

"Rick, it's me," she smiled at her reflection in the glass partition.

He was alarmed, "What's up? What's happened? Has something gone wrong?"

"Shut up and listen!" she snapped, "I've just had a visit and – you were right he is a weirdo! But here's the thing Rick, they're so desperate for that sword back it must be worth a great deal more than the measly few hundred you gave me! And don't think you can wriggle out of it this time! I want my share of the profit and I'm not taking no for an answer!"

©2007 Cara Aldous

Chapter 14

Entwined in Jack's arms, Rose tried to imagine what sort of future they would have together. The stifling heat of the nights had cooled considerably as autumn crept closer yet it was still uncomfortably hot; she couldn't think straight. Jack moaned in his sleep as she pulled herself free and he rolled over, his back to her. She looked at his outline through the darkness; at his broad tanned shoulders and ran her finger down his spine. She marvelled at the power she had over another human being as he shivered. He remained in a deep and peaceful sleep and she watched him awhile.

They had returned home after much deliberating at the shop. She had resigned herself to a future shared; though this was not how she had hoped it would be. Jack opened up to her and spoke for the first time about his own hopes and dreams; and about his past. It made for grim hearing. His childhood was a story of poverty and drunkenness and it was small wonder he had escaped it by immersing himself in a world of make-believe. Many great actors have had some damage or hardship in their lives, it was a pity he had not put it to good use but instead drifted from job to job. Soon he became known as unreliable and difficult to work with and so tried independent movies. The Indie Directors were surprised that he had never broken into mainstream when they saw his performances but soon came to realise why when they too experienced his unpredictability.

Unsurprisingly Rose featured heavily in his future plans. She should have been excited but her heart felt weighted down with the enormity of it all; she would be accountable for this damaged man forever. Whilst she prepared supper he had sat at the table, watching contentedly. She felt responsible for him; for his happiness and his welfare. The feelings overwhelmed her and she had to be careful not to betray her thoughts. If he saw it in her face he chose to ignore it. Not for the first time she felt doomed to a life of fear and regret. Not fear of Jack, strangely enough; but those he had deceived. Roland hung over their heads like a dark cloud; Jack had duped his employer into believing he had delivered the promised sword and Mr Roland was a powerful man. It was only a matter of time before they realised the sword the police were holding was not the Sword of Aramoth.

They had fallen exhaustedly into bed soon after eating. The moments when Jack made slow, satisfying love to her were times she could immerse herself in the present and forget the problems of the past and future. Moans of ecstasy had escaped her lips so easily, belying her true feelings. At the beginning of their relationship he had scared her a little with his unflinching belief that their love had spanned centuries, yet she had so desperately wanted to believe it too. He had been relentless in his pursuit of her and she had found it exciting. But when he finally had her his sheer intensity threatened to destroy it all.

She had eagerly opened herself up to him; anticipating his passion and affection for her. But what she had expected to happen failed to materialise. The love she thought she felt, muddled and confused with yearning for her perfect man, was raw. Stripped bare it failed to stand up to close scrutiny. She believed she had loved him; at first. But now, with so much history between them, in such a short space of time and with so many lies and recriminations, it was difficult to know what she felt anymore. Apart from numb. She knew that however misguided, his love for her was here and now; and it was real. It was the only solid thing she had to hold onto and it had to be enough. For now.

On his part Jack no longer tried to live in the past. He had seemed to shun Blackheart since they got back together. In fact he was scared of the Pirate; she was sure of it. He had given up on his ancestor; he had made her a solemn promise. So perhaps they could have a future after all and with the past firmly back in its rightful place; behind them; they could begin anew and look to a more hopeful future for both of them. Destruction is drawn to those who invite it through their damaged view of the world. They must both start to think positively about life. It was their only chance.

She watched as he slept, listening to his steady breathing. He slept peacefully, free from the torment he endured while awake. She knew; he thought she didn't but it wasn't difficult to see. His struggle to remain composed at times of stress concerned her and she worried he might be seriously ill. He was almost certainly confused and tortured at times but with her friends and neighbours watching closely she dared not think about it for long. For once he slept soundly by her side, safe in the knowledge that she would never leave him. Rose sighed wishing she could love him the way he loved her. She turned away from him and soon fell into a deep and troubled sleep...

"...Come to me,
My lover, my mate,
Soon we shall be,
At one in our fate..."

Flashing blades and the sound of clashing swords and cutlasses filled her with dread. The blur of fighting men became clearer and Jack and Babe came into focus, fighting with cricket bats. They metamorphosed into men Rose did not recognise; yet unmistakably pirates. She fought to open her eyes but couldn't. She watched as the eighteenth century ghosts surrounded her. Her body felt heavy and she strained with the effort to move. She tried to cry out to Jack, sensing him beside her; tried to reach out and touch him, begging for him to bring her back to the real world. But the nightmare continued.

©2007 Cara Aldous

The men closed in on her yet she could not see their faces nor hear their voices. The dream was as vivid as the one which had brought forth Jack into her living world and she prayed that this was not another omen. She felt powerless as the men bore down on her and squeezed her eyes tightly shut. When she opened them again the men were fighting as though she were not there. The pirates fought with a violence that shook her soul until not a single enemy was left standing. They stood looking down on the dead men and Rose was forced to look too.

Naval men in blue coats lay dead at her feet in a pool of scarlet. She tried to move back but the oozing blood touched her bare toes. She stepped back further but still it seeped through her feet. The long red dress which she wore hung in the blood no matter how high she gathered the skirts. It crept up her dress, staining it a darker and deeper crimson. Frantically she pulled the hem up and began to scrub it between her stinging fingers. The pirates circled her, closing in menacingly; their cutlasses held aloft, their rasping breaths hot on her face. Looking up she saw the familiar outline of Captain Blackheart. The notorious captain threw back his head and laughed, deep and hard. The pirates were almost upon her, large and threatening. They seemed taller or perhaps she was smaller; shrinking with terror.

There was a flash of lightening and a clash of blades and the pirates lunged at her; their raised cutlasses aimed at her throat. They plunged them deep and hard. She plummeted through the nightmare, hurtling fast into a dark abyss where Jack stood, arms outstretched, waiting for her; smiling up at her.

Black Nightmares to Scarlet Dreams

Her eyes flickered open. She was staring into a dark, murderous face but this was no pirate. He held aloft a sword which seemed to weigh heavy in his outstretched arms as they shook to keep control. This was no dream; he was very, very real. She tried to scream but no sound escaped her open mouth and she was frozen in terror, unable to move even the smallest muscle. The man stared back at her his eyes wide, startled by the wakefulness of his victim. He staggered forward and she saw the glint of the blade as it fell toward her.

She shut her eyes, praying for salvation. *CLASH!* The sound of metal upon metal forced her to open her eyes again. Another sword blocked the offending blade with such force it quivered. With a skilful swish it threw the sword from the hands of the man and away from her, sending both reeling to the floor. Gaining control she sat up and scrambled out of bed, pressing her back into the wall. Jack was struggling with the intruder, throwing him to the floor again and again. Rose watched as they fought, punches flying and she let out a small scream as Jack was knocked crashing into the wardrobe. But he sprung back quickly and landed a punch squarely on the jaw of the man who slumped down hard onto the floor.

A horrible, sickening silence descended as Jack sunk down onto the bed. He wiped the back of his hand across his face and, as he pulled it away, Rose saw blood glistening in the gloom. She stumbled forward and switched on the bedside light. He turned and she saw blood trickling from the side of his mouth. He smiled at her. Sobbing with a mixture of relief and shock she flung her arms around him and buried her face in his shoulder. He turned to her and lifted her face to his; kissing her tenderly then he placed a strong, protecting arm around her and pulled her close.

"Who…who is he?" she whispered hoarsely.

"Don't worry, honey, he can't hurt you now. It's over," he mumbled into her hair.

He reached down, picking up his sword from the floor and wiped the blood on his shirt. He placed it down on its point and spun it round and round. The blade shone in the yellow light and softly hummed as the hilt whirred through his fingers. Abruptly he stopped, holding it up to show her. The golden phoenix like the one carved into the oak glinted and gleamed. Hands shaking she took it from him; the Sword of Aramoth had come home to its mistress and Jack had delivered it as promised.

Chapter 15

Glad to get away Rose disappeared downstairs to make some tea and to think. Stopping outside Sam's door she wondered if she should knock to check that her friend was okay but thought better of it. Sam had obviously slept through it and it was better she stay out of it. She would only insist they call the police anyway and Jack had been very clear on that score when Rose had picked up the phone.

"I know him," was all he would say.

He had refused to elaborate any more so she left him alone with the man. It wouldn't be long before he was fully awake; she could hear his groans as she padded down the stairs. She was pretty sure he worked for Roland. Perhaps finally it would be over; though her instincts told her this unlikely. The man had tried to kill her and she was still very shaken up by it. Why her and not Jack? Or had he thought she was Jack? She guessed it was difficult to tell in the dark just who was who; especially wrapped inside a duvet.

Jack sat on the edge of the bed and unscrewed the hilt of the Sword of Aramoth. He was just going through the motions really; he already had an idea of what he would find. The man climbed up onto the bed and lay, exhausted, beside him clutching his head. Jack nodded at him; a friendly acknowledgement in the circumstances. The two men knew one another but this didn't make them the best of friends; far from it.

"Hey, Artie – How you feeling?"

"Like crap! What did you hit me with?" Artie Ribald felt the bump growing on the top of his head.

"My fist but you fell back. Knocked yourself out on the edge of the bed I guess." Jack shrugged.

Artie watched as he finished unscrewing the handle, carefully placing it on the bed. He peered inside the hollowed out centre. It held a small, modern lined note but Jack wasn't surprised. Artie was though.

"You mean to say that this goddamn sword we've all been chasing is useless? We nearly got ourselves killed – and for what? A pretty sword – that's it?" Artie was incensed.

Jack chuckled to himself, "Always hoped it would be empty. Just have to tell Rose all this was for nothing. She's not going to like it though – she'll think Roland will still come after us!"

*

Black Nightmares to Scarlet Dreams

Rose watched the kettle come to the boil, her hand resting on the handle. She wanted to feel the heat and steam on her fingers; to warm through her hands. She felt cold standing alone in the kitchen in the early hours; the heat of the night now turned to the chill of early morning. She jumped when she felt a kiss on her cheek. She hadn't realised Jack was standing behind her until he slipped his arms around her waist. She looked up at him, waiting for him to confirm what she already knew. His face gave little away as he shook his head. She turned back to the kettle and began to pour the boiling water into the mugs in front of her and smiled. At last Roland would be off their backs; without the map he would have to stop his incessant search of the unobtainable. Her father would have been pleased.

"Oh well," she said breezily, "That's that then…"

Jack dropped his hands to his sides and stepped away from her. He was staring at her with a strange look in his eyes. She waited for him to speak. In the still quietness of the hour Rose looked into the eyes of a man she thought she was finally getting to know but saw once more the stranger looking back at her. She had been kidding herself it would work; they both had. Neither of them had any idea who the real person was behind the other. In that moment she knew she may at last have a chance to be free of him. Careful not to give anything away she lowered her gaze and turned back to the task of making tea. The hairs stood up on the back of her neck as his eyes bore into her. Mustering all her courage she spun around to face him. She would force the issue and have it out with him once and for all.

"What?" she snapped.

The sharp tone to her voice surprised him and he stumbled back. He looked at her accusingly and sadly shook his head. He tried to turn away but she grabbed his arm and pulled him to her. The suddenness of her gesture unbalanced him. The darkness which had finally begun to lift after the night before now descended thicker and faster than it had ever done before.

"...Leave her be,
Come to me,
Black turns night,
And all be right..."

"What?" she spoke again, this time softer; trying to break through the darkening clouds.

"You knew," he frowned, tears forming, "All this time you knew it wouldn't be there. You knew the sword would be useless to Roland without the map yet you said nothing! Where is it Rose?"

Rose lifted her face to his. She searched his eyes for some warmth but found ice. His face was closed of any sign that he loved her. Instead he scowled and sulked. She wanted to break through the torment as she had so many times before but she was afraid; even if she could it would doom her to a lifetime of regret. She must resist the urge to help him; whatever the cause of his illness the cure was not something she alone could offer; Jack needed professional help. Sam and Aubrey had been right all along.

He took her by the shoulders and shook her so hard she thought she would faint. "Where the hell is it? Where's the map, Rose?"

Frightened, she broke free from his grasp and crossed quickly to the other side of the table. Realisation dawned and she was afraid. She moved quickly; she wasn't going to give him the opportunity to attack her. Her eyes shone as she smiled defiantly; show your fear and they have you. Bullies thrive on fear, that's how they control you. She had read that once in a magazine article on wife-beating. It was all too clear; in a fit of rage she had seen him for what he really was. He was a bully. He had tried to wear her down, tried to run her life; well not anymore. She edged her way slowly round to the kitchen doorway.

"I haven't the faintest idea what you're bloody talking about! What map?" not needing a reply she continued, angrily, "Anyway – did you honestly think, after all these years, these centuries it would still be there anyway? That's if ever it was there! Did you? Cos if that's the case then you're a bigger idiot than your boss is!"

"Of course I didn't think it would be there!" he shouted back at her, "But if you knew it wasn't then how come you didn't say? Every time I mentioned the map, you always changed the subject. I always assumed you were scared if it was there you'd never see your sword again. But, you knew all along it wasn't, didn't you? How else would you explain this...?" He held up a small piece of paper. "'Ha ha! Joke's on you!' it says and it's written by you, Rose...."

She faltered, "Oh...For God's sake Jack! I've had enough of this! I've had enough of you trying to control me – trying to scare me – and trying to run my life! Well, here's the news: I'm not afraid anymore! Do you understand? You don't scare me any more – you or Blackheart!"

"Oh, really? We'll soon see about that!" he rushed toward her. Instinctively she crouched to the floor, her hands covering her face from the onslaught.

Jack staggered back, his knees buckling as he realised what he had become, "Oh my God! I never meant..." he whispered. He leaned his head against the table.

"Maybe...maybe there never was a map – have you thought of that?" Rose pitied him; he looked pathetic.

"I...I'm so sorry, honey," his voice was muffled as he spoke into his hands, gripping the edge of the table hard, "I would never hurt you Rose; I thought you knew that."

The hurt in his voice tore at her heart but she remained motionless and expressionless. If she broke now there really would be no going back. It was over. She bit her lip as she listened to his muffled sobs. He lifted his face to look at her and she guessed he wanted her to go to him and hold him and cover him with soothing kisses as always but she stood firm. He got to his feet and moved around the table, holding onto it for support, until he faced her.

She wasn't afraid anymore. He stood so close to her she could feel his pain. She placed a hand on his chest and felt him shudder. With all her will she pushed him gently from her. He sat down hard against the edge of the table. She moved to the window. Dawn was beginning to break. Birds sang happily in the trees, unaware of the night's events, their song deafening. With her back to him and her mind closed to his torment she folded her arms.

"Just go," she said dully.

He made no sound. She waited for his protests but none came. When she turned around, ready to face another barrage of pleas she found she was alone. He had gone; slipping out without a sound. The back door stood wide open and she shivered in the chill of the early morning air. She stood, drinking in the silence, wiping away all doubts. It was for the best; for both of them. She knew he wouldn't bother her again. They would still be neighbours; maybe eventually they could even be friends.

"Goodbye, Jack, my first love" she whispered as a solitary tear fell down her cheek, "My true love...."

*

It was ten o'clock before Sam came home. She walked in through the unlocked back door and found Rose sitting at the table sipping tea and chatting to a strange man. She instinctively braced herself for one of Jack's cruel remarks. She had spent the night with Aubrey and Jack was bound to take the piss out of the whole fantastic experience as usual. She wanted it over with. Rose turned and smiled at her and she nodded back nervously. She went to the kitchen door and peered up the stairs; no sound came from the bedroom or bathroom. She turned and frowned at Rose.

"He's gone," her friend replied, still smiling, "It's over."

"And you're okay with that?" Sam asked hesitantly.

"Absolutely," Rose laughed.

Sam took a deep breath and blew it out in relief.

"Couldn't agree more," Rose replied, laughing, "This is Artie by the way, Artie Ribald; he knows Jack…"

Artie smiled at Sam and nodded by way of hello. His mouth was full of toast and he slurped his coffee hungrily. He placed a hand on the back of his head and gingerly fingered an angry red lump poking through his dark hair. Accepting that having strange men in the house was becoming the norm Sam went over to the pot and poured out a mug of over-brewed tea before sitting down with them. Having learnt from past mistakes she waited for Rose to explain more. She didn't have long to wait.

"Artie works for Mr Roland – the same man Jack does; or did should I say. It seems Jack's been a naughty boy! He wanted the sword for himself and if Artie hadn't come looking for it I doubt Jack would ever have told me he had it. Seems his plan all along was to get the sword and take it back home to America. God Sam, I've been so stupid! Jack is completely insane! I think he might've hurt me if I stayed with him too much longer," Rose took a deep breath, "So this morning I told him just what I thought about him and that I wanted him gone – and he went!"

Sam frowned; this was a bit too much to take in, "Just like that?"

Rose nodded, "Just like that!"

"I would definitely say you had a lucky escape," Artie said through a mouthful of toast, "He may be nothin' more than a B movie actor – and a bad one at that! But he sure as hell is nuts! If you hadn't 'a been there Rose, I reckon I would've been dead!"

Sam shivered and glanced fearfully out of the window. The three sat in silence, sipping their drinks, Rose and Sam contemplating Jack's rôle in their lives. It was the most bizarre and surreal experience to date; even having breakfast with your burglar seemed normal next to what had happened so far. Rose missed out the part about Artie's place in the nightmare; Sam would only fret and besides, she felt perfectly safe with him. They listened to the noises of the morning; to the hum of an early lawnmower, the birds' mid-morning chorus, the sound of letters dropping through the letterbox, the meowing of a cat. Two familiar black heads sat outside the back door and stared at them through the glass. Smiling, Sam jumped up and opened the door to let Aubrey in.

"Guess what!" he was almost jumping with glee, "Guess who I've just seen – Jack Bracken or Jon Black or whatever his bloody name is! Anyway, he's gone!"

"Yes, we know, Rose told him to go and he left here this morning…" Sam kissed him much to Rose's surprise.

"Did you Rose? Well done," He looked quizzically at Artie as he continued, "Anyway, he's not just left you – he's left full stop!"

Rose stood up, "What do you mean?"

"I saw him leaving his house about half an hour ago carrying a large backpack. And – this was the really bizarre thing – he was crying!"

"Crying?" Rose bit her lip to keep her own tears at bay. The emotions of the morning crashed over her in waves.

Aubrey chuckled and nodded, "Yes, like a baby!"

Chapter 16

By the middle of October the cold air had enveloped the country and crisp mornings full of mist replaced the oppressive heat of summer. Several days of heavy rain had slowly begun to penetrate the parched earth and the luscious green that England is so famed for had started to emerge from its heavy slumber. Autumn had been delayed for so long that the over-burdened trees were grateful to drop their load quickly and soon the leaf-covered streets hid all signs of that heady, drought enforced period.

Jack Bracken had been gone for over a month and there had been no word from him; not even a phone call. He had utterly vanished. Rose had heard nothing; no hello or explanation. It worried her deeply that he should just disappear off the face of the earth so quickly and quietly. She was afraid he might return at any moment. She was also afraid he wouldn't. He darted in and out of her head at least once a day and she

©2007 Cara Aldous

realised that breaking up with him had been the hardest thing she'd ever had to do. She still had feelings for him and a dread which she could not shake; he might possibly be dead.

She tried to busy herself with the refitting and auditing of her shop; bringing in new stock and rearranging the old. A new alarm system had been speedily installed at the insistence of both Sam and Aubrey. Aubrey had proved quite an asset, even helping out by financing the installation of her new security. Overwhelmed by his generosity and no longer wanting sole responsibility of the shop, she had gratefully accepted his kind offer. He promised to be a silent partner but she wouldn't hear of it. He was already proving to be a shrewd businessman and had brought in a great deal of new orders for her authentic stock. He had busied himself setting up a website where people could buy her range online. Financially things were looking up for both of them.

The Sword of Aramoth was back with its rightful owner and in the shop. For safe-keeping it was mounted in a brand new glass-fronted counter. The glass was toughened; smash-proof and the steel doors at the back of the display were fitted with a sturdy lock. The key was kept in a secret compartment in the back of the till and no-one apart from Rose knew where it was; not even Aubrey had access without her permission. The countertop was bare except for the till which sat at one end. The sword lay along a glass shelf in the centre of the display underneath which was draped the flag from The Phoenix. A book sat open at a double-paged drawing of the ship along with a small description of its two notorious Captains. Rose was making small cards which gave a potted history of her ancestor and strategically placing them around the relics of hers and Jack's family history.

The light switches had been sensibly moved to the front of the shop, just inside the door so that on unlocking and locking up Rose would no longer be in a dark, forbidding place. The darkness still spooked her and now that the sword was back she was more afraid than ever. Though she could not pinpoint any reason for this fear, the last time she had tried to ignore her senses Jack Bracken had entered her life along with Captain Blackheart.

She worried the Sword of Aramoth beckoned to Jack and she feared the day he would come back to claim it. If he returned she knew that her resolve would desert her again and she would be under his spell for eternity. She was fragile and never again would she have the strength to resist him; as a fan is obsessed with her idol so Rose had become obsessed with the man who had been her first love. Now that he was gone he was fast becoming the ideal man once more.

"What shall I do with these?" Aubrey's voice penetrated her thoughts and she gladly welcomed the interruption.

"Over there please Aubrey, by the others."

She watched him as he worked and smiled; carefully he placed the pile of flags he was carrying onto the floor and began one by one to attach them to the hanging display. She had few reservations about working with him and, now that he was there, felt safe having him around. She hummed gently to herself as she finished off a card explaining the symbols on Rosie Scarlet and Blackheart's pirate flag; black heart and scarlet woman.

Aubrey listened to Rose's sweet tune and smiled; she still had a long way to go but it did seem that she was finally beginning to get her life back together after Jack Bracken aka Jon Black had turned her world upside down. Rose had gradually told of his strange moods and behaviour and it had made Aubrey very uneasy. It was obvious to all who had met him that Jack was mentally unstable. Aubrey had often sensed it was only a matter of time before the man exploded. Yet he felt ashamed. If he had been more understanding and more of a man he could have stopped Jack's self-destruction. He didn't quite know how or why but he identified with him on some levels; Rose had explained about the sadness of his childhood. Jack had told her how desolate he felt growing up. Aubrey could wholly identify with that; Rose too. The three of them were not so different and only a fine line separated them all from normality and insanity.

Sam had become Aubrey's stability. She consoled Aubrey by the only means she knew how; in bed. Yet after their love-making they often talked for hours with such intense feelings of intimacy that Aubrey had come to understand how such intense feelings of love could confuse a mind like Jack's. This someway went toward explaining his erratic moodswings. With such strength of love and passion it was a struggle to refrain from becoming manic in behaviour and a man in turmoil could so easily be tipped over the edge.

Black Nightmares to Scarlet Dreams

Aubrey finished hanging up the flags and got to his feet with little effort. Sam's love had done wonders for his waistline. He had also taken to walking more and more and thought nothing of a brisk pace to town and back. He still wore the same clothes although his belts were tighter, and combed his hair the same way but, with time and patience, he knew eventually he would change; for Sam, for love and for the best.

"What do you want me to do next?" he leaned on the counter and grinned at Rose.

"Um, I think that's all the stock isn't it? You're too quick you know! Better be careful or you'll do yourself out of a job!" she laughed.

"Oh don't you worry about that – I can always find something to do!" he laughed back and with a wink disappeared into the stockroom.

Rose watched him as he went out the back, a spring in his step. It was amazing how much of a transformation he had made since he and Sam had become serious. They were so in love Rose caught herself several times thinking about Jack. Her feelings puzzled her and she asked herself time and again if she still loved Jack. This simply added to her bewilderment over his behaviour.

Some days his mood had changed with each passing hour and many times his temper would throw her off balance. But he never actually lost his temper with her; not until that last day. She swallowed hard. It was all she could do most days to stop herself from bursting into tears. But if she reminded herself of his possessiveness and jealousy and the claustrophobic hold he had over her she could just about stop the pain from engulfing her completely. She had to remind herself that besides being incredibly loving he had also been over-protective and overbearing just like Mother had.

In fact, the more she thought about it, the more she knew deep down that if they had stayed together it would have been awful. It didn't stop her from worrying about him though. Even Aubrey showed signs of concern for him and Sam. Once they knew the extent of his troubled life they both felt sorry for him. The house had remained locked and empty since the day he left. Even his agent had not heard from him and she too was very concerned for his safety. Everyone thought the same as Rose, although they didn't actually say it; he was quite possibly dead.

"Rose!" Aubrey cried out excitedly from the back, rushing in he held up a roll of paper in front of her. "Look what I found! I mean, I doubt it's real or anything – can't be! But it's really interesting all the same…"

He unrolled the yellowing paper carefully, spreading it out on the glass-top counter. Rose looked carefully at it. It was very old parchment and contained an intricate map. The small scribbled calligraphy on it was barely legible but she knew what it was. It was the cause of all the fuss and the root of all Jack's problems.

"It's a map!" Aubrey chuckled gleefully.

"Yes it's a map." Rose said flatly, "The supposed whereabouts of Blackheart's buried treasure. Where did you find it?"

"Tucked behind a load of books was a small box. And in the box…"

"In the box," Rose interrupted, "Amongst some papers was this…"

"But, if you knew, why didn't you say before? I mean, this is what they have been looking for isn't it –Jon, uh Jack, and Roland?" Aubrey frowned, it was impossible to read Rose sometimes.

Rose nodded sadly, "I tried to forget about it! I should have been more honest with Jack…"

Fighting back the tears she leaned over the piece of parchment. As they pored over the ancient map Rose sighed hard; how could such an insignificant looking thing be the cause of so much heartache? Both Jack and Roland had wanted it; but both for very different reasons. Jack had told her once that something else was buried along with the treasure; something evil. Rose had refused to listen. Such things only belonged in films and fantasy.

He said that if the evil was unleashed it would make Roland the most powerful, richest and indestructible man in the world. She had refused to believe it then and could not allow herself to even think it now. It was much too frightening to even contemplate the implications of such a thing in existence. She hated horror stories and films and wasn't about to star in her own.

She turned to Aubrey, "Do you think it's authentic?"

Aubrey shrugged, "Probably not, but I'm no expert. A complete load of rubbish I expect but might be worth something; if only because of its age. I should imagine if this map was ever deciphered and the place of the treasure discovered it will be found to be long gone. I don't expect it even exists anymore – most likely a car park or something!"

"I wonder," Rose murmured, "I wonder if he'd buy it anyway and end this or, at least...It could save Jack..."

*

Rose walked home alone; Sam had met them after work when she and Aubrey headed off to the pub. They invited Rose to join them but she declined. Before she changed her mind there was something she had to do. As soon as she got in, she grabbed the phone and sat on the stairs, with the receiver in one hand and the map in the other. On the bottom stair the phonebook rested open at the page upon which she had written Artie Ribald's number.

"Never know when you might need me," he had said to her before he left, "My job here is done - for now."

Rose hoped she wouldn't ever need him. After all he had tried to kill her. But she had seen compassion in his eyes when he heard how distraught Jack had been. Aubrey's description of Jack leaving with tears streaming down his face had moved them all. Especially, it seemed, Artie.

The phone rang several times before it was answered. Artie sounded suspicious when he heard Rose's voice, not recognising her at first. Once he realised who she was his tone changed; and he became more cheerful and friendly.

"What can I do for you Rose?"

"Well, it's more what I can do for you really, Artie…" Her heart thumped.

"Oh?" he was intrigued, "Found Jack have you?"

Rose's voice caught, "No, no sign…No, Artie it's the map…"

"Didn't think you would. Rumour has it he's been 'disappeared'……Wait - map? What map?"

"The one you've all been searching for?" she held her breath.

Silence.

"It's just that, well, I…I've found it! Does Roland still want it?" her words came out in a rush.

"Does he ever!" Artie hesitated, "You sure about this Rose?"

"I...I think so..." She sighed inwardly.

Replacing the receiver with trembling hands Rose looked down at the map. She bit her lip, hoping she was doing the right thing at last. If she could sell the thing to Roland maybe Jack would be safe. The map had been with her father's belongings; among the papers he had stored in the loft. Rose doubted it was the original but it may be of some historical interest to Roland if nothing else and it might buy Jack some time. If her father had known how much trouble the sword and map would cause he probably would have destroyed them both. She faltered; he had hidden it from her, she didn't even know it existed until after his death. He thought they were out of harm's way.

All of this was her fault; if she hadn't been so naïve and caught up in all the romance surrounding the heirloom neither the sword nor map would ever have come to Roland's attention. And Jack would never have had reason to come to England and her. Perhaps if Jack did come back she could help him. The sale of the map could make things right; Jack would be safe. She made a silent promise to him wherever he was; she would try to make it right.

Chapter 17

Rose checked her bag for the umpteenth time, making sure the map was in there. She had slept very little that night, wondering if she had done the right thing by phoning Artie. If she were completely honest she hardly knew him; but what she did know was that Jack had trusted him. As that was the only thing she had to go on she had to trust him too, he was Jack's only hope. By selling the map to Roland the hassle could end once and for all. Artie's words echoed through her head; what if Jack had been 'disappeared' already and it was too late? She couldn't think like that. She had to believe he was still alive. She wanted to believe he would come back to her for she knew now that she did still love him. She wanted the chance to put things right.

Someone had been inside Jack's house the night before. She desperately wanted it to be him. A light had come on out the back of the houses and she had been tempted to investigate but something had stopped her. Instead she had waited and listened to the noises coming from inside; someone was banging about loudly. They didn't stay long and the sound of the door slamming had brought Rose to her window. Peering out onto the quiet street she could see nothing in the yellow glare of the streetlights at first. Then, ever so slightly, she made out the shape of someone running down the road.

Even in the false shadows of an autumn night she knew, with a sinking heart, it was not Jack. Fireworks exploding overhead had made her jump, causing her to scream. Halloween had frightened her more than ever this year; it heralded the beginning of darker days and longer nights and she felt more low and miserable than ever. The nights were eerie with the threat of something darker. Something that spooked her, making her keep the lights blazing every night.

She checked her watch, it was lunchtime but she wasn't hungry. She went into the kitchen anyway to make a cup of tea and keep busy. She was to meet Roland at three o'clock at the posh hotel in town; The Rotchley. Artie had told her to come alone but she knew that was unwise and told Sam about the meeting.

"I'm coming with you!" Sam had insisted.

Rose made no objection, not even when Aubrey had insisted coming along too. Even if they stayed outside, close by, at least they would be near at hand should something go wrong. Rose tried to sip her tea casually but the sudden ring of the phone soon destroyed the fake calm. Answering it with shaking hands the first thing that crossed her mind; that always crossed her mind; was Jack. She hoped Artie wasn't calling to cancel. Her stomach lurched as she placed the receiver to her ear.

"Hi Rose! Really sorry but I can't make it this afternoon." Sam's strained voice made her heart sink. "Have to do overtime again – last minute and I can't get out of it! Sorry, but Aubrey will still be there. See you later, and be careful!"

Rose wasn't too concerned by this but when Aubrey too cancelled only minutes later alarm bells began to ring; it was as though some evil force was at work. She shuddered as she tried to remain calm, playing it down.

Aubrey was incensed, "…It's this bloody time of year – if I had my way I'd cancel bonfire night! The cats are running up and down the curtains and circling the room like the wall of death! I have to take one of them to the vet …God only knows what state they'd be in if I left them!"

Rose assured him she would be fine. He had assumed Sam was still going with her and she saw little point in correcting him; he would only try to stop her. Perhaps it was a sign; it was much better if they didn't get involved she reasoned and besides at least now she could ask about Jack. Whenever she tried to broach the subject Sam would fly off the handle. Aubrey seemed to understand her wanting to know he was safe but Sam didn't; she still blamed him for nearly ruining their friendship. She wouldn't understand that Rose still loved Jack. He was her first love and she would never forget him. She was also scared he would be her only love; doomed to a life of loneliness without him and it

©2007 Cara Aldous

was partly because of this that she longed to have him back in her life. But mostly it was because she still loved him; deep love is blind and she would forgive him his faults and welcome him back with open arms. The map would help her do this, so long as he was still alive.

Chapter 18

At two-thirty that afternoon Rose stood on the front steps of the Rotchley Hotel. She glanced at her watch; it was only a few minutes since she had last looked. She was too early. Butterflies swarmed around her stomach and she felt hot and sticky. She ran a hand over the back of her neck. Her cold hands cooled her down a little but as soon as she pulled them away the heat flooded over her once more. Her hands trembled as she held them up in front of her face. Her heart raced and she breathed in slow, deep breaths as she tried to calm her nerves. The ever present panic bubbled beneath the surface as she struggled to keep it in check.

Not now! She prayed, *not now!*

With heavy legs she stepped slowly up to the front entrance and pushed her way in through the revolving doors. A friendly porter showed Rose up to the penthouse suite and Mr Roland. He gushed about how the

American had booked the whole floor for the autumn. In the lift she kept grasping her neck, her palms, cold through fear, cooling her just enough each time. She rushed through the doors as they swished open and hurried up to the door of the suite with just a backward glance at the bemused porter.

Inside the room was decorated with taste and understatement in a way that oozed class and money. The wallpaper was just a hint of green, the subtle patterns varying shades. A plush velvet green upholstered sofa with fine gold brocade stood central to an oak coffee table upon which sat a silver tray of fine bone china cups and saucers, matching teapot, sugar bowl and milk jug. A man was sitting in the centre of the sofa, his arms spread wide along the back of the seat, his legs crossed. He wore a well-tailored suit of dusky silk blue and a crisp white shirt. Gold cufflinks with an onyx black letter R fastened his sleeves and a silk tie of a deeper shade of blue finished it all off to perfection.

As Rose drew closer he sat up attentively and placed a manicured hand carefully on each leg so as not to crease the suit. Rose swallowed hard as she tried to smile but it turned into more of a grimace. He grimaced back at her then relaxed into a grin.

"My dear Miss Scarlet, we meet at long last…" he smiled, showing a row of neat white teeth.

He motioned for her to sit but Rose felt it was more of an order than a request. So she nodded by way of reply and sat opposite on a chair that matched the sofa for class but not comfort. She forced a smile as he poured tea for them both, using a strainer to catch the leaves. She sipped the sickly sweet scented brew and hoped that her dislike for it was not visibly noticeable and studied the man before her.

Roman Roland was not as Rose had imagined him at all. He was American but it was very apparent that he was also of Italian descent. This was a bit of a surprise; she had always imagined a big, brash Stetson-wearing Texan. The small, wiry, American-Italian before her was something she hadn't bargained for. She didn't trust him. His deep brown skin matched the colour of the curtains and both oozed luxury but for all his money and charm he lacked charisma. He studied her for an unnerving time like a bird watching a wriggling worm; his long beaky nose wrinkled as she blushed. He hardly seemed to blink and she looked away.

They sat, awkwardly, in silence for several minutes. Rose perched stiffly on the edge of the seat; her bag clutched tightly to her, wondering how and if she could safely tell him she had changed her mind. Real or not she wouldn't sell him the map. If there was any shred of truth in the myth about the evil buried with the treasure this was one man who didn't need any more. Jack had been right about one thing; Roland was a horrible man. She would have to find another way to help Jack.

"So, my dear Rose – can I call you Rose?" he smiled at her, holding her gaze, "Artie told me you might have something of interest for me?"

"I…" Rose faltered; how could she get out of there? "I might have." She sounded like a petulant child.

"Please, relax…" he leaned back on the sofa, "I think perhaps; my false reputation precedes me…"

"Your reputation certainly precedes you," Rose snorted, "I think I made a mistake in coming here..."

"Oh?" he smiled, clearly pleased at her discomfort.

"Yes –you ordered Jack to steal my sword! You started all this! And you sent Artie to kill me!"

"Kill you?" he began to laugh, getting louder and louder.

"I'm glad you find it funny!" Rose was nearing tears, "All I can say is you're lucky I haven't been to the police!"

He stopped. "And what would you tell the police, hmmm? You have your sword and, unless I'm very much mistaken, you are most definitely alive. I cannot be responsible for the action of my employees, even if they are a little…….. misguided. I merely employ them, I do not ask by which methods they will obtain what I am looking for."

"But if you hadn't been so desperate to get the Sword of Aramoth!" Rose looked at him steadily, "You know if you had asked I might have sold it to you and saved everyone the hassle!"

"But, my dear woman, I did ask," he replied calmly, picking an invisible thread off his jacket.

"When? I've never even met you before today!" Rose stared at him, trying to work out what he was thinking, "I think I would remember if I had!"

"Oh, I grant you I did not ask you in person but many people in my employ have asked to buy the sword on my behalf – many times.

And each time you refused. You even turned down Mr Drummond's more than generous offer; I had really high hopes for him too. Jon Black was my last hope before it was too late."

Rose felt sick; Rick had been a phoney. So many times he had visited her shop and told her of his longing to own such a magnificent sword; a true specimen of centuries past. So often he had told her how lucky she was to have such a family heirloom. It had turned into a joke between them; each time he would make her an offer, she would turn it down. And all the time he had been seriously trying to buy it for Roland. It was little wonder he too had disappeared, if this was the type of person he did business with.

"So," she had to know, "Where is Jack?"

"Jon Black is no longer my concern. I admit he was something of...a loose cannon, an error for which I have paid expensively. But no matter," he sighed lightly, a smile tugging at his lips, "He will no longer be a bother to either of us again. You have my word."

Rose shuddered; finally admitting to herself that she still loved Jack was too little too late. Nothing else mattered any more; he wouldn't have hurt her she realised that now. He was unorthodox, certainly, but he had given her a reason to live again. For the first time since Mother's death she had looked forward to each day thanks to him. It was as though a great weight had lifted from her shoulders when Jack entered her life. He had renewed her interest in life and the living. But she had mistaken true love for fear and she had retaliated by pushing away the only man who could ever really love her. If what Roland said was true then Jack was dead and she had lost the only person who had ever truly touched her soul. Without him she was lost.

"But enough of Jon Black," Roland, sensing her discomfort, moved the conversation up a pace, "Tell me about your pirate shop and how you became interested."

Falteringly at first Rose began flatly to tell of her discovery of the Sword of Aramoth. Then, as she began to talk of Rosie Scarlet and Captain Blackheart, she began to relax. As the story of The Phoenix and its Captain's exploits unfolded she began to relax even more; it was her favourite subject and although he probably already knew plenty of the history he didn't attempt to interrupt. When she finished they sat in quiet contemplation. He sipped his tea absently, almost as if she wasn't there. Rose took a gulp of hers but found it cold so carefully placed it back on the tray. She watched as he drained his cup, placing it carefully by the side of hers.

"So, Miss Scarlet, now you have told me your story, I will tell you mine…"

Rose stifled a yawn and checked her watch; an hour and a half had passed. An hour and a half during which she had told her story and he told his. His beginnings had been promising; the son of Italian immigrants, of honour and families, of hard work and ambition; it all made for a riveting story. But the narrative soon turned to how he had made his money; after Harvard he had worked many jobs and made several investments; blah-blah-blah. Her eyes glazed over and she heard very little until he began to talk of his hobby; eighteenth century antiquities, in particular anything nautical. What began as a hobby collecting a few cutlasses and pistols, the odd map or flag; soon turned into obsession once he discovered the story of The Phoenix and her notorious Captains.

Rose sat forward at the mention of Captain Rosie Scarlet; just listening to another mention her name gave her a surge of misplaced pride. He spoke of her likeness to her ancestor and then began to lament the likeness that Jack had for Blackheart.

"So why did you choose him? I mean, you had seen him before; you must've known he wasn't right – mentally, I mean?"

Sadly, Roland shook his head.

"So why choose him in the first place? He had no connection to Blackheart as far as you were concerned. Or had someone told you about him?"

"No, no, nothing so simple," he shook his head again, "Jon Black was a dead cert for a man like me wanting an actor to play the part of an evil pirate. You know – ask no questions...."

"Blackheart's ancestor you mean?" Rose frowned, "You wanted someone to pretend to be his ancestor?"

"No, actually, what I originally wanted was for an actor to pretend he was Blackheart himself."

His words chilled; if only he had realised the mistake he was making in choosing Jack. She waited for him to continue.

"When we met I could hardly believe my eyes! There, standing in front of me was the truest likeness of Blackheart I could ever have hoped for! I was so eager to employ him that I did not question his past. I believed him one hundred per cent when he insisted he had no idea who Blackheart was."

"But he did know, only too well, he was a true descendent." Rose said sadly.

Roland sank back morosely, his head low, "Yes, I know now that he was indeed."

Rose watched him as he gathered his thoughts and composure. He had been hit just as hard as the rest of them by Jack's decline into insanity but as all he had lost was money she could feel no pity for him. With all his education and fortune he couldn't see what the rest of them had; Jon Black was already a very disturbed man when they met and Roland had inadvertently tipped him over the edge.

Pity Jack, she thought ruefully, *Pity what you made him!*

His eyes narrowed as he looked up at her and she turned away; afraid he might read her thoughts. He'd never understand her love for a man like Jack. She looked toward the window at the darkening sky and checked her watch; it was nearly six - time to leave. But first she had to know what had happened to him; what had Roland meant when he said that Jack would no longer be a bother to them?

"Black is a true descendent alright – I had him checked out after he double-crossed me. Too late I know but there you are. Anyway, Blackheart had a brother it seems, a blacksmith by the name of Davey Bracken who lived quietly in a small English village along with his wife and child; until Blackheart was hung that is. The whole of England were talking of the notorious Captain, Davey knew it would only be a matter of time before the connection with his brother was discovered. So with his family in tow he moved around the country, eventually setting sail for New England and a new life."

"So Jack really is descended from Blackheart and the sword really is his; I was so wrong." Rose murmured to herself.

©2007 Cara Aldous

Chapter 19

Roland sat forward excitedly. "Actually, my dear, as the direct descendent of Scarlet and Blackheart's child you are the true owner of the sword and Black has no right to anything. In fact, even life itself is much too good for him!"

Rose waited, captivated yet horrified as Roland talked about Jon Black and how, in his insane mind he came to believe he really was Jack Bracken; Blackheart the Pirate. He spoke as if she were no longer in the room; Jack's pitfalls and failings his only focus. He had little idea that Jack had opened up to her and told her everything in an effort to be closer to her. It was only when he reached the part where Jack was supposed to seduce her in order to obtain the sword that she listened properly, even joining in at times to correct the smallest of details. As they discussed the events which culminated in her and Jack becoming lovers a clearer picture of the public and personal differences of Jon

Black became apparent. The man Roland had met was the actor Jon Black yet Rose had seen a very different side of him; she had seen Jack - the true Bracken descendent. He came from a more honest stock of men; the brother of Captain Blackheart – Davey Bracken.

She felt ashamed for ever doubting Jack when Roland told of his anger, wanting him to continue his deception when he felt there was no longer any need. She knew the reason was their love wasn't a fraud to Jack; it had developed into something real and true. When he told her he loved her he meant it. With a heavy heart she realised too late that Jack hadn't been the one who wanted to con her; he had simply been employed to do so. And when he met her, once they got to know one another, he fell in love. That was the only thing he was guilty of; laying bare his emotions.

She swallowed hard the lump in her throat and remembered his tears as he pleaded with her and told her he would never hurt her. Her own tears threatened to belie her calm exterior. It was true Jack had demons to fight but everyone has some dark secret they wrestle with on a daily basis. No-one is completely free from the pain of their past. She of all people should know that. She had been so desperate to break free from a love that scared her that she had hurt him deeply. She prayed Jack would forgive her.

She closed her eyes and ears to the futility of it all; even selling the map now wouldn't bring Jack back to her. Roland had hinted that she would never see her lover again and, hard though it was, she believed him. He had proved to be a very nasty man who got what he wanted one way or another. The opportunity to put things right had been cruelly snatched from her by the rich, oppressive bully who sat before her. A sudden urge to scream and shout, rant and rave at the man responsible for organizing the appearance and then, undoubtedly, the disappearance of Jack Bracken welled up inside her. She had the urge to leap up and start raining blows down on his perfectly styled head. The sudden ringing of the telephone brought her abruptly to her senses. Hastily Roland snatched the receiver from its base.

"Speak to me!" he barked into the mouthpiece.

Rose watched closely as he smiled a short apology to her then moved quickly into the bedroom, leaving the door ajar. She moved to the window and peered out into the darkness in silent deliberation as she listened to the muffled words. Whoever had phoned was being told off in no uncertain terms. She shook her head and wondered what to do next. A tear escaped and slowly trickled down her cheek onto her hand. More followed then more and she turned her face upward to the sky as fireworks exploded across her view, lighting up the city below in a multitude of colours.

At the sound of the door opening she didn't turn instead wiped her hand across her wet face, holding back the sobs with a deep intake of breath. A loud cough behind her made her spin round sharply; it was Artie. Knocked off-balance she opened her mouth to speak but he placed his finger to his lips. She nodded, letting him know with her eyes that she understood. He looked toward the bedroom where they could hear Roland pacing as he continued to berate the caller. They both froze as without warning the door was pushed shut. Artie smiled wide and moved quickly so that he was only inches from Rose. He leaned forward and whispered in her ear.

"Good job he wants some privacy," he indicated toward the closed door, "Now's your chance…"

"Artie," Rose whispered urgently, "Artie – its Jack…he…he's…"

"I know, Rose, I know, now shush or he'll be wise to us." He indicated the closed door again this time with more emphasis.

"I don't care, not anymore! Without Jack…"

"Listen, hun, without Jack you wouldn't be in this mess!" Artie whispered through gritted teeth, "He knew what he was getting into. When you work for a man like Roland you expect trouble – especially when you double-cross him! Besides Jack didn't feel a thing…"

Rose put a hand to her mouth; inside she was screaming, "My God! My God! It was you! You killed Jack?"

Artie shook his head, "Not me honey, not guilty this time. Listen, we don't have a whole lotta time. You've got to leave…"

"I know…I was just going…"

"No, not just the hotel, I mean leave. Your home, this city, get away as far from here as possible where no-one knows you. And don't tell a soul where you are. You hear me? Not a soul – no friends, no family, no-one! Or you'll be joining your boyfriend."

Rose nodded numbly as Artie picked up her bag and wrapped her coat around her shoulders. Her head spun with all of the information she had been given in the short space of a few hours. She had learned plenty but only one thing stuck in her mind; Jack was dead. Shakily she moved toward the door as Artie held onto her, almost pushing her out into the corridor. They stopped when the bedroom floor creaked and Rose held her breath. The muffled tones from the next room continued heatedly and they both heaved a sigh of relief. She turned and Artie winked at her like a kindly uncle.

"You gonna be okay honey?" he asked in hushed tones.

Rose smiled back at him weakly, "No, but I guess I will be. Will I see you again?"

Artie shook his head, "Nope, not if I can help it. Hey, don't worry, you'll be fine. You'll see!"

"I wish I could believe that…"

The muffled voice stopped suddenly and they heard a beep as the line was disconnected. Roland had finished his call. Artie turned to her and gave her a small shove.

"Run!" he hissed, "Run as fast as you can and don't stop, don't look back! GO!"

*

The driver slung Rose's case into the boot and slammed it shut. Rose sat on the back seat and stared out of the window at the oak. It stood forlornly in the dark autumn night, its branches bare and bark damp. The carving, a lasting reminder of Jack; a legacy left behind by her lover, looked eerie in the shadowy streetlight. She didn't have a clue how she had got home so quickly or even how she had left the hotel without

Roland coming after her. At every step she had looked over her shoulder. She knew Artie didn't want her to go home but she had to; she had to pack some things and she had to say goodbye.

But the house was empty and had been trashed. She feared for Sam's safety but, noticing the phone flashing up a message she played it back; relieved at hearing an assurance that her friend was okay. Sam was merely at a bonfire party with work colleagues as well as Aubrey. So he had relented and left his cats after all. Rose was glad. At least it meant they were both safe. She had toyed with the idea of leaving a note the whole time she was packing but thought better of it. Roland was a nasty piece of work and her friends would be in grave danger if they knew where she was. No; better ignorant and safe than knowledgeable and dead. Like Jack.

She watched the houses pass by, the familiarity surreal and dreamlike, the taxi driver chattering about the dangers of fireworks and she smiled and nodded not really listening. As they pulled onto the High Street and past her shop she allowed herself a final look. A pang of apprehension gripped her as she thought about her sword. Leaning her head against the window she fought the urge to stop and collect it. To carry a large sword would only draw attention and it was best that no-one noticed her leaving. She could slip quietly away knowing that the one thing Roland really wanted was safely tucked into the inside pocket of her suitcase; the map was going with her for insurance.

*

©2007 Cara Aldous

Jack hid in the darkness of the shop and watched the taxi pass by. Rose had looked straight through him as though he were invisible; that was good. He made his way to the counter with ease and fumbled in the till for the key to the cabinet. Unlocking the doors he shook as his fingers touched the hilt of the sword. He followed the contours of the phoenix and marvelled at the way it glinted in the half light. His eyes shone with pleasure as he lifted it carefully from its resting place.

"Come to daddy," he whispered as he held the Sword of Aramoth aloft.

A noise at the front of the shop brought him to the window and he smiled knowingly; it was time to go. The hitman was waiting for him. He must have seen him enter the shop and it was only a matter of time before he followed. Jack picked up the petrol can he had brought with him and sprinkled the dark pungent liquid around the shop. He soaked the flags and clothes first then the rest. He toyed with the idea of taking a few more of the swords with him but knew carrying just the one would be hard enough in itself. Not the weight; he could manage that with little effort. No; it was a dangerous weapon and he risked being arrested if noticed.

He pulled The Phoenix's Jolly Roger from the cabinet and wrapped it around the sword. Then he wrapped them both in his jacket. He placed it comfortably under his arm and stood behind the door. Carefully he tied a small damp cloth around his nose and mouth which he had soaked under the tap in the small back kitchen. Lighting a match he threw it onto the drenched cloth and it ignited almost immediately. He had telephoned the fire brigade only a few minutes ago and could hear their sirens as the flames took hold. He watched sadly as Rose's life and history began to disappear up in smoke. A new chapter must begin now; for both of them.

The hit man shone a tiny red light in through the window, searching for his target. Jack realised with mounting horror that it was the infra-red sight of a gun and the hairs rose on the back of his neck. The fire engines were drawing closer and in desperation he offered up a plea to Blackheart for one last time.

"I cannot repay you with the vengeance you seek nor will I destroy those whose ancestors destroyed you!" he muttered, "But give me my life and I will continue the true line of Brackens – Help me to live and I will make her mine and together the Brackens shall rise once more!"

"...Yo ho, yo ho ho,
Take my sword and away you go,
Sink that ship,
Dash that head,
Feed the sharks with the wretched dead..."

©2007 Cara Aldous

Chapter 20

The train rushed through the early morning mist, drawing into the station with a whistle before shuddering to a hissing halt. Rose gazed anxiously around as she reached her foot up the steep step into the carriage, stretching her leg over the huge gap between platform and train. She moved steadily down the aisle, stopping at a vacant table and stored her case in the rack above her head. She shuffled awkwardly along the seat toward the window just as the train creaked and groaned and shunted along. It began to move faster, the station disappearing slowly and the view becoming nothing more than a blur of earthy colours as the train gathered speed. Rose sat back in her seat and studied the ticket in her hand; one way to Welmley-On-Sea. It was a destination she knew well, remembered fondly from childhood summers of past. The journey she knew off by heart making her feel safe and warm just as she had all those years ago as a carefree child.

Black Nightmares to Scarlet Dreams

Neither parent could drive; few people did in those days as cars were deemed luxury items and therefore not necessary for every day life. One or two families in Oak Grove owned cars but most preferred public transport which seemed more reliable and less expensive back then. Several of the men worked in town and caught the bus but many worked locally in the High Street and surrounding areas so walked to work. Even some mothers worked part-time in the local shops and supermarket or were dinner-ladies at the local primary school. Rose's Mother, however, remained at home; keeping the house spotless and the cupboards filled with home-baked cakes and breads whilst her father worked in the neighbouring city and commuted every week day by train.

He spent the weekends at home but did not have a great deal of time for his wife and so pottered about in the garden and his shed where the young Rose would find him whistling happily as he tinkered with various plants and seeds. Together they wasted many a happy hour busy doing nothing as Rose asked question after question and her father answered patiently and carefully until finally Mother would drag her off to go shopping in town.

Often Mother would be angry at the hours her husband worked and vented her anger by muttering under her breath as she moved about the household doing chores. Rose, being her only audience would listen both horrified and enthralled as Mother lamented woefully that he was probably having an affair as working late was a perfect excuse.

But even as a child Rose knew this to be untrue; her father worked long and hard and was up at the crack of dawn to catch his train on time and home by seven every single evening. Not once was he late and, on the odd occasions when Mother had rung the office he would answer his extension immediately.

It seemed to the adult Rose looking back that her Mother had almost wanted him to have an affair so that, in some absurd way, it would relieve the tedium. With no job description other than housewife and her life teetering on the edge of boredom it must have been a lonely existence for her particularly once Rose had started school.

A mass of blurred dark grey clouds filled the sky outside followed by hard drops of rain splattering intermittently on the pane. The rain began to fall faster, rattling against the glass and Rose shivered as she pulled her coat tightly around her shoulders. Autumn was fast hurrying toward winter and she wondered if she was mad to go to one of the loneliest places on earth; the British seaside at winter season.

She pulled her bag onto her lap and began to rummage around for some gum or a mint to freshen her mouth. Her hand touched on an unfamiliar object and she pulled it out. A crumpled pack of Jack's cigarettes fell on her lap and she gulped as the sadness caught in her throat. Swallowing hard she fought back the threatening tears. Leaning back in her seat she closed her eyes and a tear escaped. She let it fall as her thoughts turned to him; had he been just as alone and afraid as she was now? Had the end been quick and painless? Or had he suffered, fighting with his demons to the very end?

The motion of the train rocked her gently from side to side and she drifted off to sleep with the clickety-click-clickety-clack running through her head, the rush of raindrops against the glass an accompanying percussion.

Walking from the station to the Sea Front was short and painless but upon reaching the row of familiar boarding houses it became surreal. She faltered at the foot of each set of steps that individually led to a house. They stood silent and foreboding in the grey outline of the sky and most were closed for the season. The rain had subsided but another downpour threatened as the clouds grew darker.

She finally came to a halt at the bottom of a set of steps which were more memorable than any of the others and which led up to an unforgettably tall, higgledy-piggledy grey brick house. It was Gothic in appearance and had always scared the young Rose. Nothing had really changed. The front door had a thousand coats of the same yellow paint and the crumbling window frames were held together by as many coats again. A sign in the window informed passers-by that they were still open for business and had vacancies. Rose stepped onto the bottom step.

This had been their family holiday residence ever since Rose could remember. A small Bed and Breakfast it was not the Hotel Mother had boasted so many times to neighbours about but it held a lot of happy memories for them all. It was the one time her father spent every waking hour for a whole week with his wife and daughter; it was a yearly treat for them all.

She took another step. The frontage had hardly changed in all this time; Rose's last visit being when she was sixteen. The only difference she could tell was a small sign advertising TV's and ensuite in every room. Rose smiled as she remembered the shared bathroom which she had frequently scurried to and from especially during her shy teenage years. She thought back to their last visit; sweet sixteen and, literally in Rose's case, never been kissed. It was on that very porch she had experienced the whole messy business of teenage angst and her first love.

She chuckled to herself as she heard the ghost of her father laughing when he caught the two young lovers in a passionate embrace. He was returning from his evening stroll along the front and had found her acute embarrassment sweet and wonderful. Mother, on the other hand had not been quite so forgiving and had forbidden Rose to ever see the boy again. It's funny but most people remember the full name of their first boyfriend; they remember every minute detail about them. Yet Rose could not even remember what he had looked like. When she tried to picture the two of them cuddling in the porch all she could visualise were her and Jack.

She shivered as the wind lifted her coat and she pulled it tightly together with her free hand. Her other clutched the suitcase tightly; it was heavy, weighing her down. She felt tired and miserable and longed to be in before the storm hit. She took another step but stopped; what if she had been followed? She glanced fearfully around the deserted street. If Roland or his people had done their research half as well as Jack had then they would know that she had visited Welmley on family holidays. Or if they did not know for sure it would only be a matter of time before one of her neighbours innocently gave the game away. Mrs Simkin would be sure to remember, after all Mother had bragged to her so often. To stay in the same B&B in the same seaside town would be incredibly dumb. She saw now how stupid she had been in coming to Welmley-On-Sea at all. She turned and stepped back down onto the path then crossed the road to the promenade; she had to think.

The sea was darkening like the sky and the waves crashed onto the rocks which jutted out either end of the bay. Along one side were the high, grey stone cliffs, sheltered by the large rocks which took the full force of the battering sea. And standing on top of the cliffs was the large anonymous hotel, grey as the cliffs beneath. It stood serenely, looking down onto the beach below; the tide now fully in and only the tips of the protruding rocks she had climbed as a child could be seen above the huge waves. The white foaming mass threw up vast sprays of salt water into the air and her face stung as it carried on the wind. It was perfect; an anonymous hotel for an anonymous guest.

*

He watched her from a distance biding his time; if he were to go to her now it would spoil everything. He had to be sure it really was her for one thing; her outline was not familiar in the blur of rain and sea. He could not focus his eyes clearly. He must wait. He gazed up to the hotel that she had been studying for some time; it was large enough to hide them both. Thunder cracked overhead as she hurried along the front to the path that led up the cliff. He must find another way; he could not let her see him. He smiled. Soon he would reveal himself to her and then he could begin the arduous task he had set out to do. Once it was over he

©2007 Cara Aldous

would be free. Free from Roland, free from Blackheart. One last job and it would all be over; for ever.

Chapter 21

Rose had eaten an ample and satisfactory lunch; her appetite surprising her with its ferocity. Even in mourning she had managed to eat a bowl of leek and potato soup, a main course of lamb cutlets and a dessert of treacle tart and custard. Returning to her room full and warm she unpacked, leaving the map in its hiding place, and placed the case on top of the wardrobe.

With a sudden urge to be outdoors she wandered down to the foyer and followed the paving out and down onto the narrow cliff path which led to the beach below. The tide had turned and the sea sat way out on the horizon. The rain had stopped and the sky brightened a little but dusk was only a few hours away. She climbed down the steep path and felt glad she had the foresight to change from heeled boots into trainers. She wished though that she had changed into something a bit warmer than trousers and shirt. Her coat, though thick, was more trendy than practical; although its two buttons were fastened it still flapped annoyingly in the wind. She tugged it close to her as she clambered down.

The beach was deserted as she stepped onto the damp sand, not even a dog-walker in sight on such a bleak and cheerless late afternoon. She looked into the distance at the hazy line of water against sky then strode off purposefully toward the rocks which jutted out from the sand, free now from the retreated sea. The rocks loomed tall and silent in the fading light as she looked up, wondering at their majesty. Something caught her eye; somebody was standing on the uppermost point of the top rock. He appeared to be scanning the horizon but turned and focused on Rose; the lenses on his binoculars glinting in the insipid light.

Rose stopped and her heart began to pump furiously as it pounded her chest. It could be a hitman sent by Roland to find the map and finish things once and for all. If it was then like a fly to a web she was walking right into the trap. Reason deserted her as she drew closer, curiosity prevailing over common sense. As her assailant became clearer she could see it was a young man. Her heart somersaulted as she recognised the outline of his silhouette. She could just make out his mop of dark hair tousled even more by the wind. He reached up and pushed it out of his eyes in such a familiar manner that she could visualise his memorable lop-sided grin as though she were looking at a photograph.

At this her pace quickened until she was running along the sand, all caution abandoned; thrown carelessly to the strong gusts. She called his name as she began to race toward him and he looked down on her from his elevated position.

"Jack! Jack!"

On reaching the base of the rocks she clambered up onto the smaller ones then climbed recklessly over the larger, more slippery ones. Her feet slipped; sliding over the slimy moss covered surfaces. She had to drop her gaze from her beloved to stop herself from falling. Finally she stood on the largest rock below his to get her bearings. She felt disorientated at first as she stumbled around the flat grey platform of slate. She looked up to where he should have been, strained her eyes, searching the skyline. But he was gone. She frowned, deeply troubled; turning around and around, scanning the horizon. Any sight of him, any trace had disappeared as suddenly as he had materialised. Her heart plummeted as she sat down heavily on the hard, cold stone.

Did I imagine it? She asked herself, *was it him; was it Jack?*

Perhaps it had been a hallucination; maybe in her grief what she had seen was nothing more than a mirage, conjured up by her overwrought imagination. Or perhaps…Perhaps it had been his ghost, come to warn her of her own impending doom. And she had frightened him off in her craziness to get to him.

She shivered, realising the rain had started falling once more; the fine mist soaking through her coat and shirt. The sea had begun to creep in, getting gradually closer to the rocks and to her. If she did not move soon she would be trapped and laid to rest in a watery grave. A poetic end to one so consumed by an obsession with pirates, perhaps, but not one she actually relished.

Dusk had fallen quickly and she knew she had been irresponsible staying on the beach for so long. Self-preservation kicked in as she hurriedly made her way back and began the slow, arduous task of climbing up to the hotel path. After her impulsive behaviour on the rocks Rose climbed carefully, thoughts of Jack running through her head. She wanted to believe she had seen him; wanted to so badly but if they had been reunited she doubted if their meeting would have been a happy one. After all, the last time they saw one another she had unceremoniously dumped him. She had been so cold and cruel, so out of character.

If only they could turn back time; if only they could replay that moment again. The second time around she would hold him and wipe his tears away and tell him she loved him and that of course she knew he would never hurt her. If only she could rewind the whole thing and wipe the memory away; for she was one hundred percent sure now that she did still love him.

As she reached the steep incline near the top she dug her toes in and leaned forward, bending almost double as she climbed up. The downward climb had been easy and she resolved to explore further in the morning in the hope of finding an easier ascent.

"Here, honey, give me your hand," a familiar accented voice spoke softly as an equally familiar hand was thrust out to her.

She looked up, "Jack! It was you!"

With one huge burst of energy she grabbed onto him as she surged forward. Together they pushed and pulled so hard that Rose fell into Jack's arms at the top of the cliff. He gripped her tightly, holding her so close to him that she could barely breath. But she didn't care; this was the second chance she had prayed for.

They laughed and cried and spoke simultaneously so that neither could hear a word the other said. Quickly they fell into a companionable silence, simply hugging one another. Rose put her face up to his and kissed his lips so tenderly he shuddered. He responded at first then sadly, very gently pulled away.

"Rose," he pleaded, "There's something I need to tell you."

*

Because of the quiet of the autumn/winter season Rose had been able to move rooms easily and they were able to book into a double suite. They shared a long soak in a hot bath sipping whisky from the minibar. Afterwards Rose sat huddled up on the bed as the wind howled outside and the rain lashed against the window. She shivered, her naked body covered in goosebumps and Jack wrapped her in a warm hotel bathrobe. Wrapping a thick towel around his own waist he sat next to her and took her hands in his, staring intently at her.

His dark green eyes were warm and tender and inviting and she wanted desperately for him to take her in his arms and make love to her. She wriggled free from his grip and encircled her arms around his waist, sliding her fingers over the tucked edge of his towel to work it free. He stopped her, taking her hands in his again and placed them in her lap then stood to tighten the towel firmly.

"Rose, I need to tell you something…" he began.

She placed her finger on his lips to stop him. "Ssshhh, my love," she urged, standing and pressing her lips to his, "I love you; that's all that matters…"

"And I love you too, honey, but…" he responded to her kiss but quickly pulled away again. "Rose, I'm going to tell you something which you're not gonna like but I have to tell you all the same – you do understand don't you? If I don't tell you you're gonna find out anyway and then it could destroy us…"

"Jack! Please; I can't bear anymore of this, I just can't!" she turned her face so as not to show the tears that formed.

He moved to her side and, cupping her face in his hands kissed her tears away. Not for the first time in his company Rose felt uneasy. She had an idea what he was going to say but wished he didn't always feel this need to offload everything in the face of all that had passed between them.

"There's no need," she begged, "Jack, I love you…"

"And I love you too," he kissed her, "But, Rose…I have to…It's your store…"

"My store?" Rose straightened up, puzzled, "Oh, you mean my shop."

"I'm so sorry, but I had to do it," his face crumpled and he leaned into her.

She held him close and stroked his hair soothingly, wondering where all this was leading.

"I had to pretend, you see. I had to make them think I was inside."

Rose pulled his face up to look at her, searching as she tried to make sense of what he was telling her. He looked troubled and worried and she smiled at him to reassure him. She nodded and he took this as a sign that it was okay to continue.

"I had to make them think I was dead," he said, trembling, "I went to the store and waited inside a while. I didn't know what else to do; where else to go. I slept rough a while after we…After you…Well, anyhow when I knew someone was after me I went to the store. The guy followed me. I knew he was there. He waited outside and I couldn't remember if there was a back way. But I found there wasn't. So, I waited and waited. He was watching the place and I knew I couldn't just run – wouldn't get the chance….Then I had this crazy idea that if the place was on fire, I could get out. You know; under the confusion. Anyway, I used my lighter and some of the flags. Shame though; I really liked what you done to the place. Some nice touches." He added ruefully.

"Aubrey," Rose said numbly.

"Anyhow," he continued, avoiding her eyes, "It went up quicker than I expected. It really took hold. The fire department came. There were sirens and flashing lights. I hid behind the door and when they came in; the smoke was thick and burned my throat and eyes but I got out. The guy didn't see me, no one saw me…"

Rose tried but could not stop the sob as it escaped her lips. She released her grip on him and covered her face in her hands. Her shoulders shook with the force of her tears and her heartache. The man she loved was safe but her shop, bought by the money given her by the only other man she had ever loved was gone; destroyed in the process.

"*Don't worry, darling,*" she heard her father's voice. His words, tender and soothing, washed over her and she held her face up to the ceiling and gasped.

"Don't worry, baby," Jack said equally tender and soothing, "We can rebuild it. Oh God, Rose, I'm so sorry."

A mixture of relief and anguish washed over her and she fell into his arms. He kissed her tentatively, unsure of her reaction. She responded, kissing him urgently and forcing him back onto the bed. Slowly she moved until her body covered his and they began to explore each other as though for the first time.

*

Jack lay peacefully by her side. Rose watched as his chest rhythmically rose and fell as he slept soundly. She felt comforted by his presence and knew that no matter what happened now they had each other and no-one was going to come between them again. She was deeply upset by the loss of her livelihood for it was more to her than that; much, much more. It was her father's legacy and she had lost all but the map. The yellowed paper still safely tucked inside the pocket of her case. She hadn't told Jack that she had it. Nor had she told him about her real reason for meeting with Roland, only of Artie and how he had helped her. Something about the map still troubled her and she worried it would come between them again.

"I think Artie hates Roland as much as I do," Jack told her, "He hates what the man stands for. At least they're off my case now. After all, I'm dead." He laughed.

He explained how he had followed her onto the train but lost her at first at the station. This worried her; if Jack could follow without her knowing, who else had? She pushed this thought to the back of her mind and wondered instead what on earth she was going to do now. She turned over and pushed her back against Jack. He moaned and moved so that the curve of his body spooned into hers and placed an arm around her, nuzzling his head into the back of her neck. She smiled as a warm feeling swept over her. One thing was for certain; whatever happened it would happen with Jack by her side. So long as he was with her nothing could hurt her.

©2007 Cara Aldous

Chapter 22

Rose smiled tenderly as she left Jack sleeping and went down to breakfast. His revelations of the night before, in the sobering cold-light of day swam in her head and she could only manage a cup of tea. The waitress hovered around, hoping Rose would change her mind and go for the full English. Rose felt sick; the whole of her father's possessions which he had kept safely hidden were now gone; destroyed in the fire.

Jack had not mentioned the sword and Rose hoped against hope that it had survived the inferno. After all it had endured all sorts over the years; the battles of The Phoenix, handed down generation after generation, hidden in a dusty loft until Rose, in her vain stupidity had displayed it proudly and shown it off to all who entered her shop. That's how Roland had discovered its whereabouts. If only she had not discovered it. If only she had heeded Mother's warnings and got a proper job; forgot about Pirates.

    Her mobile beeped and she reached into her pocket. A message flashed up from Sam. Quietly she left the dining room and strolled outside into the watery sunshine to read it. Sam was desperate to know if Rose was alright. She and Aubrey had been frantic when they heard of the fire and were afraid that Rose had been inside but were assured by the police that no bodies had been found. What with that and the house having been turned upside down, they had feared the worst. Rose texted a quick reply to assure her friend she was alive and well.

    Not really paying attention where she was going, she found herself walking down the small cliff-top road toward the town. It was a small seaside village which had a few new single houses tacked on the edge of the old but without taking anything away from its quaintness. The ancient houses stood in rows with narrow streets and cobbled stones. The worn narrow roads wound around and in and out through the streets forming narrow passages like a maze. The village steeped down from the cliffs and Rose followed one of the paths into the labyrinth of alleys and passageways, stopping to look in the windows of the closed shops shut up for the winter; empty and silent through the lack of holiday-makers.

    The path led toward the seafront and she followed it absently until it turned off, darting down into another alleyway. She walked steadily along the darkening passage which began to lead up a slight incline. At the top was a formation of small cottages and standing at the front of them was a shop with an open sign hung on its door. Curious,

©2007 Cara Aldous

Rose pushed it open and stepped inside to an accompaniment of a tinkling bell.

It was as though she had stepped into her own shop. She had to pause to take a breath. A display of pirate memorabilia hung around the walls and flags hung from the ceiling; an exhibit of pirate ferocity and pride in all its glory adorned every inch of the building. Central to the whole thing was a large wooden bird fixed to a pillar. Rose moved closer for better inspection. It was a ship's figurehead with the body of a woman, the head of a bird and enormous wings stretching out behind. Its beak gaped open to show a dagger-shaped tongue surrounded by a row of sharp little teeth. Rose knew she had seen this before; she had gazed out at it from her bedroom window, and seen it a hundred times on the hilt of her sword. Excitement mounting she reached out to run her fingers over the Phoenix.

"Beauty ain't she?" a gruff voice from behind made her jump.

She turned to see a man leaning on the counter. He smiled at her. A dark beard hugged his chin and he wore a navy cap. He was almost a typical looking local sailor, many of whom the young Rose had seen sitting outside the pub on the quayside most summer evenings, regaling tourists with their stories of the sea. Yet this man seemed both out of place and at home in the wonderful little replica of her shop. With his attire and chiselled features he reminded her of a young Errol Flynn in Captain Blood.

"This place – it's just like mine is - was," she stammered.

"Was?" he smiled a friendly smile that melted her heart.

"Yes, I don't have it any more. But everything here; it's practically identical!" she twirled around in wonderment then stopped, embarrassed at her foolishness.

The man chuckled and came forward.

"John Batcher at your service," he offered a callus-rough hand.

"Rose," she replied coyly as he took her hand in his. She looked up at the figurehead again. "Can you tell me about it?"

"Why yes, of course! It belonged to a pirate ship called The Phoenix, captained by two of the most notorious captains to sail the high seas. Everyone feared them, even their own crew it's said. Their names were…"

"Rosie Scarlet and Jack Bracken also known as Blackheart," Rose's heart skipped a beat.

"Yes, I thought you might know of them," John said eagerly.

Rose smiled, embarrassed, "Oh only a little. I've never seen anything like this…"

John replied with a nod and a bow. He was extremely proud of his collection and began to tell his tales of how he came by many of the items in his possession. Rose listened quietly and patiently but she was certain that most of his stories were no more than that; fabricated for a tourist audience. Because of her own, now extinct, collection she knew all the collector fairs and websites where avid enthusiasts bought and sold the most bizarre things. She felt sure that John had obtained his figurehead this way and not, as he said, washed up in the bay.

There was, however, one piece of information that did stir her interest; Rosie and Blackheart had lived in Welmley-On-Sea for a time and their picture had been painted by a local artist. It had to be the one Aubrey had found on the internet and the postcard she had stolen from Jack too.

"…It's in the Maritime Museum of Pirates and Smugglers down on the front," John explained, "The actual painting! We were really lucky to get it – nearly went overseas to a rich American! It's a remarkable thing to see; come take a look sometime."

"I would but isn't it closed? This is out of season now, isn't it?" Rose sighed.

"You'd be right about that but it won't be closed for long!" John replied, dangling a large bunch of keys in front of her, "If you got time I can show you now, if you like."

*

The Maritime museum was a large square building on the seafront. It stood separately from the other seaside shops and cafes. A faded board indicated that this was the 'Welmley Maritime Museum of Pyrates and Smugglers'. John unlocked the small door cut into the side of one of the larger wooden panels and stepped inside, holding the door back for her to follow. Silently he turned and led her along a dark, winding corridor toward a small room. He stopped outside the door and, flicking on the light, stepped to one side, stretching out an arm into the room with a grin.

Rose stepped past him into the room and stopped in her tracks. Hung on the wall was a large canvas. It was a picture Rose had seen before; of The Phoenix's two Captains but at this scale it took her breath away. John stood by her side and let out a deep breath with a whistle. He looked from the painting to Rose and back again, several times. Each time he pointed at her but could say nothing. Rose barely noticed she was too busy scrutinising the face of Blackheart; her Jack.

"My God! I know I thought you looked a bit like her but this is uncanny!" John finally found his voice, "It's you - it really is you!"

"Yes, isn't she beautiful?"

They both turned to see Jack standing in the open doorway, smiling at them. From behind his back he pulled a sword as he went to Rose and knelt before her. A multitude of emotions threatened to overwhelm her as she recognised the Sword of Aramoth in all its glory.

"For you," Jack said as he placed it over his arm, returning it to her once more.

Very carefully Rose took it from him, letting it stand by her side. She turned back to the picture and Jack stood next to her, a protective arm around her waist. John gazed in amazement at the doubles mimicking the stance of those in the portrait. The moment he had waited for all these years had finally happened yet he was speechless. This was going to be one hell of a reunion party!

©2007 Cara Aldous

Chapter 23

"I think it's time I introduced myself," John stepped forward, placing himself between them and the picture. He looked from Rose to Jack then up at the painting again. He coughed as he noisily cleared his throat.

"I am John Batcher, descendant of Jolly-Johnny the cabin-boy."

Rose and Jack exchanged puzzled looks.

Jack raised an enquiring eyebrow, "And?" he said.

"And," John scratched his beard, "Don't you realise? I thought you knew all about The Phoenix?"

"Not everything," Rose replied, still puzzled.

"Only about Blackheart and Rosie, really," added Jack. "And the Sword of Aramoth, obviously!"

John sighed exasperatedly, "Jolly-Johnny was the cabin-boy aboard The Phoenix the night of the mutiny! It was him who left the sword with Blackheart and Rosie. The mutineers were so angry when they found what he had done that they made him walk the plank!"

"But if he was a child and walked the plank... Then, how can you be descended from him?" Rose frowned.

"Because," answered John irritably, "He didn't die – he swam ashore somewhere off the Caribbean coast. From there he was rescued by a merchant ship what brought him here – to Welmley!"

"I think it's time we introduced ourselves," Jack said to Rose and, turning to John held out his hand, "Jack Bracken, descendant of Blackheart the pirate at your service."

He shook John's hand and bowed his head with a nod.

"I knew it! I knew it!" John almost jumped with excitement.

"And this," Jack put an arm around Rose and pulled her toward him, "Is Rose Scarlet, descendant of Captain Rosie Scarlet, of The Phoenix."

*

An hour later the three of them were making their way to a pub supposedly frequented by the Pirates centuries ago. John walked on ahead to lead the way while Rose and Jack followed closely behind, deep in thought. John led them down several alleys, through twists and turns until they came to a set of steps leading down onto the beach. They followed until he turned off suddenly without warning and disappeared. Jack made to shout out but Rose placed a hand on his arm. John had returned and waited until they reached the bottom of the steps before revealing all. He held up a hand and waved dramatically toward a concealed doorway cut into the rock, grinning up at the obvious pub sign that hung above it.

"The Jolly Roger," read Jack, "Are you serious?"

Inside was dark and gloomy and Rose had to blink until her eyes became accustomed to the dimness. Large bench tables were crammed around the walls which men sat at drinking, talking quietly amongst themselves. Smaller round tables were scattered to fill in the gaps and some men sat at these too. Rose scanned around but could see no other women other than the barmaid who stood behind the large central bar, wiping a glass with such vigour Rose felt sure it would break.

The barmaid stared suspiciously at Rose as she brushed back her bleached blond hair with the tea towel still in her hand, but on catching Jack's eye she stopped and smiled shyly. Rose pushed her red curls out of her face, she could feel Jack's arm pressed comfortably in her back and she smiled up at him for reassurance. Jack kissed her cheek and gently pushed her forward until they both stood at the bar alongside John.

"These are the true descendants of Captains Scarlet and Blackheart of the pirate ship The Phoenix," he announced proudly, "This is May."

Silence fell as the regulars momentarily studied the new arrivals before turning back to their drinking and talking. The barmaid scowled at Rose who returned a nervous smile.

"Now then, May," said John scolding her, "Don't frighten off our distinguished guests!"

She started to protest but John held up a hand to silence her; an obviously much used signal between them.

"I know you always thought you were related to Captain Rosie Scarlet but I did tell you that wasn't so, didn't I?"

"And I always told you I wasn't related to her," she spat nodding at Rose, "I am related to his lover – you know that! You've seen the picture!"

"Yes, well, that's a discussion for another day. I mean it!" John held up his hand again as she began to protest, "These are my guests so not another word!"

His eyes twinkled as she nodded sullenly and, reaching for a pewter mug, began to pump beer into it. She placed it on the counter in front of John as he ordered two more. Rose wished he had asked her first; beer was not a favourite of hers and she could do with something much stronger and containing less gas. She suddenly became very aware that she was still holding the sword and moved in closer to Jack, hiding it between them. He took it from her, bearing the heavy weight as though it were just a light stick; his muscles rippled beneath his shirt and jacket. Rose flashed her eyes jealously as the barmaid gazed admiringly at Jack with her huge brown eyes, leaning forward and placing his beer down gently with a show of cleavage.

As Jack reached forward to pick up his drink their fingers touched. He recoiled as though she had given him a huge electric shock. Rose glared at her threateningly and May slammed another glass of beer down on the bar, this time spilling it. John beckoned them to a table in the corner and Rose followed gladly, pulling Jack with her.

"To hide the sword," she whispered in reply to his quizzical look.

She sipped her warm beer and shuddered; the bitter taste made her screw up her face and Jack laughed loudly at her discomfort. Frowning she began asking John questions about the painting and the figurehead. He in turn asked about the sword and how they came to be reunited. All the weeks of confusion and hurt and anger which had built up inside began to mingle with her jealousy. As she talked she took gulps of beer and was amazed at how quickly she became accustomed to the taste. Another round of drinks loosened her tongue a little more and she told of Mr Roland and his search for buried treasure. She told of Jack's part in the story including his real identity. Jack shot her a warning look as she spoke his real name aloud. Ignoring his increasing agitation and warming to her subject she began to explain about the map and how it had been hidden in the sword for centuries and removed by her father for safe keeping.

"Oh my, that's funny," John laughed, "Now that really is in the realms of fantasy!"

Spurred on by her audience Rose revealed how she now had the map, back at the hotel. John fell silent as Jack leapt to his feet, and she knew she had gone too far. He stood over her, staring down at her, his anger burning. She deliberately avoided looking at him and carried on with her tale, unable to stop until she had finally said all the things she wanted to say. John was fascinated by her account of everything that had happened since the night Jack had come into her life. Jack sat back down, trying to hush her but she ignored him and carried on, wanting to get it off her chest once and for all. She felt if it were all out in the open then they could start afresh. For his part John encouraged her by returning to the bar for another round of beers to help loosen her tongue further. She gladly paused to take several gulps, the alcohol sitting warmly inside her washing away her cares. She was aware she was becoming louder and louder but felt exhilarated by her new found confidence.

"...And he burnt down my shop!" she yelled, flinging her red hair defiantly.

Jack tried to hush her again. He took the half full glass of beer from her but she snatched it back and held it tightly. Her eyes shone as the anger erupted.

"You walked into my life through my nightmares!" she spat viciously, "I was doing just fine on my own until you came along! Why Jack? Why? What did I ever do to you?"

"You did nothing," he said quietly, "Stop, honey, it's the drink..."

"Oh, that's it, isn't it? You want to avenge your precious Blackheart! I'm right, aren't I? Go on, admit it! Admit that you wanted the sword and the treasure for yourself! Admit it!"

*

"...Black turns to Scarlet, Scarlet to Black,
The season's in turmoil, time to come back,
Black, back, Black, back,

©2007 Cara Aldous

Back to his true love, never look back..."

The dark cloud descended quicker than it had ever done before and Jack jumped to his feet, his head pounding. The sword clattered noisily to the ground. Silence fell over the whole pub as Rose got unsteadily to her feet. The two lovers stood facing one another, Rose with fists clenched; Jack dark and brooding, his green eyes cold and defensive.

"Come on, Rose, Jack," John implored, rising slowly, trying to diffuse the situation.

"He's not interested in me. He's only interested in my ancestor and what she did to his," Rose narrowed her eyes. "He destroyed my shop and took my sword and no doubt would've taken the map too if he'd known about it!"

"Blackheart was hung for his crimes, and deservedly so; he was a cruel and callous man. But Rosie escaped because she carried his child, and only for this reason. She told the authorities that the child was not his in order to save her skin." Jack growled menacingly.

"No, that's not true! It…it can't be!" Rose felt deflated; the beer and arguing combining to make her head swim.

"It is true, I'm afraid," John shook his head sadly, "Records show that she did deny the child was his. If she had admitted carrying Blackheart's baby…Well, let's just say the powers that be would not have wanted his son and heir to live. They would have destroyed her too."

"That's what destroyed him. She destroyed him; he lived and died for her. Well, I sure as hell wouldn't let a woman do that to me. Not even you Rose."

Sadly and slowly Jack turned and began to make his way through the tables to the door. The demons soared through his mind and he could hear Blackheart's voice goading him, telling him to destroy Rose. Fighting the urge to hurt her, to squeeze the life from her he knew he had to get away.

"Jack!" Rose screamed after him; but he was gone.

*

May stood silently at the bar carefully polishing a glass as though her life depended on it, hoping no one had heard her whispers. She looked longingly at the disappearing back of Jack Bracken then turned her stare toward Rose Scarlet. She bent her head, her hair falling over her eyes, hiding her hatred for the woman before her. Her scowl was quickly replaced with a defiant smile at John as he frowned.

One day soon they would be reunited; then and only then would the true love prophecy be fulfilled. She took the pitcher of beer that she had given Jack; her special brew, and carefully poured it away. It wouldn't do for someone else to drink it; she wasn't sure what effect it would have on another person. But the effect it had on Jack had been perfect and the whispered spell had fuelled the argument between him and Rose. The first phase of her plan had worked better than she had dared to imagine. For now she would have to tread very carefully and ever so slowly.

©2007 Cara Aldous

Chapter 24

Sam felt relieved then angry at her friend's text message. At least she was alive and okay but where she was exactly was anybody's guess. She wanted to rush round to Aubrey's straight away to tell him. But first she had to set the newly installed burglar alarm, carefully locking each window, and check the backdoor was locked properly too. Aubrey had insisted on the burglar alarm. He too had one installed after the break-ins. Sam shuddered as she thought back to the evening they'd found both their homes ransacked. Rose and Jack were both missing presumed…Even now she dare to only think it in a whisper; dead.

Sam trembled, her nerves destroyed since that night. She didn't like Jack but still, she didn't want him dead; just out of their lives so that things could get back to normal and life could resume its same-old-same-old boring routine. A routine she would no longer complain about if only

Rose was here and Jack was safe but gone. Then, and only then, everything could go back to the way it was before. But it just seemed so impossible that things would ever be the same again.

Aubrey opened his front door a crack, the chain pulled taught. As soon as he saw Sam he quickly shut the door, unhooked the chain and let her in. Once Sam was inside he closed the door and slipped the chain back on, drawing across both top and bottom bolts just to make doubly sure they were safe. Sam sighed deeply; even Aubrey was shook up to the point he dared not go outside. The shop, having been destroyed in the fire, remained boarded up. Neither of them could bear to go there anymore.

Their homes had been ransacked yet nothing had been taken and, other than the disappearance of their friend, it was obvious that the perpetrators had not found what they were looking for and so, logically, would not return. Still, it was better to be safe than sorry and the security on their homes gave them both peace of mind. The extra locks and alarms would be a lasting reminder of their association with Jack Bracken.

Sam followed Aubrey along the dark hallway, with the dreary 1950's style wallpaper and dark wood stairs, into his small back room. Rose's own home had been opened up, both front and back rooms made into one which, along with the apple-white walls and pale furnishings, gave theirs a much more light and airy feel. Sam felt much more at ease in Aubrey's place than hers especially as she was alone now. Rattling around in the large, open room at night made her very uneasy and she had taken to sleeping at Aubrey's now.

She sank down into the large armchair which was usually only for him but he seemed not to mind Sam using it. She waited while he offered the usual drinks and snacks, declining each and every one individually, knowing that was the way things were done at Aubrey's until slowly he settled himself on a stiff-backed dining chair and waited patiently.

"I've had a text from Rose," she began. "On the mobile," she added by way of explanation.

She always felt the need to explain everything to him like he was simple and, being so in love, he usually indulged her. This time, however, his nerves were so frazzled by the recent events that his temper flared.

"I do know what a bloody mobile is you know!" he snapped, "I'm not a complete idiot!"

Taken aback, Sam shut up. They sat in silence for a while neither knowing quite how to break through the awkward embarrassment of the moment. Finally Aubrey's cats – the black twins – bounded indoors clattering through the catflap and juddering to a halt by Aubrey's feet. Both looked triumphant as though each believed he had won the race. Sam began to giggle and soon Aubrey too joined in, tittering at first before exploding into a loud and hearty laugh. Sam screeched and cackled raucously, the tears pouring down her cheeks and she gasped for breath suddenly aware that she was crying.

Great sobs racked her body as she wailed uncontrollably; all the pent up rage and anger, hurt and pain finally bursting through her hardened façade. Aubrey, shocked momentarily into silence, perched on the arm of her chair and placed a comforting arm around her.

"Oh my God, Aubrey," she gasped, pointlessly wiping the flowing tears, "What are we going to do?"

"About what, my love?" he asked softly.

She looked up at him through drenched eyelashes. Slowly she moved her face up to his so that it was only inches away. Instead of responding in the way men usually did in that circumstance, with a kiss, Aubrey merely remained where he was, motionless and smiling; he never made the first move. Sam sighed, moving closer, and kissed him on the lips. The kiss was like an electric shock which seemed to jolt him into life. He held her tightly and kissed her hard on the mouth, only pulling back for air out of concern for her. But when she reached up and pulled him back down he responded with equal fervour.

*

Several hours later as they lay in one another's arms, wrapped in the crisp white sheets of Aubrey's bed, Sam finally felt safe. Wallowing in her satisfaction of their love-making she thought back to their first time. She had been pleasantly surprised by his expertise as a lover. Thinking he would be a 'missionary' man she had been both shocked and delighted when he did things to her that she had only ever dreamt about. He took great pains to give her pleasure before he allowed himself to give in to the ecstasy of the moment.

As they lay together now, holding one other tightly Sam read Rose's message out word for word; Aubrey liked things to be precise. Once infuriated by this type of person Sam now felt she could easily live with his ways. With the promise of nightly orgasms she could live with anything. She could even live with Aubrey's cats and all his peculiar ways, which were not actually peculiar just orderly and precise.

They lay in quiet contemplation; Sam nestling into his arms which enveloped her protectively. Aubrey was deep in thought so Sam stayed quiet, thinking about how they could help Rose; they had to try at least. With Aubrey's help she was sure they could find out where Rose was. It was only a matter of time before the person who broke into their houses and burned down the shop found her anyway and they owed it to her to try to help. Sam shivered at the thought that Rose could still be in danger. Aubrey kissed her forehead gently.

"You okay my love?" he asked, genuinely concerned.

Sam nodded as a tear escaped and slipped silently down her cheek. She buried her face in his neck as more tears threatened. She gulped them down, trying to think positively; to think about helping Rose. It was almost as if she were mourning her friend.

"Just worried about Rose," she sniffed, her voice muffled.

"I know, I know," he murmured, stroking her hair, "I've been thinking about her too. I think I may be able to work out where she is. But I'll need your help."

She lifted her face to him and gave a watery smile.

"I don't see how I can help but I'll try..." she replied.

Black Nightmares to Scarlet Dreams

*

Within minutes of being on the internet Aubrey had found several possibilities of where Rose might be. Sam marvelled at his dexterity with a keyboard and modem. Who would think to look at this strange little man that he had such hidden depths? She watched him intently as he studied the screen; first thing tomorrow she would take him shopping and get his haircut. She had been amazed to discover that he was living in a timewarp simply because he had no idea of how to get out of it. She was even more surprised to discover that he was the same age as Jack. Though his body underneath the pressed shirt, clean vest and nylon trousers definitely bore witness to this, the clothes swamped him and belied his true age.

Now, as they sat together at his computer, she watched enthralled as his fingers typed quickly and nimbly, guiding them through many websites, bringing up maps and pictures so fast that Sam hardly had time to take it all in before the next page popped up. Finally with a few well-placed questions and confident taps at the keyboard, Aubrey turned to face her. His grin stretched from ear to ear.

"There! This is the most likely," he motioned at the screen with a flourish of his hand.

Sam peered closely at the map in front of her. At first she was unsure at what she was supposed to be looking at but suddenly the name of a very familiar place jumped out at her. It was on the coast and was as familiar to her as it was to Rose. As a young teen she had once been invited along on the annual Scarlet holiday as company for Rose.

"Welmley-On-Sea," she almost shouted with excitement, "Of course! It has to be..."

Chapter 25

It was to be a long wait for the train. Sam had been so keen to get to Welmley-On-Sea that she had insisted they leave immediately. She was extremely cross when Aubrey had insisted on packing and had become incensed when he had then insisted on wasting yet more time by asking Barbara Knox to feed his cats whilst he was away.

Barbara had refused at first, on the grounds that she did not want any involvement whatsoever with Rose or Jack. But Aubrey had assured her they were not involved and explained that as she was the only person he trusted he knew she would look after his cats properly. He told her he would be happier knowing they would be in her safe hands. Flattered into accepting she nonetheless warned Aubrey about getting involved with obvious trouble-makers. Aubrey thanked her and told her he would be careful before finally climbing into their waiting taxi where Sam sat impatiently strumming her fingers against the window.

A shower of rain fell as the taxi made its way into town. Once at the station they booked their tickets for the next train to Welmley-On-Sea. Unfortunately, because it was winter and the tourist trade fell off during the months September through to April, the trains to that particular area of coast only ran twice a day and they had missed the first train. In her anger and frustration, Sam felt this was simply ridiculous and proceeded to tell the booking clerk in no uncertain terms how the service should be run. Aubrey had to apologise which made her even angrier but he placated her with the promise of having his hair cut and agreeing to let her take him clothes shopping. This calmed her down a little and she immediately bought several style magazines for men, to leaf through as they waited for their train.

She soon found the perfect style to suit Aubrey's face and bone-structure and excitedly showed it to him. Not knowing whether it was nice or nasty, fashionable or unfashionable, he simply smiled at her and nodded. That was a green light as far as Sam was concerned and with several hours to kill she insisted they visit the men's hair salon across the road from the station to see if they could fit him in there and then.

"As you pointed out, we've got loads of time," she reasoned.

He couldn't really argue so it was he found himself sitting at one of those funny looking sinks as he leaned back into the basin. The young trainee roughly washed his hair ready for the cut. When asked if he wanted conditioner, Aubrey realised he was completely out of his depth. He had been happy to let Sam have free reign in choosing a style for him but, as the stylist snipped away and discussed the weather and holidays, he became more and more miserable. With his hair layered and styled in a kind of tousled effect which he desperately tried to flatten down, they emerged from the salon with ten minutes to spare.

The train breezed into the station as they gathered their things together, Aubrey reaching for Sam's smart, new designer case.

"I'm glad you made me pack," she said sheepishly as they boarded.

Aubrey smiled and nodded as he took her case and pushed it into the rack above their seats. He pushed his own small battered brown suitcase in beside it and noted how they looked odd together. A bit like him and Sam, he thought with a smile. She smiled back at him as he took off his coat, catching a glimpse of his reflection in the window. His haircut took years off him, he had to admit, and it was a style he would never have had the nerve to ask for himself. The stylist did look at Aubrey a little oddly when Sam had told him what she wanted. Aubrey had simply nodded and sat down quickly before he changed his mind. But now he was glad that Sam had dragged him in there and vowed to let her take him clothes shopping too as soon as she liked.

*

As the countryside sped by Aubrey pulled out of his pocket an A-Z of Welmley-On-Sea and the surrounding areas and spread it on the table in front of them.

"What's that for?" asked Sam, busily munching her way through a large bag of crisps she had bought on the way back to the station.

"Well, it's so we can find Rose. If she isn't at Welmley-On-Sea, she could be staying here," he pointed to a small village.

"Leckton," Sam read aloud, "Why there?"

"Didn't you read anything from the sites I showed you?" He sighed and rolled his eyes but he was only teasing so she shrugged playfully by way of reply.

"Jack Bracken – the original one, not our American friend," he paused to allow Sam to interrupt before continuing. However, she was silent and he was more than a little taken aback by her lack of usual venom toward Jack.

"The Brackens were from Leckton. The family lived there in fact until Blackheart's capture. It's rumoured that Blackheart is buried there in an unmarked grave. That it was the last act his brother performed for him before turning his back on both the family name and birthplace."

"So why would Rose go there? I mean, surely she's trying to escape the Bracken family, isn't she? I know I would want to be as far away as possible from any connection to that man!"

Aubrey smiled, "Yes, yes, I know you would but Rose," he paused, "Well, she loves him, doesn't she? Anyway, he's not the reason she might go there. Captain Rosie Scarlet was also born there. It's rumoured they knew each other well before he captured her. They possibly even played together as children."

"Bloody hell, that's quite romantic really!" Sam sounded surprised, "Blackheart and Scarlet grew up together and almost died together. She had his child and now, all these centuries later, descendants of their offspring and his brother's offspring get together. Makes you wonder, doesn't it?"

"Doesn't it just," he agreed, "Anyway, it was in Leckton where it all began and, who knows - perhaps Rose is hoping it will finally all end there."

©2007 Cara Aldous

Chapter 26

Rose sat quietly in the car, staring out of the window. She had tried unsuccessfully to calm Jack down and talk him out of making this journey, but he had refused to listen. He was agitated about the map and, seemingly wanting to prove something he insisted she accompany him. Her hesitation seemed to upset him even more. He had looked up at her through his lashes, his green eyes shining with sorrow as he confused her apprehension of facing the past with fear of him.

She had little choice but to join him in the hire car. She tried to hide her uneasiness by leaping in with such vigour that it shot his mood from low to high in an instant. His mood manically lifted so fast it scared her as he broke into a huge grin and leapt in beside her. He kissed her and hugged her so tight she thought her ribs would crush and pierce her already fragile heart. But she was too scared to protest lest it tip him back the other way; back into the abyss of depression. With horror mounting she realised that she was still frightened and always would be; not of him but of his terrible moods. She knew it was no basis for a stable relationship.

He was ill; she accepted that now. His moods dropped down into the depths of despair but also lifted so quickly into a manic high that it terrified her. He played off her moods and reactions and it pained her to think she might be the cause of these episodes. He was – what; a manic depressive? She knew very little about mental illness but he was without doubt plainly ill.

"Don't you want to know where we're going?" his words broke into her thoughts.

She smiled, "Wherever we're going, I'm sure I'll like it," she replied quietly. She knew exactly where they were headed; it was a place she had considered visiting many times since she had arrived at Welmley.

He frowned, "Oh I'm not so sure you'll like it exactly. It's a little village that's very significant to both of us - you and me."

Flustered by her silence he continued, "It's a little village called Leckton. Heard of it?"

No reply.

"It's the birthplace of Rosie Scarlet and Jack Bracken."

Rose sighed, visibly irritated by his naïvety. She couldn't help it; she did not want to hear any more about Rosie Scarlet and Blackheart. They were the past and should remain dead and buried and at peace. If

Jack continued dragging them up all the time they would never be free of their ancestors. She wanted to scream loudly. But, afraid of his reaction if she did she said nothing. They sat in silence as the car hummed steadily along the country lanes.

Finally Jack could stand no more, "Look Rose, what the hell is the matter with you? If it's about last night…"

"Yes, it is about last night!" she snapped, "Last night and every other day and night since we met. And even before that – it's about every bloody night and every bloody day of my whole damn life!"

They continued on in silence, Rose fighting back bitter tears as Jack's face, set and determined, hid the turmoil within. Finally he could stand no more and carelessly pulled over to the side of the road, bumping the car dangerously up onto the verge. Aware that they were in the middle of the countryside, in the middle of nowhere, Rose began to have a panic attack like nothing she'd experienced before. She stared wildly around for a sign of someone, anyone who might help her. Jack sat back in his seat and thumped the steering wheel hard with his fist causing the horn to sound and Rose to jump even more. Her breathing became faster and faster as her head began to swim. She fumbled with the door, trying desperately to push it open but her sweaty fingers couldn't grip the handle.

"What the hell's wrong with you Rose?" Jack spat angrily, reaching over and pushing open the door for her. "What are you so afraid of?"

"You." It came out in such a whisper that Rose wasn't even sure she had said it.

"Me?" his voice was hoarse and he rubbed his face, "Why?"

"I...I don't know," she desperately wanted to reach out to him. She could see he was in pain but so was she. She wanted him to reach out for her but knew he wouldn't.

"Am I really that terrifying?" he spoke more to himself than Rose, "Have I played the part too long? Have I finally begun to believe in it myself? Because if that's the case, then boy! Have I lost the plot! God, my head hurts!"

"...Yo ho...."

He began to rub his hands through his hair, pressing his fingers hard into his eyes. Rose watched him, numbly. Did he really believe he was Blackheart? Did she? Was that why she was so afraid of him? Sighing deeply Jack switched the engine on and turned up the volume on the radio as loud as it would go. He slammed the car into reverse and slid off the verge with a squeal of wheels before crunching the gear lever into first and accelerating hard away. Rose barely had time to close her door properly.

"...Yo ho ho..."

*

They would go to Leckton and maybe there they could talk but right now his head pounded and he had a job to stay focused; he didn't want to hear anything Rose had to say. He wanted them to be together forever but forever was a long time and he knew, deep down, they were no more made for each other than Blackheart and Rosie had been. Those two had been bad news for one another from the start. They were both selfish and nasty people; both evil. The two had parted with animosity and he knew that soon he and Rose would also part. It was only a matter of time before the curse fucked his head up completely. But he wouldn't let Blackheart win – not without a fight. He could see the village up ahead; soon he would have some answers; they both would.

"...Find the dead,
Reap what ye sow,
Bury it deep,
Now yours to keep,
Ye pirate Black will never sleep..."

*

The small village of Leckton was a few miles from Welmley-On-Sea and, at any other time, a pleasant drive through the open countryside and dwindling farms. Fields were barren and empty, ready for winter, but in spring and the subsequent summer they would be resplendent with the multi-colours of nature instead of the blandness of it. The village itself could only be glimpsed briefly as the road twisted and turned, disappearing behind hedges which sprung up here and there; hidden too by a small wood. Leckton wood was reportedly thousands of years old though Jack doubted if this were actually true. Many of the trees now would be saplings of the ancient ones, mere seedlings compared to their ancestors. No different really to him and Rose. He turned the car round a sharp bend which brought them face to face with a sign informing them that they were indeed entering Leckton which only welcomed safe drivers.

Jack laughed loudly then stopped, aware that once more he had made Rose quite literally jump. He pulled up sharply, parking by the side of the old church and looked up at the ancient bell tower, wondering if these were the same bells that rang out the news of Blackheart's hanging. Without checking to see if Rose was coming with him, he got out of the car and headed for the graveyard.

He walked carefully in and out the graves, looking at the names on the headstones. Many were crumbling and old and few were legible. The churchyard itself was well tended, the grass cut regularly and weeds kept at bay. He read the names he could make out, his search becoming more and more frantic until finally he found the name he had been searching for. Out of reverence he knelt, lost in thought. He clasped his hands together just as his God-fearing Grandmother had taught the young Jack and began to pray, hoping it was not too late for this lost soul.

Rose watched as he wandered aimlessly around the graves, stumbling as he checked each and every one. She wasn't in the least surprised when he stopped but completely taken aback when he knelt down in prayer. Surely he couldn't be? She crept closer but was still too far to make out the name. She moved in closer, one eye on Jack and the other on the headstone.

"It's not who you think it is," Jack remained kneeling, his head still bowed.

"Sorry?" Rose stood behind him.

"It's not Blackheart – I don't think they buried blaggards, murderers and pirates on sacred ground - do you?" he got to his feet.

"I…I…No, no they didn't," she smiled. "So, who is it?"

"This is the resting place of Jeremiah Black, father of Jonathan Black and Jack Bracken. Blackheart shamed the Bracken family name so they changed it to Black. They say Jeremiah's soul was as dark as his youngest son's but that's another story!" he replied hotly.

Rose blushed and turned away, embarrassed. She spotted another grave nearby bearing the name of Black and turned, leaning over to rub across the name with her hand. Jack followed, frowning at the headstone. There was a single year on it which was unusual but not uncommon. It was clear that there had been no other name or date for although the stone was old it was not cracked or chipped and any other carving would have weathered the same as the others.

"Black - Seventeen Hundred and forty-five," she read out loud. "Jack! That's the same year Blackheart was hung!"

Jack frowned then shrugged and turned, walking away. "A mark of respect from his family, I would guess – but empty and pointless! Just like everything has been!"

She stood by the grave and watched as he made his way back to the car. She swallowed hard, trying to think. If the Bracken or Black family were buried there she was pretty sure the Scarlets would be too. Carefully she picked her way through the crumbling stones, looking at each one in turn. One stone box had started to crumble away leaving large gaps around the joins. Rose shuddered at the blackness within, trying not to think about what was inside.

"It's only dust," she reminded herself as she stopped to read the name.

After a fruitless search Rose abandoned her hunt and picked her way carefully back through the graves, taking care not to tread on any. At the car she found Jack sitting on the bonnet having a cigarette. He squinted up at her through the smoky haze. She deliberately avoided his eye as she got into the passenger seat and quietly closed the door. She watched him out the corner of her eye as he flicked the butt away but, instead of getting into the car like she expected, he remained sitting with his head bowed. Her anger flared at his childlike behaviour as she flung the door open and marched round to face him.

"What the hell is wrong with you?" she demanded.

He turned to look at her then smiled and shook his head, twisting away from her intense stare.

"God, Jack! You're such a… such a… Aargh!" she screamed, exasperated by his lack of reaction.

He fixed his deep green eyes on her. "I'm what?" he asked menacingly.

"You're so fucking infuriating!" she sighed, the anger subsiding.

They stood looking at one another for some time; neither speaking nor moving, but each knowing that this really was the end. Neither wanted to say the words, both clinging onto the last few dying embers of their love. A love that could well have spanned centuries but, ultimately, would destroy them. Not soulmates; lust peppered with love. They couldn't live with one another and they couldn't live without. But if they stayed together they were in great danger of destroying each another. If they had lived; would Rosie and Blackheart's love have survived? Rose doubted it. Rosie Scarlet had proved to be a scheming, selfish bitch who renounced her man to save her own neck. They would have murdered one another eventually.

Jack's unnatural obsession with the pirate was eating him up. It had already killed their relationship and Rose worried that it was also killing him. By parting he had a chance; she was only too aware that his headaches were at their worst whenever he was with her. The other evening in the pub he had been in agony; his face twisted in pain and torment. With each venomous word she threw at him he had visibly winced as though she had stuck him with needles. Only when he looked at the barmaid did the darkness and hurting momentarily lift from his face.

Maybe he could find peace with her. She, Rose, would always have a connection with Jack; Rosie Scarlet and Blackheart would always be a part of them. And she would always be thankful that he had been her first love and had finally broken the spell. At last she felt free and alive; she could and would love again. Of that she was certain. She had learned perfection didn't exist, only an acceptance of flaws. In time she felt sure she would meet someone and settle down. She could be happy and Jack had given her that.

©2007 Cara Aldous

Chapter 27

Jack pulled carefully over to the side of the road and switched the engine off. For several minutes they sat in silence looking out to sea through the grimy windscreen. Ignoring Rose he got out and leaned over the rail looking down at the rock pools and funnels of water left by the eroding sea.

It was some time before Rose joined him. First he heard the car door slam then he was aware of her standing next to him, her gaze burning a hole in the back of his head. He knew she hated and loved him in equal amounts. He knew this; he had always known it but only now, that it was finally over, could he admit it. The pain at the realisation she was afraid of him; thinking him even capable of hurting her wounded him deeply. It was a wound he was sure would never mend. He sighed long and hard before turning to her.

"Why, Rose?" he asked softly.

Rose sniffed, her eyes watering in the cold wind howling along the coast. Her first instinct was to turn and run. Yet she so desperately wanted to understand him. The confusion of emotions that had run through her from their very first meeting right up to now bubbled dangerously close to the surface. It would only be a matter of time before they manifested into one huge panic attack and she did not want Jack to see her like that. Yes, he could be gentle. Yes, he could be kind. But he was also controlling. And showing her emotional vulnerability would give him a new power over her. One she was not sure she would ever be able to break free from. Their relationship was over for good; it had to be.

"I don't know, Jack," she said, "I'm not sure. Only that…" she faltered.

He looked into her eyes, his own full of tenderness and concern, and she had to turn away.

"All my life," her voice wavered and she swallowed hard to contain the rising emotion, "All my life I have had someone telling me what to do; where to go; what to eat; what to like and what to dislike. My whole life has been run by someone else. First there was Mother, God rest her soul, she tried her best, I know, but my best was never good enough. I was the great disappointment of her life. When Dad died I felt so alone. She didn't care how I felt, didn't even ask. Just organised the funeral, didn't ask what I might like only what she wanted! We didn't have hymns, you know, no music; nothing! All that was there was a handful of people and a few words. Hollow, meaningless words! I wanted to say something but I couldn't upset her! It didn't matter how much I was hurting! Huh! What did she know? What did she know about the 'Scarlet' women? She was only one by marriage, not a real one! Not like me!" her voice cracked and she gasped back the tears.

Jack put his arm around her shoulders but she shrugged him off as she wiped her face with the back of her sleeve. She staggered away from him a little as she fumbled in her pocket for the screwed up tissue she knew would be in there; was always in there. Jack watched as she blew her nose and smiled a watery smile at him.

"I'm sorry you had a horrible time, I had no idea," he began.

"Why would you? You don't even know me – All you know about is a legend of a time long gone. It's just rumour; the facts we'll never know for sure. How can we?" she looked at him imploringly.

Having no idea what she wanted from him he had to give it one more try, "Yes, it's legend and yes, it was long ago. But I believe that they loved one another, in their own way. Blackheart died for Rosie. I also believe that, deep down, you still love me. Somewhere in your heart there is some love for me. I have to believe that!"

Rose smiled and shook her head, "Don't you see? You're no different from her – Mother - telling me how I should feel; that I should love you. Don't I have a say in how I feel?"

The tide was coming into the small bay now. Waves rushed in and out, taking any debris left by day-trippers back out to sea; cleansing the sand of all trace of them. Jack shook his head at the sadness of it all.

At the pollution by the visitors and the pollution of Rose's heart and soul by the very people that were supposed to love her.

She was just as damaged as he was. Her pain was no different from his. Yet all he wanted was to love and be loved and he knew this would save him. Rose, on the other hand, was drowning in too much love. She could only be saved by becoming free from all those she believed to be in control of her; and that included him.

"What…What about Sam? She's been with you for years. The two of you are like sisters – she said so," he clutched desperately at straws; a drowning man.

"Sam?" she scoffed and his heart sank, "Sam is just as bad! Oh sure, we've been friends for a lifetime but only because Mother liked her. I had no say in whether I wanted this friendship! We were thrown together yet we've got nothing in common, not really. She's used me over the years just like everyone else…"

"Rose; don't, please!" Jack grabbed her, looking imploringly at her. This was too much for even him to bare, "I can't let you pull apart a friendship that has been the only solid thing in your life. Sam was there when you needed her; you told me so many times. And though she and I never really saw eye to eye I always knew, deep down, that one day we would grow to tolerate one another through our mutual love for you. And now…" he shook his head sadly.

"Now I've finally seen the light!" Rose shrugged him off and stepped back, gripping the rail hard. "Yes, Sam has been there for me through hard times, when I had no-one else. So what? Am I supposed to be eternally grateful for that? I've been there for her too, you know. I kept my family home for her. I wanted to sell it and move into a flat in town but, oh no! That wasn't a good idea; don't sell Rose, she said, you know it makes sense to keep the house. We can do it up as we want, we can have parties every weekend and we can have boyfriends to stay too. Great! Yeah! We did up the house – as she wanted. She had the parties! And as for boyfriends staying, well! She had a different one each month but when I wanted one to stay - you! Well, you know what she was like about that! No, Jack, Sam is okay but she's just as controlling as Mother was and you are…"

He turned his head away as Rose continued, "Admit it, if you're honest, you have been telling me what to do since you arrived. The way you set me up from the start with the carving and the projector – that was a really nasty thing to do too!"

Jack hung his head, "I'm sorry Rose; I was just doing my job. And it was before I really knew you, before I fell in love with you."

"I know, Jack. But you could have told me afterwards. You could have explained it all to me. But instead you kept on lying…"

"I know, and I'm real sorry but I'm not sure how many more times I have to say it before you start believing me."

Rose held his face close to hers, "Jack, look at me, what do you see?"

He gazed at her thoughtfully, "I see a beautiful woman who had everything and has now lost it thanks to me."

"No, Jack! No! That's what you think you see. What you really see is a frightened, lonely woman who, whilst clutching at straws, grabbed hold of love with both hands and held on for dear life. I wanted to believe, like you did, that we could be as in love as Rosie and Blackheart were but, really! Do you honestly think they were as in love as all that? At the first sign of trouble Rosie saved her own skin and let his be damned!"

They moved closer together and stood, holding onto one another for one last time. Each deep in their own thoughts and each wondering what fate had in store for them now. In his head Jack was forming plans to return to his homeland. He had been away too long and it was time to give up the acting and the pretending and get a real job; one that had regular hours with regular pay.

"Do you think we have more than one soulmate in life?" he asked her.

"I hope so, Jack," she replied, "I hope so."

Rose too was making plans and hers involved one person. She would live alone, make her own decisions, do her own thing, and enjoy every minute of it.

"Jack," she stood back from him, "What happened to my sword?"

"Your sword? I don't understand – you have it, I gave it to you and left it with you at the pub."

"Yes, yes, but," she faltered, "When it all began I mean. How did you steal it?"

"Me?" he half laughed, half gasped, "You still think I stole it? Rose, honey, it really wasn't me, you know. It was that Drummond guy…"

"Rick! But - why?" Rose felt her knees buckle and grabbed the rail for support.

"When you left the shop after finding that 'body' I was supposed to go in and collect it. But you ran out and down the road to his place so quickly and there were just too many people about. I was just trying to figure what to do next when Drummond came back alone and went inside. I couldn't believe it when the guy strolled out with the sword in his hand and calmly put it in the trunk of his car." He laughed and rubbed his face, "I was just going to speak to him when you joined him in the street. I had to get away then before the cops showed. I'm sorry, Baby, I thought you knew."

Rose wasn't really surprised, "But, well okay, you've said how he did it. But why? What did he have to gain? Surely Roland couldn't offer him the sort of money that would make a guy betray his friend. I mean, he watched me fall to pieces when I discovered it gone….And all the time it was outside, in his car, only a short distance from me…"

Jack shook his head, "You don't get it Rose, do you? You have a very valuable item in the Sword of Aramoth. Roland has been searching for it for years and he was willing to pay a hell of a lot of money for it too! He even posted a reward on the net for anyone with information about it to contact him. How do you think he found out you had it in the first place?"

The anger surged through her and she shook, "Rick Drummond is a bastard! One day I hope he'll get what's due to him!"

"Oh, he'll get that alright! And much, much more! You don't double-cross a guy like Roland and get away with it so easily. I should know that!" Jack smiled, "If I know Roland he's mad at losing the sword and the map and with you disappearing like that, he'll need someone to take his anger out on."

©2007 Cara Aldous

Chapter 28

Sam and Aubrey stood in the grounds of the cliff-top hotel, swept away by the magnificent view across the bay. Several ships and boats sat majestically on the waves, not really seeming to move yet skimming across the horizon. Whilst Sam admired the view and thought romantically of the pirate ships that had sailed those very seas centuries ago, Aubrey looked at his watch; it had been ages since Rose had left with Jack. When they arrived the receptionist had explained that the couple had left in a hire car.

Even though he now thought Jack was probably misunderstood; he mistrusted the man and was worried he might harm Rose. They both turned suddenly at the sound of tires crunching gravel as Jack pulled slowly into a parking space close up to the edge of the cliff.

"Dangerous idiot!" muttered Aubrey as Sam ran toward Rose stepping out from the passenger side.

"Hey, Aubrey!" Jack called out, genuinely pleased to see them.

Aubrey nodded curtly and walked quickly over to Rose and Sam having a very heated conversation.

"Aubrey, tell her!" Sam pleaded, "She says she wants to sell up.

Aubrey frowned, "What do you mean, sell up? Sell up what exactly?"

"Sell up everything," Rose stared hard at Aubrey; he looked so different.

"And do what?" demanded Sam.

"Anything I want! Anything at all!" Rose flung her arms wide, dancing around much to the amusement of Jack and Aubrey. Even Sam found it hard to stifle a giggle.

"Oh Rose, you idiot! I've been worried sick about you!" Sam caught her friends arm, "Just stop for one minute will you! You can't sell! You just can't! I won't let you do anything that daft – you're not thinking straight!"

Rose stopped and raised her eyebrows at Sam before turning to Jack. He shrugged and nodded, understanding their earlier conversation. Sam frowned at Rose and glared at Jack whilst Aubrey stood quietly waiting for Rose to reply.

"I am thinking straight for the first time in my life and I am going to sell up and move here!" Rose said quietly before turning and walking back into the hotel.

*

Aubrey and Sam had booked into a double room. Sam wanted to share all about her new found love with her oldest and closest friend. But

Rose disappeared upstairs before Sam had chance to catch up with her. The receptionist had refused to tell Sam what her room number was so she sulked all the way up to their room. Throwing herself down onto the bed she brooded over Rose's revelations as she watched Aubrey unpack. He carefully put their things away in his usual neat and methodical way, removing each item individually from the case. She had thought this would irritate her but was surprised to discover that she actually liked the way he did things for her. She could never usually be bothered and would normally live out of her suitcase. It would be nice to pull something from a drawer or closet easily without rummaging around for a change.

    She focused her mind on more pressing things; like how she was going to talk Rose out of selling their home. And how on earth was she going to persuade Rose to start again with the shop? After all, Aubrey did need the job. Especially now they were together. She voiced her concerns aloud and, even though she was aware it sounded more like selfish whining than concern for her friend, was unable to stop.

    Aubrey waited patiently until he was certain she had finished. He too thought it nothing more than self pity but he also understood how scared Rose's plans must have made Sam feel. For the first time in years the two of them were going in completely different directions. If this really was what Rose wanted and not the whim of a violent and controlling man then it was something she would not and should not be talked out of.

Aubrey felt he had to tread very carefully where Sam and Rose were concerned or it could all blow up causing irrevocable damage to his own new and exciting relationship with Sam.

"Sam, my love," he began cautiously, "Don't worry. If Rose has decided to sell – and, let's face it, it's a big if – then we'll be okay. You still have your job and I have my gardening work. My house is my own and I have no mortgage to worry about. And you'll still see her, of course you will," he added hastily.

"How do you know?" she demanded before breaking down, sobbing uncontrollably.

*

Rose stared out of the window at the sea. It was calm and still with a solitary ship sailing slowly across the horizon. It was a bit like watching a clock; you don't actually see the hands move but you know they do because time moves on just like the ship. Time was moving on for Rose too and she was glad that Jack had not come back to their room.

He had muttered something about going for a walk. She looked down at the spot where the car park ended and the path down to the beach began. As she gazed out, Jack's head bobbed into view and then slowly, as he pulled himself up the steep incline, the rest of him followed. She sighed; he was extremely handsome and her heart did a little flip as he pushed his hair out of his face. Maybe she did still love him a little bit, but was it enough? Even before she asked she already knew the answer. She turned away and picked up her mobile, scrolling down through the phone book. She pressed the button to dial and waited as it rung. It was answered quite quickly.

"Hello? It's me, Rose. Can we meet? It...It's important – I have something to tell you..."

Chapter 29

The sun was watery and the sky remarkably clear for a late November lunchtime. A strong wind whipped up the sand and the far-out tide left a large wet-sand expanse which made the beach appear even more barren than usual in its winter quiet. From outside the pub appeared deserted and Rose wondered, not for the first time, how on earth it survived the onslaught of a crashing, angry sea during those dark and stormy nights. The sign creaked and groaned with every gust, each swing threatening to send the wooden board high into the sky.

Rose pulled her woollen hat down over her ears as she pushed the door. It gave way easily, helped along by the weather. It was a lot harder though to shut against the elements and Rose had to lean all her weight into it. Breathless, she removed her hat and loosened her coat as she looked around her.

May leaned on the bar day-dreaming. On sight of Rose she grasped a glass and started polishing furiously, concentrating on an imagined blemish. Blushing deep crimson as Rose approached the bar she tried desperately to pretend not to see her at first. Instead she kept her eyes focused on the glass and did not look up until she heard a loud and obvious cough. Smiling, she met Rose's gaze with a steady and closed face and waited. She didn't have to wait long.

"Is John here?" Rose demanded.

May looked bored, "Not yet," she answered.

"Well, what time does he normally get here?" Rose asked, irritated.

May shrugged, "When he gets here."

"Yes, but what time is that?" Rose's voice became higher as her anger welled.

May shrugged, unperturbed by Rose. She ran a hand through her wavy blonde hair. Every time the door opened both of them looked toward it expectantly. Rose hoping to see John's friendly smile, May hoping to see the handsome figure that was Jack Bracken.

May longed to see the man destined to be her lover. All she had to do was work harder to get him away from the clutches of the red-headed bitch in front of her. She narrowed her eyes as she turned her attention to Rose. Rose was a beautiful woman, that was something she couldn't deny, but there seemed to be a sadness surrounding her. Sadness she had sensed the last time too, even though the ungrateful bitch had been accompanied by Jack. Even when he touched her it had made no change in her mood. If anything, he had seemed to make her worse. May frowned; maybe the magic was stronger than she had anticipated. She shivered and scrutinised her competition even closer. Yes, the sadness was still there but there was something else; something stronger and growing by the minute.

But before she could work out what exactly the door opened and John entered the inn. He strolled to the bar and ordered his usual pint before taking Rose by the arm and ushering her to a table in the far corner. May bristled that Rose had not ordered a drink. After all, who comes into a pub and doesn't order a drink? But what really burned her was that Jack had very obviously not been invited. She moved along the bar nearer to them, pretending to rearrange the bottles, straining to hear some snippet of their conversation. All she could make out was the odd word but not once, and she was very sure of this; not once did they mention Jack. She smiled and hummed happily to herself; soon he would be hers and they would finally live happily ever after.

Rose sat huddled in the corner of the inn. John drank slowly and listened to her plans for her new future. Now and again he nodded courteously but Rose's heart sank as she realised that he was only being polite and had no intention of helping her as she had hoped.

"…And," she finished, "I thought, obviously, of you and your shop?"

John downed the last few gulps of beer as he considered his answer.

"That is a lot for a man to think about Rose," he replied carefully, "And I will have to think long and hard before I can give you a definite answer…"

Rose smiled weakly, "Oh, of course! I never thought for one minute you would – or could – give me an answer today!" she lied.

John smiled warmly, aware of her disappointment. "Now, Rose," he said kindly, "I haven't said no! It's just – well, it's a big decision; you understand?"

Rose nodded and turned her attention to the bar and to May who seemed to be listening to every word. She cursed her stupidity at choosing the one place the staff hated her. It definitely was not a welcoming inn, she thought ruefully. The only time she had seen the scowl change to a smile was when May flirted with Jack. If only she knew. Rose smiled at her.

May turned away, cursing under her breath. What a bitch! She was bored of their conversation anyway. Her ears had pricked up at talk of a permanent move to Welmley but her hopes had been dashed when she realised it would only be Rose; there had been no talk about Jack at all. Maybe they were tired of each other. Maybe he had finally seen sense and dumped her. Or maybe…She hardly dared hope. The gift had been passed down to her through generations and she knew that she had abused her powers.

The spell she had cast was wrong, she knew. The love potion she had administered the other night was so wrong, but she couldn't stop herself. It was only a little shove in the right direction, that's all it was.

Goosebumps shivered down her spine as the wind howled outside. She was a white witch but had used dark magic. If it all back-fired she would only have herself to blame. And no-one knew; no-one but her and whatever unholy god she had conjured up. Jack would be hers, one way or the other, and soon.

The spell had been cast and it had brought him to these shores, albeit to the wrong woman. But that was just a minor glitch; together with the potion he had drunk and the incantations she recited night after night under the cloak of darkness, it was only a matter of time before he realised that she, May, was his one and only true love.

"Yo ho,

Yo ho ho,

Leave my man and away you go..."

*

Rose left the bar in a much less optimistic mood than the one she had arrived in. Her dreams of buying into John's shop with the insurance money she hoped to get from the fire were dashed. Quite understandably John had been reluctant to commit to anything. In fact, he had been so uncomfortable he visibly squirmed in his seat and she felt compelled to leave him in peace. She knew why he was reluctant; Jack. He was a loose cannon; he had stolen her sword, tried to make her believe she was going mad, and burned down her shop. He had managed to wreck any future plans she had. They had parted awkwardly and she wasn't even certain he understood they had split for good this time. Nothing concrete had been said; no words of goodbye exchanged. All she was left with was a feeling of confusion; had they actually split up?

She stopped at the foot of the rocks where she had seen Jack watching over her; that first night in Welmley-on-Sea. He cared about her, she knew that. But he was controlling and unpredictable. He was very jealous and possessive. She didn't even know if he was living legally in this country or whether he would have to go back to the States soon; it would certainly solve a few things if he was deported.

She sat on the nearest rock. It was damp and covered in little barnacles. It reminded her of the hull of a ship. She gazed out to sea; there was a mist over the horizon and she could hardly distinguish between the sea and sky. She wondered if any vessels were out there, alone in the haze, and her thoughts turned to the pirate ships and how magnificent they must have looked as they sailed out of the fog. She shivered and pulled her coat around her. The Phoenix with its bird-like figure-head must have looked truly beautiful as well as sinister, shrouded in a swirl of fog. She could almost see it sailing into view, almost touch it. Her heart quickened and she breathed in great gulps of cold, damp air. Her palms sweated and she fumbled to open her coat buttons. She sat alone and quiet as the turning tide crept in around her, and tried to steady her breath against the gentle rhythm of the waves. Her legs were jelly and she couldn't stand; she would have to wait out her panic as her dreams and future plans disintegrated.

Chapter 30

Jack crouched behind the large rock watching silently. He had been there all morning, contemplating his future; fighting with the growing number of demons swirling through his head. Rose hadn't seen him, preoccupied with her own thoughts when she'd passed by. He'd instinctively hidden and now watched as she struggled to calm her breathing. She thought he didn't know about her panic attacks but he had known from the beginning. The panic which bubbled furiously under the surface had made his job of scaring her and controlling her easy. As he sat and watched her struggle now with her own demons he felt only remorse and pity; his love for her locked away where it could no longer hurt him.

He too suffered anxiety and it was no laughing matter. It had ruined his once promising career; that was how he came to be involved in such a ludicrous job. When Roland had approached him, at first he had laughed at the idea. It was incredible, not to mention downright cruel, to make someone think they were going out of their mind. To use a person's suffering in such a cold and calculating way just for a sword was despicable. Yet he had been party to it from the beginning. It pained him to watch her struggling and, quietly he made his way back along the beach. It was ironic that in the end he was losing his sanity; poetic justice some might say.

Jack had walked those rocks and beach so many times since his arrival that he knew the place almost as well as his home town. He had wandered along alleys and passageways which led up and down, in and around the small coastal village. He imagined Blackheart, sailing the majestic Phoenix into the harbour and mooring her alongside other, lesser vessels. The man must have had nerves of steal to enter the town as often as he did. It seemed strange to think he may have wandered the very streets that Jack now walked. Though Blackheart and his crew belonged in the town; many grew up there, Jack did not. It seemed to him there was no need to be there anymore.

The threat from Roland was less pressing. Maybe he had been frightened off by the involvement of the police after the shop burned down. Or maybe, as a businessman, he had simply thought the pursuit of the Sword of Aramoth no longer a viable option and so simply walked away. Whatever the reason, there had been no sign of anyone remotely connected to Roland at Welmley. Jack had a strong feeling that Rose was safe now, as long as she remained there. The ghost of her ancestors would see to that; she belonged there with them.

With no thought as to where he was going, Jack found himself standing outside the pirate museum. The door was wide open. John had told them that he rarely came to the museum during the winter months. And when he did it was only to check things, then he would leave as quickly as he could. Jack hadn't seen why he was so scared but Rose had been frightened of the place too.

"Truth be told, the damn place gives me the creeps in these cold and dark days. I reckon the ghosts of the crew of The Phoenix haunts it!" John had tried to laugh it off.

Carefully and quietly as he could Jack stepped inside; a light shone from the far end of the passage which led to the room containing the paintings. Jack hoped and prayed that Rose had not given John the map as she had drunkenly promised, and still had it in her possession. That kind of insurance was hard to come by and she needed it in case Roland had decided to pursue her. Maybe he was inside the museum. Though John had poured scorn on the existence of any treasure, Jack still partly believed in it. It would be the one thing that Roland might pursue. And maybe something which others might kill for. He inhaled deeply as he thought of the man sent to kill him. By now they would know that no bodies had been discovered in the burned remains of Rose's shop. If the man was a professional he would want to finish the job; and fast.

His pace slowed as he moved cautiously along the corridor until he could see inside the room. Hiding behind the door he watched as a woman came into view. It was the barmaid from The Jolly Roger. She had stared him down the other night and this had unnerved him; very few people could do that. He felt inexplicably drawn to her yet she was nothing like his usual type. He shrugged; maybe it was time for a change.

*

May was aware Jack had been watching her for some time. She resisted the urge to turn around, remaining quiet and still as she hummed softly. She studied one of the paintings intently as though looking at it for the first time. But over the years she had spent many an hour standing on that very spot, studying every minute detail. She held her breath as she heard Jack approach her. Still she kept her gaze on the painting. He stood beside her and scrutinized her in much the same way that she had him. She could feel his hot breath on her cheek and longed to turn and face him but still she remained facing the painting.

"Who is it?" he asked, breaking the silence at last.

"Don't you know?" she replied coolly.

He considered for a moment, "Not another damn ancestor?" he laughed.

She smiled and turned to face him. He stopped laughing. They were only inches apart, their lips almost touching. He lowered his head and cleared his throat. He gazed up at her through his lashes and she melted in an instant. Her legs turned to jelly and a host of butterflies fluttered inside her as his deep green eyes pierced her soul. She flashed him a smile; putting a hand out to steady herself softly she touched his chest and felt him quiver beneath his thin jacket. She breathed in his smell, using all her white energy to calm the turbulent waters within them both.

"Who, uh, who is she?" he stammered as he broke away, turning his gaze on the painting.

"You mean you don't recognise her, Jack?" she breathed.

He shook his head and turned back to face her. She smiled and stepped away from him. "Can't you see the likeness?" she asked as she stood alongside the picture, "I mean, she isn't blonde, but then nor am I really…" she laughed and widened her eyes in mock horror.

He grinned and studied the two women carefully for the first time. The one in the portrait was dark haired but had flashing brown eyes just like the barmaid. Her dress was that of a serving wench and her smile showed defiance.

"Looks like she had spirit," he commented.

May smiled. "Oh, she had that alright! But," she hesitated, "Don't you know who she is? Really, you have no idea - None at all?"

He shrugged apologetically and looked hard at the picture then back to her. "Should I?" he asked.

"Oh, Jack," she sighed, "You didn't do your homework very well at all, did you? Blackheart sailed the seas with Rosie Scarlet but really he didn't love her. He loved May the barmaid - her…"

Jack frowned as she pointed at the painting. "No," he shook his head, "I believe you're mistaken, um, May too, isn't it?"

She nodded, happy that he remembered her name. It was a start. She moved to his side so that their fingers touched together lightly. She hoped that last nights incantation had worked; it must have been what brought him to her. Now it was down to her to make the spells come together. She tilted her face to look at him.

"Oh, I'm not mistaken, Jack," she whispered, "She was his mistress. She loved him and, when the time came, she would've died for him too. Only her family kept her from him. After Blackheart had been captured she wanted to die too. But her father locked her in the inn and forbade her ever to see him again…either in this life or the next!" She laughed, "Like she ever could after he had been hanged! Anyway, afterwards, when things quietened down she retrieved his body with the help of some of the crew from The Phoenix – seems they felt some remorse over what they had done and wanted to save their own souls by helping him. Rumour has it he's buried in the graveyard, over at Leckton."

"I saw a grave there – you mean, it is his?" Jack rubbed his face, he looked tired.

"Well, so they say," she wanted to kiss him, "I don't know if it really is him though. But May loved him, more than that bitch Scarlet did. May would've happily died alongside him! She wasn't ashamed to be associated with Blackheart and neither was she afraid to tell anyone who would listen about her love for him! No, she loved him deeply and truly and she was loyal to the end. I'm very like her..."

She reached up and planted a kiss on his cheek. At first he was surprised; completely overwhelmed as she brushed his lips with hers. Then, overcome by the urge to hold her and kiss her properly, he swept her up in his arms, kissing her urgently on the mouth. She responded as his tongue delved and probed. But as he began to pull at her jumper she pulled away.

"Not now, my love, not here," she whispered.

"When then? Where?" he demanded as he pawed and pulled at her clothes. His eyes were empty, devoid of all emotion.

One of her buttons was ripped open and she had to push him away, "Soon." She promised, trying to remain in control.

She left quickly; almost running down the corridor as she held onto the walls for fear her legs would buckle under her. The spell was strong and she had to stop it; but she was in much too deep. She was no longer in control of it; it was in control of her. Whatever devil she had manifested to work its dark magic for her would not relinquish its hold over Jack quite so easily. She felt afraid; it also held her own soul in its grasp and she had no idea how much longer she could contain it. If only her Grandmother were still alive; her white magic had been good and strong and between them they could have banished the evil entity back to hell; for that must surely be from where it had come.

©2007 Cara Aldous

Chapter 31

From the uppermost point in Welmley; the cliff-top hotel car-park, Rose looked out across the bay. The sky was a clear watery blue and the sun, low and pale, swept up over the horizon. No ships or sailing boats littered the surface today and the dark waters looked foreboding and treacherous in their stillness. The beach below was yellow and smooth with not a footprint or mark on its silky surface. Rose loved this time of day; early winter mornings were, she had come to realise, wonderfully deserted. With no holiday-makers to take a pre-breakfast stroll and very few locals with the time or inclination to admire the view, Rose relished the quiet and isolated Welmley-On-Sea that she had fallen in love with.

    She smiled and surveyed her surroundings with a new and mounting excitement. This was to be her home. No; this was her home and for as long as she was happy here; she had a feeling that might just be for ever. It was all thanks to John. John had helped to make her plans real. He had helped her to love again. They had met up in The Jolly Roger one evening with Sam and Aubrey. They had sat together at the bar and let the conversation flow over them. They had chatted about small, meaningless things which somehow turned to her staying in Welmley.

"I'm not really sure what I'm going to do, to be honest," she had shot a look at Jack sitting by himself but he had ignored her so she continued, "I would like to stay but it's more a question of what I'll do for a living."

John could no longer contain his mounting excitement, "The shop – it's yours! If you still want it, that is?"

She had been happy; happy that she could move on without guilt or remorse. With not having to rely on Sam or Jack she had felt carefree making her own decisions. She had felt a little responsible for Jack but May had her sights set on him and Rose said a silent thank-you to her for that. Although their parting had been drawn out and difficult, they still remained close, and she felt more than a little responsible for him. He wasn't showing any signs of going home to America but maybe he would one day.

How does that saying go? Rose thought *Keep your friends close and your enemies closer?*

She had chuckled and caught Jack's eye then. She had thought she'd seen a smile flicker across his face but it was hard to tell. She had wished he would move on but something held him there; something stopped him from going home yet she knew he had desperately wanted to go; he had told her when he collected his things from the hotel. More than anything he had wanted to step onto safe, American soil and never ever leave it again.

She remembered how time had stopped that evening not so long ago; it was several very long minutes before she was able to find her voice and much, much longer before she could clearly hear anything else at all. Sam and Aubrey had clapped and cheered as the whole bar joined in and they toasted Rose, John, and their future together. And, when she had finally turned to see his reaction, she found that Jack had gone; slipped quietly away. In his own way he had given her his blessing.

*

"Rose…"

She remained lost in her thoughts, looking out over the deep blue sea. He stood by her side and together they silently watched the edge of the waves lapping at the beach. They listened as the gulls circled overhead, and felt the chill wind of winter blow through their hair and blast against their faces. Rose's eyes streamed in the icy air and she dared not turn to look at him in case he mistook them for tears. But when curiosity forced her to glance at him she saw that he too had wet cheeks, stung by the cold. She wiped her face and turned against the wind and he too turned so that he was sheltering her from the brutal elements.

She smiled, "Sorry, John."

"Don't be," he looked concerned, "I think the bride is allowed to be a little emotional on her wedding day…"

"But Jack," she began.

He touched her face as she faltered. "He's okay – just came to wish us well, apparently," John turned and nodded, "And I believe him. He's with May now and she'll see he's alright. He just wants a few words; that's all…"

Rose tried to object but John gently shushed her, "I think he just wants to say a proper goodbye."

John walked back toward the hotel and stood in the entrance. Inside the reception blared out noisily and happily; sounds of chinking champagne glasses and loud bursts of laughter emanating from within. John stood patiently, watching as Jack moved stiffly to Rose's side. He resisted the urge to run to her as she put a hand up to her mouth to hide her anguish. He too had noticed it, they all had; Jack Bracken was a mere shadow of his former self.

*

Rose couldn't help a small gasp escaping her lips; Jack's eyes looked hollow; dark circles around them. His eyelids drooped and he slurred his words yet he was not drunk. When he had arrived at the church with May it appeared he had been drinking heavily but she had assured them all he did not touch alcohol anymore. Rose had been concerned he might make trouble but he had sat at the back as quiet as a mouse throughout the entire ceremony.

Standing in front of her now he seemed ill and withdrawn. She reached out a hand to trace his scar but he gripped her wrist tightly to stop her. The force of his grasp unnerved her; his strength belied his appearance and it threw her off-balance as it stirred up memories of the happier times they had shared together. He gritted his teeth as he lowered her arm. Letting go she dropped it to her side.

"I…I understand, Rose, that you don't…don't…love me anymore," he struggled to get his words out, "I know…now…you never really did. And I…didn't…love you either. I thought it was love but..."

It had been hard to say those things but they had to be said. At last he could let her go and move on. Rose had John and he had May. He turned toward the hotel; he could see May watching from the window, worried and concerned. John had a similar look on his face too. Jack managed a short laugh before a racking cough shook his body.

Concerned, Rose held out her arms to him and he moved into her as she hugged him closely. After a brief time they pulled apart and stood, silent and reflective, facing their futures. It started to rain but still they stood at the edge of the cliff their backs to the tossing, turbulent sea. Their tears flowed freely, hidden by the raindrops as they both began to shake with emotion. They touched their fingers together as they silently said their goodbyes.

Rose walked back to her husband, the celebrations of their marriage, and the beginnings of a new and happier life. Theirs had been a whirlwind romance to say the least and her friends had warned against such a rushed decision. But Rose knew it was what she wanted and, unable to wait a moment longer, John had managed to organise the magical ceremony for Christmas Eve. The local vicar had been most helpful and all of their family and friends had pulled together to sort out the reception.

Rose smiled as she held out her hands to John and he swept her up in his arms. He twirled her around and hugged her tightly.

"Hey! I can't breathe!" she laughed.

Reluctantly, he loosened his grip, "I just can't believe how lucky I am! I don't ever want to let you go!"

"Well, you'll have to if I'm going to run the shop and you the museum! We can't be in two places at once," she grinned.

"Yes, well there's plenty of time for that but right now, Mrs Batcher, I am going to have a dance with you and hug you as tight as I like!" he grinned back.

"Oh you are, are you? We'll see about that – do you know how much this dress cost?" she teased playfully.

"Sod the bloody dress! I'm going to rip it off you tonight anyway!" he laughed as he made a grab for her.

Rose screamed and ran into the reception, their friends and neighbours laughing and pointing; joining in the fun. Throwing her hands up in mock horror as John caught her, Rose spied Jack leaving quietly with May.

Goodbye Jack, take care. I hope you find peace one day soon.

A slow and beautiful ballad started playing as Mr and Mrs John Batcher began their first dance together. She felt secure in his arms as he

©2007 Cara Aldous

waltzed her around the dance floor. She smiled dreamily at Sam and Aubrey as they passed by. She was pretty certain there would be another wedding soon. Finally Sam would see an engagement through and actually wear a wedding dress. But for now Rose wanted to savour the moment and live her own special day so that she could remember it all, second by second. It was everything she could have wished for and more.

Chapter 32

Welmley-On-Sea shone brightly with tiny twinkling coloured and white lights. In every home in every window stood a tree of varying sizes and colours; some real, some artificial. Rooms were decorated with colourful bunting and shiny decorations just like every other town in England. Even the usual dark corners had been lit up by the festive lights hung by the local council. And though the beach was shrouded in its normal night blackness there was one small part which glowed warmth and cheer on a dark December night.

The Jolly Roger was filled with the sound of happy voices and chinking glasses. It was the busiest time for the quiet, out-of-the-way inn. The busiest it had been in centuries. May stood behind the bar serving quickly and efficiently. As the newly appointed landlady she was flushed at the successful way in which she had tempted more customers into her little pub. The door opened and more blew in with a gust of wind which whipped the sand inside.

"Shut the bloody door!" thundered out a chorus, followed by raucous laughter.

May joined in and giggled as she deftly threw the coins into her till. Takings would be the best ever and later, after she rested, she would count it with her love by her side and they would talk again of their own impending wedding in the New Year.

"You okay, honey?" Jack placed an arm around her waist and kissed her gently on the neck. "Need a hand?"

She shook her head and returned his kiss before turning her attentions once more to her busy bar. She was worried about him; his moods were dark but not menacing and she was only too aware how ill he looked and sounded to all that knew him. Some had openly showed their horror at Rose and John's wedding. Their wedding had been nice but not as nice as hers and Jack's would be.

Jack sat hunched up at the bar; he had long given up trying to focus on the conversations in the pub. Instead he thought about Rose and her marriage to John. Sitting in the back of the church he had desperately wanted to stop it; had tried frantically to stand up and make his objections heard. She had married hastily and he was sure she would come to regret it. His mother had.

He breathed deep and long, his chest painful with all the anguish and hurt. He cursed Blackheart under his breath and winced as the pain in his head intensified. Once his relationship with Rose was over he had felt sure the headaches would stop. But they hadn't. Being around May helped a little; he knew what she was. But she was good; white. Thank God she didn't delve into the dark powers. He shivered as the cold fingers of death toyed with him. Even though he sat near the large, roaring open-fire he remained frozen to the core.

*

Rose hummed softly to herself as she wound the tinsel round and through the branches of the large tree which stood in their tiny front room. The cottage glowed with the heat of a hearty fire raging in the hearth and Rose felt warmed and comforted in her new little house by the sea. A lot had happened this year and she was looking forward to spending her first Christmas as a married woman; the first of many.

She glanced at her watch; eight-thirty. The reception had finished only an hour and a half ago and she felt as though she were floating on air. John had carried her over the thresh-hold and they had collapsed, giggling in the hallway. When he opened the door to the front room she had cried, overjoyed with emotion as she saw the cosy fire freshly lit and the real fir tree awaiting decoration. There was even a box of tinsel and baubles by the sofa as well as lights and other Christmas trinkets.

"My mother's," John had offered by way of explanation, "We can get our own next year."

But Rose didn't care; they belonged to her now too. She had rushed upstairs to get changed so that she could get decorating but John had raced up behind her; he had other plans before the Christmas festivities began. He knew once Rose started it would be midnight before they got to bed and by then they would both be too exhausted for anything else.

Rose hummed Carols as she began again to hang baubles onto branches, wrapping tiny silver bells through the tinsel. Sam and Aubrey were staying for Christmas at the cliff-top hotel. She hoped they would stay for the New Year too so that they could all attend Jack and May's wedding together. It had been a huge surprise when Jack had told her about him and May; she thought at first it was in retaliation of her and John's marriage.

May had done all the running in their relationship and kept his head filled with Blackheart and pirates. Jack needed to be away from that; he should be back in America. By rights he should be going by his proper name now too. She worried that May was a bad influence and hoped he would see sense and soon. She would always feel responsible for him and a part of her would always love him. But John was her lover and her best friend and he was nothing like Jack.

She pushed all thoughts of Jack from her head as John entered the room carrying two mugs of steaming hot tea. He handed one to her and kissed her on the nose. She giggled and responded by kissing him hard on the lips.

"Looking good, Rose," he murmured into her hair.

"What, me or the tree?" she laughed.

"Both," he replied and grabbed her around the waist.

"Careful, you'll spill my tea!" she warned jokingly, "And we've got loads to do before tomorrow! This tree, presents, supper…"

"The tree is nearly done, we wrapped the presents yesterday and supper is waiting to go in the oven." He pulled her close and kissed her long and gently.

"Well, what am I going to do then?" she asked, slightly breathless.

Silently he took her by the hand and led her upstairs to their bedroom. The lights on the tree twinkled and the fire crackled behind its guard. Outside the sea crashed onto the beach as the storm whipped it into a fury. Rose shivered in ecstasy as her moans were drowned out by the howling wind.

*

May locked the door on the final reluctant customer and heaved a happy sigh of relief that their busiest night was finally over. The till was ready to burst at the seams and she grinned as she began to clear the tables. Jack sat at the end of the bar and watched her work. He muttered an offer of help but she refused, motioning him to sit quietly at the end of the bar.

"You stay there, my love," she cooed, "I'll finish up quick as I can then we can have a Christmas Eve supper my old Gran would be proud of!"

If he took his attention off her for just one minute he lost his focus and it took him a while to remember where he was. So he watched her fixedly. Besides it made his head hurt if he turned his gaze away from her for too long. The hold she had over him was mesmerising and he found her beauty captivating. His whole body craved her and he cried out for her in the night when the dreams came; the dreams of Blackheart and Rosie Scarlet and The Phoenix. Why he had begun to dream of these things God only knew but it gave him an insight into what had scared Rose so much. He was the one who had brought her nightmares; the instigator of her dreams. Now he was on the receiving end and it scared him. Blackheart haunted his every sleeping and waking hour.

Once upstairs Jack performed his nightly ritual to rid himself of the curse of Blackheart using the Sword of Aramoth; Rose had given it to him as an early wedding present. She had said it was a parting gift, something to remember her by, yet he had given her nothing in return.

"Oh, you've given me a lot, lot more Jack," she had replied when he voiced his concerns, "You've given me the strength to live my life the way I want."

Sweat trickled down his forehead and glistened on his bare back and chest as he concentrated on wielding the sword. He was Blackheart the pirate and he fought hard against his enemies. The demons and devils swooped down on him, round and around.

May sat in the darkened kitchen lit only by the glow of an open fire in the hearth. A large black pot sat above the flames and she stirred the bubbling stew absently as she poured over a large book on the wooden table. Jack's behaviour was becoming more and more erratic and paranoid. She knew she would have to stop giving him the potion soon but she was afraid. Once they were married she would definitely stop the spells and incantations and put away her books for good. She would contact all the white witches she knew and ask for their help. But if she did it now, she could risk losing him for good.

She loved Jack so deeply it hurt to see him in such turmoil. But she could not take any chances; if it didn't kill him to stop the magic abruptly then it would certainly kill his love for her. May stood to lose a great deal if things went wrong now, not least the man she had loved her entire life; the man in the portrait at the museum. The man whose features she had studied and imprinted in her mind, whose face she saw each time she closed her eyes. And now the man whose face she saw each time she opened them.

Carefully she spooned several spoonfuls of the stew into a bowl then from her pocket she pulled a small, purple bottle and poured a few drops into the bowl, stirring it in.

"Jack, my love," she called, "Supper's ready."

She closed the book and placed it back on top of the dresser. Soon her love would enter the kitchen and they would eat together. Then they would go to bed and have a long, glorious night of love-making. Absently she dipped her finger into his stew and sucked it thoughtfully. The room began to swim as the kitchen door flew open and Jack stepped into the room. He stood with the sword in his hand, dressed in all his pirate finery. Demons sat on his shoulders as he strode toward her. He grabbed her roughly and pushed her onto the table.

"Jack!" she tried to push him away but he was too strong.

He kissed her so hard she could taste blood; her lip, split and sore she pulled away.

"Jon! Jon Black! It's me – May!"

He staggered back and sunk into a chair, exhausted. With huge rasping breathes he tried to fill his lungs as his chest threatened to implode. May quickly fetched him a glass of water which he gratefully gulped down. As his breathing steadied he smiled weakly.

"What…what happened?"

"Nothing, my love - nothing for you to worry about. You blacked out, that's all." Quickly she cleared the dishes, throwing the stew into the bin.

"Honey, we haven't eaten yet," he objected.

"I'll do you some cheese on toast. This stew tasted a bit off. In fact, it's all been a bit off lately. That's why you've been feeling so ill I reckon. Well, no more. From tomorrow I'll make sure you get fresh, good food and we'll make you well again, Jon," she smiled and wiped her bleeding lip, "We'll make you Jon again."

THE END

Black Nightmares to Scarlet Dreams

www.ingramcontent.com/pod-product-compliance
Ingram Content Group UK Ltd.
Pitfield, Milton Keynes, MK11 3LW, UK
UKHW041258180426
11947UKWH00008B/548